LUNA KAYNE

CRY WOLFE

Cry Wolfe by Luna Kayne

Book cover design: Pretty Little Design Co.

Cover model photographer: Wander Aguiar

Cover model: Michael Martin

Editor: Caroline Knecht

ISBN (eBook) 978-1-989366-40-0

ISBN (paperback) 978-1-989366-39-4

Luna Kayne, Kayne Publishing

CHAPTER 1
MARCUS

You are not safe.

You only feel safe because no one has decided to target you.

People are oblivious to the threats lurking in the darkness around them. Their need for attention makes it too easy for predators to have their fill.

Those who wish to harm will never starve in today's world. Social media, the internet, and a connected society that breeds an addiction to pseudo validation is what keeps me in business—and business is booming.

From my place in the shadows, I easily spot five people I could pursue tonight. My initial assessment tells me I wouldn't break a sweat finding information on three of them, but there's one girl a mere ten meters away from me who makes my warning bells go off. I'm sure the only reason she is still alive is because no one has taken a depraved interest in her—yet.

She's lucky I'm here for someone else.

Tonight I'm hunting someone who is a little more elusive than your run-of-the-mill pick-me girl.

This one is more of a challenge.

The group on the street across from the alley I'm lurking in disperses to their various venues, and I return my attention to the building I'm casing. There isn't anything flashy about it. There isn't even a business name posted on the outside, just a picture of a raven with an intricate symbol on its body above the door. Inside those doors is Ravenous, a membership-only lifestyle club of sorts, owned and operated by Alexandra Loren.

So far, I've gone unnoticed every time I've been here. I've walked down the street on numerous evenings. I glance over to the bench where I sometimes sit eating pizza. A couple of weeks ago, and while using fake ID, I brazenly walked through the front doors on a new-member night to have a look around. I got close enough to the woman I'm after to smell her perfume when she stepped around me to greet an acquaintance of hers.

Tonight is different though.

This is the night I will make myself known.

I've watched Alexandra Loren for just over three weeks now, and tonight is the night she will see me.

I could wait until her club closes and her clients and employees trickle out, leaving her helpless and alone, but I want to make a point.

And that point is that she is vulnerable—always.

If I want something, there is nothing that will stop me. There is no time, no place where she will be safe from me.

Laughter draws my attention as a couple walks arm-in-arm down the sidewalk toward me. The man whispers something in the woman's ear at the same time he runs the tip of his finger between the lapels of her jacket, and she shudders, dipping her head toward him with a mischievous smile on her face.

I know before they stop in front of Ravenous that this is where they're headed. The coat cinched around her waist goes to her mid-thigh, and it is longer than whatever she is wearing underneath. It's no longer acceptable to make assumptions about people by how they are dressed, but profiling is literally my bread and butter, and the collar buckled around her neck tells me that they aren't interested in the bakery one block over.

Sure enough, they stop at the door and knock. The man already has his phone out of his pocket when the bouncer opens the door. He taps the screen a few times, then holds the face out and allows the employee to scan whatever is on the screen. The bouncer looks up from his device, seemingly happy with what he sees, and asks for identification.

In the darkness, I smile to myself at the stringent security measures. While they are impressive, they won't stop me.

I could easily follow them in and ask to sign up for a membership, but I've already decided the back door is going to be easier.

This way, I'll avoid showing identification. When I arrived on new-member night, it was an open house. My fake ID got me through the doors, but signing up for a membership is another thing entirely. They would take a picture, put me in their database, and find out rather quickly that I am not who I say I am.

No. My way leaves no footprints behind.

I walk farther into the shadows and down the back alley to the employee door. I was down here a little over a year ago when my employer, Noah, and his girlfriend, Hazel, got into some trouble at the club, and I was asked to bring the car around to the back. So I know my way.

While I waited for them to come out, I noticed something at the back door that I filed away at the time.

Now, I'm hoping what I witnessed has become a habit that the employees have taken for granted.

I only have to wait another ten minutes in the warm

evening air before the metal door grates open with a high-pitched groan that carries down the alley.

A woman steps outside and bends over to retrieve a brick lying along the wall. She props it against the frame to keep the door from closing completely—just like I noticed someone do last time.

She pats the pocket of her jacket, then hunches over in the telltale stance of someone who is trying to light their cigarette in the open air. Then she tilts her head back and exhales a puff of smoke.

She steals one final glance at the door to make sure the brick is secure, then starts to walk away, no doubt to keep the cigarette smoke from entering the club and giving her smoke break away.

I didn't realize my breathing had turned shallow while I hid and watched her. There's another one who could simply vanish without a trace.

I inhale a deep breath to steady myself before I step toward the back door, but I freeze at the very edge of a dark corner when a man opens the door to join her. He jogs down the alley asking for a cigarette.

That was close.

The guy doesn't bother to look back when the door clangs against the brick; his attention is fully on the woman he's trying to catch up to.

When they are far enough away, I stride to the door and peek through the gap to see if anyone is close by. Another benefit of entering now is that most of the employees are out on the floor since it is the busiest time of the evening.

The back area is deserted.

I clench my teeth to brace myself for the patience I'm about to need as I pry the door open at a painstakingly slow pace to avoid the scraping sound it makes.

At the same time the heavy door becomes sluggish, the very start of a creak acts as a warning. Unchecked, it will soon turn into the loud grating sound I heard earlier. I have a couple more inches to go before I'm able to fit my body through the opening, so I push the door up and toward its hinges to alleviate some of the stress. Then I try again. It opens the last little bit without a sound, and I slip through and into the club.

When the door finally rests quietly against the brick once again, I take a step back and look around the area.

Now I'm relying on chance and luck to get me what I want. I've never been back here, this close to Alexandra's office, the space where she should feel safe.

If someone saw me now, that would be it. I have no reason to be here. The chance I might be discovered sends a surge of adrenaline through me, which settles into my nerve endings, making me feel close to giddy with anticipation.

This is probably something I should discuss with my therapist at my next appointment.

I prowl down the hall, away from the muffled music coming from behind one of the doors, until I get to an open area. There are some numbered rooms to my left, followed by a row of sofas in a sitting area. A quick peek behind door number three tells me this is some type of private or holding room.

I'm startled by a sound in the distance, and three large strides bring me to a new area. As I pass a partially open door, an office desk catches my attention, and I slip in, closing the door behind me to buy myself some time.

A woman's fragrance dominates the area, and I circle the desk to confirm this is the office I'm looking for. A framed photo of Alexandra and a man I know to be Emilia's father sit near the monitor. I saw a similar photo of the man a few months ago, when I dropped in with Noah to visit with Joshua at the home he shares with Emilia. Since I know Adam has passed, it leaves only Alexandra who would have this on her desk since they were partners in all ways.

Catching sight of a purse tucked between a bookcase and the wall, I make my way over, tugging at filing cabinets that open easily on my way across the room. Whether or not this is her office, this is Alexandra's purse. I don't take anything out, but I do make a point of leaving it open on top of the shelf so she knows I've been through it.

Then I return to her desk, remove a yellow rose from the inside pocket of my jacket, place its long stem in a pencil holder, and move it to the center of the desk.

I grab a smartphone from beside a keyboard on my way down into the seat behind the desk.

From the outside, Alexandra looks like she's a challenge, which serves her well. It would deter anyone who isn't fully committed to getting close to her.

Unluckily for her, I am not that man.

I kick up my feet, crossing them at my ankles on top of her desk as I lean back in her seat and go to work unlocking her phone.

I don't get the chance to power it on.

For a brief moment, the music surges from the front, telling me the door to this back area has been opened.

I freeze, waiting to see if I've been found out so quickly.

Heels clack against the floor, the rhythmic steps growing louder as they get closer.

My breathing slows, my pulse quickens, and a smirk stretches the corner of my mouth.

Then the door opens, and her eyes meet mine. Alexandra pauses. Her knuckles go white around the file folder she's holding, and she stills with one foot frozen in the air, not willing to take another step into the room.

It's subtle, but the rosy color drains from her cheeks.

I give her a moment to take everything in while I sit in silence, savoring this moment.

Victory.

Her eyes trail down to my shoes, still propped up on her desk, then move just a little bit farther until she sees the rose.

Her confusion morphs into disbelief, and she finishes her step, propping her free hand on her hip.

"Are you kidding me?" Her lips pinch together as though she's about to say my name, but she thinks better of it, instead asking, "And you are?"

Clever girl.

My smile widens in satisfaction.

"Marcus Wolfe." I stand, buttoning my jacket before I lean across the desk to shake her hand.

Alexandra takes a fraction of a second to give me the once-over, her eyes trailing the length of me then back up. Then she closes the distance, reaching her hand out, only partially reluctant to admit defeat.

I step around her desk, allowing her to take the seat that is hers, and she circles on the opposite side, setting her files down as she speaks. "I have to admit, when Joshua first challenged me to a security evaluation, I was positive he was wasting his time."

Alexandra reaches for the flower I left in her pen holder and lifts it to her nose, smiling when she inhales its scent.

It was decided ahead of time that I would be carrying a yellow rose, so she would know it was me and there was no imminent danger.

"Yet here we are," I counter, following her lead as she sits. I take the chair in front of her desk.

"Here we are." Her words sound like a realization as she glances at her purse, which is open on the shelf.

"I only opened it. Nothing is missing." I lean forward, answering the unasked question written on her face as I return her phone to her desk. "These things should either be on your person or locked up—always. Do you have time to talk now, or would you like to schedule a meeting?"

She has the good sense to look sheepish when she picks up her phone. Noah told me Alexandra was made aware of what happened to Hazel a year ago, when Paul tracked her location using her phone.

"Unfortunately, I've got to be up front in"—she taps the screen on her phone to check the time—"ten minutes. Are you free to drop by in the morning? This is important, and you'll have my undivided attention then."

I uncross my legs and shift my weight to stand when she reaches out a hand, wordlessly asking me to wait.

"Just out of curiosity, are you looking for a job?"

I raise my eyebrows, hoping she'll continue but not giving anything away.

There aren't many people close to me who really know what I do. I prefer the anonymity and privacy of minding my own business.

I'm *that* guy, the one people refer to when they say things like, "I know a guy." When in reality, they don't actually *know* me—they know *of* me.

"Are you trying to steal me away from Noah?" My tone carries a hint of humor.

Alexandra thinks I work as Noah's driver, and technically I do, but there is more to my story, and Noah has kept that to himself.

Seven years ago, my siblings and I started our own custom security company. We do everything from providing personal security to testing computer systems. We offer self-defense classes, arrange protection programs, remote monitoring, and—yes—testing current security measures against possible attack or infiltration.

I met Noah a couple of years ago, when we were looking to expand our company. We had a list of office requirements a mile long, and we worked directly with Noah and Connor Realty to discreetly secure a space.

A year and a half ago, Noah hired me to look into someone who was targeting a friend of his. We got to talking, and it turned out he owned a building that had some vacant apartments. I was taking some time off for personal reasons, so I worked part time as his driver in exchange for him covering my rent and allowing me to live there without providing any identification that would leave a trail.

But no one else knows this.

"Of course not, but if you are ever looking for an additional challenge, I would be open to adding a head of security position here." She pauses for a moment to consider her next thought before she says it. "I'm not sure how...familiar you are with our *community*, but there are those who hide among us and prey on our newer, more uneducated members."

I understand her statement better than she knows.

A part of me I'd considered lost surges back to the surface. I'm more than familiar with the lifestyle, but I don't tell her that. However, Alexandra's expression shows a hint of understanding as she looks at me.

The expression on my face must be giving me away.

I clear my throat and recover with the ghost of a smile. But I'm not sure she's buying it, so I change the subject. "I am familiar. I'll save you time—and some money. You don't need a head of security position. You have great staff, but you do need to fix a few things. We can address those tomorrow. My company would be open to offering your members a class or information session about safety."

Alexandra's face lights right up at that. "Really? Yes, please bring this up with me tomorrow."

I see why Joshua and Noah speak highly of Alexandra. She has an authentic heart, and it's obvious how genuinely she cares about the people around her.

When she taps her phone to check the clock a second time, I take it as my cue and stand, extending my hand. "I will make a note of it. I look forward to talking to you tomorrow."

We make small talk while we walk to the front. Alexandra asks me to give her best to Noah and Hazel, then points out a few things as we pass through the main area. I sense she is trying to gauge just how familiar I am with her club, but I only smile and nod.

As we approach the front door, her gaze narrows, and her forehead creases with concern. I follow her line of sight to a young woman standing at the front. She's speaking with the bouncer, who looks a little uncomfortable as he scans her ID.

She's the same girl I noticed standing outside earlier, and she fits a certain profile.

In the wild, predators won't often take risks. It's survival of the fittest. Even an apex predator won't waste their strength and stamina on hunting the strongest in the herd. They won't risk wasting their power and dwindling their reserves to eat. If an equal or greater threat should happen to come along after they've expended their energy, they would have nothing left to protect themselves with. So they stalk the herd, looking for an easy kill. They test and push at the herd's boundaries until the weakest of the group either falls out of line or is pushed out in sacrifice. Then they pounce.

This girl has fallen out of line.

"Do you mind if I handle this?" I tilt my head to Alexandra, and she takes a deep breath.

Her gaze returns to the girl, and a flash of worry settles across her face before she nods. "You may."

I straighten my jacket and approach the man at the front,

holding out my hand for the girl's ID. His eyes widen because he doesn't know me, which is another testament to Alexandra's staff.

The guy looks beyond me, and she must have nodded, because he hands over the driver's license. I waste no time holding out my hand toward the entrance to lead her out of the building.

This girl looks lost—curious, but lost and ill-prepared for what would await her inside.

It isn't lost on me that the door hasn't fully closed behind me, and I'm not surprised when I find Alexandra standing at the entrance. She feels responsible even for those who are not her paying members.

"How old are you"—I glance at the name on the driver's license—"Jennifer?" At the same time, I pull my phone out and open an app to get the information I'm sure she won't give me.

"I'm twenty-two. It says so right there." She points to the card in my hand, attempting to look put out, but the uncertainty in her tone is obvious.

I don't answer right away. I'm waiting for the truth to pop up.

When I get what I want, I return my attention to her. "You're a senior"—she pauses for a moment before she nods hesitantly, and I finish my sentence—"in high school."

She takes a deep breath. I know that look. I have a younger sister, and it's the look of someone who is trying to think fast.

I turn the screen toward her, and a selfie stares back at us. It's her standing in front of her school in a crop top and a big smile that doesn't shine in her eyes.

"How did you—"

I swipe the social media feed up to the selfie she took less than twenty minutes ago outside of the bar across the street.

It wasn't hard to find her. She tagged the bar's social media account, telling the world exactly where she was.

She drops her head and holds out her hand, silently asking for her fake ID back.

I slip it into my pocket. "Possession of false identification is illegal."

Jennifer's expression disappears at my insinuation. She further tenses when I dial a number and hold the phone to my ear.

"Are you calling the cops?" Now she glances from me to Alexandra in worry.

"No. I'm calling you a cab, and I'm sending you home. Is the address on your *identification* correct?"

"I—yes." Her tone is subdued.

When the car company answers the phone, I give them the information they need, and I charge it to the account my company holds with them.

When I disconnect, I soften my features.

I already stand taller than her. There is no need to make her feel any worse than she looks.

"Look." I gesture to the club. "This place is not off-limits to you for good, but it isn't the place for you now." I glance at Alexandra, and she nods in agreement, relaxing her posture slightly. I remove my wallet and start flipping through a few business cards until I find the one I'm looking for. "If you want to talk to anyone, about anything, even if you know full well what this place is and you are curious, call that number and tell them Marcus Wolfe sent you."

She looks at the name on the card, which is followed by the letters that indicate a doctoral degree in psychology, then sizes me up for a few seconds before reaching for it.

As Jennifer's fingers brush against mine, I wonder, for a brief moment, if I had done this years ago, would Adelaine still be alive today?

CHAPTER 2
ELLE

I've been distracted all morning.

An ominous disconnect pulls me out of the meeting I'm supposed to be paying attention to and thrusts me into an internal mess of sadness and foreboding, and I'm not sure why I have this sense of dread.

I haven't felt like this in a long time.

Eleven months and twenty-three days, to be exact. Although I've felt the odd sensation now and then. Sometimes a shudder will tickle over my skin, or I'll feel the ghost of a gaze when there is no one around. Then there is the little voice that warns me to watch my back.

I didn't sleep well last night, and that is how it always starts.

I thought I was doing better, but I'm obviously not.

I'm in a conference room eight floors up, in a staff meeting, and I have an eerie feeling I am being watched.

Not watched.

Stalked.

There was a time not long ago when I craved the rush that came with being wanted in such a base and carnal way.

Hunted, pursued by a predator who wanted to ravage and devour.

The forced clearing of a throat reminds me of my responsibilities.

"Elle?" Daniel smiles nervously from across the table when I meet his gaze. "What are your thoughts on the double-booking at The Plaza on the nineteenth?"

I steal a glance at the agenda in front of me.

Owning your own event-planning and promotions company means being accountable to both no one but yourself and everyone else because they either pay your salary or rely on you to earn theirs, and I'm slipping up.

My assistant, Natalie, enters the room and takes one of the seats along the wall. I take advantage of the distraction to review the two groups that we accidentally scheduled on the same date.

One is a sports dinner for our state team to celebrate a championship win. The other is a philanthropic event to raise money for a local animal rescue and shelter.

"Findlebauer and his team get the venue." My answer is met with a smile from Daniel because they are his clients. It also earns a groan from Julie because I've just pushed out her not-for-profit clients. I turn my attention to her with my reasoning. "Set up a meeting for this afternoon. We'll own up to our collective error, but this works in our favor and theirs." Julie's forehead wrinkles in silent question, and I elaborate. "We were originally unable to have the animals there because we couldn't get the proper permits in time. Moving the date allows the shelter to bring some of their rescues in, and we all know, when people can see and pet the animals, they donate more. There are also a couple of influencers who couldn't attend because they were away on some paid thing on the nineteenth. I can contact all of them with the new date. I have a list of available dates for The Plaza right here. The invites haven't gone out yet, so it's just a matter of making a correction on their social media accounts." Then I level my attention on Daniel because there is a price for everything. "I want some signed sports memorabilia from your clients for the animal shelter's silent auction. Work them, Daniel. Get me an experience with the team as well, like traveling to an away game as part of the unofficial team, or a day of training with the guys."

"Done." Daniel answers without hesitation. There was no way we could have spun it if it was his client who was out of luck with the venue, and he knows this. "I'll ask if a couple of the guys on the team can attend the rescue gig with The Cup for paid photo ops with the money made going to the charity in the form of a donation. It's good press for the team, especially after Manifred's DUI last month." He jots down a note before he exchanges a smile with Julie, and she seems satisfied with our solution.

"Does anyone else have anything to address?" To my staff, this is the same as me saying we're done here. When no one comes forward, I shuffle my papers into a stack. "Great. See Nat if you need time with me this afternoon." I tilt my head toward my assistant and slide my chair back to stand.

Natalie steps to my side, matching my pace as we leave the room. "Ms. Loren is in your office." My halt is abrupt, and Nat knows me so well, she answers my unasked question. "Remember you canceled on her twice last week, and you promised her you would see her for an in-office lunch today. I think she brought Thai."

"Right. Let's meet after lunch and go over the rest of our day." I hold my stride as I leave Nat at her desk, but I glance over to catch her nod of acceptance.

I enter my office to find Lexa standing at the window,

looking down eight floors to the street below. She smiles when she sees me and takes a few steps toward the food as the first wave of spicy cinnamon and coconut hits me.

"I was starting to wonder what I needed to do to see my closest friend!" Lexa grabs the wine bottle off the table and twists off the cap. I open my mouth to object, but she cuts me off. "And before you complain about alcohol in the office, remember it was you who canceled on me. We could very well be happily getting day-drunk in a restaurant like normal people." She fills our glasses and closes the distance between us, stretching her arms wide to hug me with a glass in each hand. "How are you? It's been a while."

She isn't wrong about that.

When she breaks away, I toss my papers on the shelf beside the door and accept the wine. "It has been. I'm sorry I went so long this time. We're coming out of a busy time, and I lost one of my account managers to maternity leave."

Lexa was going to take a sip of her wine, but she slows at my excuse. Her gaze narrows on my expression.

We both know that's exactly what it is: an excuse—not a legitimate reason. We aren't open twenty-four seven.

She continues her sip, then gestures to a chair, letting this line of conversation go for now.

"Maybe you should come by Ravenous one night and unwind." When I tilt my head in accusation, she quickly adds, "Just for a drink. I'll make sure we aren't approached."

Now it's my turn to take a sip of wine so I have a break to process her invitation.

I've known Alexandra for twenty years. I met her when I was nine—she was nineteen. I had tried to convince my parents I was old enough to watch myself when they went out on a date, but they wouldn't have it, and they hired her to babysit me.

Needless to say, our first encounter was a clash of wills.

I had decided I did not like her, and I did not relent until she offered to show me how to put on makeup. I was just a kid, and she took on the role of my big sister. I didn't realize it until much later, but we are a lot alike, and our similarities drew us to each other, creating a safe space for the both of us.

We both own companies. We are driven, focused, and private people.

"How is the club?" I reach for the nearest container of food, spooning some fried rice onto my plate before reaching for a lettuce wrap.

"It's good." A flash of guilt crosses her expression. It's been over a year since she lost Adam, and I know she still misses him. All she wanted was to have the club and her life with him, and he passed away too soon. Now her successes come with the bitter reminder that she isn't sharing her happiness with him. She recovers. "I'm serious. You should come by."

That makes me chuckle, and she shrugs, taking another sip and digging into her lunch.

Our similarities extend beyond our professional lives. While we are both dominant in business, we are both the opposite in our relationships.

When Lexa told me she wanted to open Ravenous, I told her it was a great idea. While I was happy for her, I never became a member. I preferred the anonymity of exploring myself around strangers, and eventually I joined a different club.

When I think about my old club, a memory floods my thoughts, and my breathing turns shallow. My chest restricts.

Lexa watches me closely. "Everything okay?"

"Yes." Now she crosses her arms. She's not buying it, so I come clean. "Well—I don't know. I think it's just been so busy, and I'm not sleeping well."

"Are you just tired or—you know—is it happening again?"

It.

My sense that something isn't right.

The last time it happened, it was a series of insignificant events: a bump in the night, missing clothing, an item not quite in the same place I left it. The sense deep in your soul that someone is attempting to claim a part of you that isn't for them.

I couldn't put my finger on it, so I told no one for a long time. I would have looked like a raving lunatic. It's hard enough being a female CEO. We are scrutinized for everything. Everything we say, every action we take, is dissected and held against us. We aren't savvy, we are conniving. We aren't entrepreneurial, we are greedy. We aren't focused, we are cold, or, my personal favorite—a bitch.

Imagine the CEO of a successful event and promotions company going around telling everyone that *something* feels off. It's nothing in particular, nothing that can't be explained away as just a woman being dramatic or delusional. Which is exactly what happened.

I broke down and called Lexa after a particularly harrowing experience. I didn't want to. She was still mourning the sudden passing of her partner. I just felt like my time was running out, and she convinced me to go to the authorities for help.

When I finally relented and contacted my local police department, my statement turned into an interrogation as soon as the officer asked me about my private life. I wasn't about to lie, so I had to tell him that I had a casual relationship with a dominant at a sex club I belonged to. After that, the atmosphere in the room changed, and I was told there was nothing they could do until they had something to go on.

In plain English: "We can't help you until you end up dead. Good luck with that. Don't let the door hit you on the way out."

I know what he thought of me. I also know he was wrong, but it tore at me just the same.

Eventually, I pulled Daniel and Nat into my office and told them most of my situation. They've been with me since the start of my company, and they were both understanding.

It wasn't long after that I learned Greg, the dominant I had started to trust at the club, had been arrested for human trafficking.

That was all I needed to hear.

I broke all ties with him, canceled my membership, and shut down that side of me. Lexa followed the trial and told me he was sentenced to almost two years, and that was the last I ever spoke about it with anyone.

After he went away, my unease slowly lifted. There have been fleeting moments of awareness, but I think every woman feels the need to look over her shoulder at some point in her life.

"I don't know. We have a few big events coming up, and I haven't been sleeping, so it's probably just that."

Lexa reaches for a pad of paper on the table. Her assessing gaze never leaves mine as she retrieves a pen from her purse and starts to write. "Listen, I'm serious. If you don't want to meet me socially at Ravenous, I get it." Neither of us have been too keen to witness the other explore her kinks. "But there is an event coming up, and I won't take no for an answer."

"No," I answer anyway.

She makes a buzzing noise before saying, "Wrong!"

Lexa clicks her pen before tossing it into her purse, and she slides the piece of paper over to me. "I know a guy who might be able to help."

"You know a guy? That sounds so portentous." I glance at the time and date, and I'm already irked because I can't immediately think of a reason not to attend. Not one Alexandra will buy anyway.

"He did some security work for me a few weeks ago. I talked him into doing a session about personal safety for my members. There's quite a lot of interest. And before you give me some lame excuse we both know isn't true, it is after hours, and it is mostly subs who have signed up."

I don't answer.

Instead, I glance at the paper.

There have been moments when I've missed being at my club. I never thought Greg was going to be anything more than temporary. Now it turns out he was the one I was supposed to stay away from, and I don't trust myself not to make that mistake again.

"Hey." Lexa leans forward. "I mean it. Get some sleep, and you're coming. At the very least, you'll learn some things about protecting yourself. Maybe the more you know, the less powerless you'll feel. I'm going to sign us both up. You're my guest." She taps the piece of paper in my hand. "This Sunday. I mean it, *Elora.*"

That makes me still.

Lexa only uses my full name when she's serious.

Everyone knows me as Elle. Even my parents call me by the shortened version. My full name is private, mine, and very few own that piece of me.

Lexa uses it when she's trying to make a point.

"Fine. I'll be there."

I can do this.

It's a harmless night out.

Greg is behind bars, and Elora is hidden safely away—maybe for good this time.

Piece of cake.

Jax straightens beside me, scanning the lounge while I set up some pamphlets on our display table. "So this is Ravenous."

I catch my older brother smiling and nodding toward the sitting area, and a couple of women perk up in their seats at his attention. Voices bleed together, a hum of obscure background noise punctuated with a surge of laughter now and then.

It's close to a full house tonight.

I pack away the rest of our material and set the bag under the table before joining him.

"This is it."

I've only seen this room a few times. Once when I was doing recon. The second and third times were when I broke in, then met with Alexandra the next morning about her company's security and her goals for the meeting we planned for tonight.

When Alexandra said there was a lot of interest in our session, I didn't think she meant this much. I expected about five to ten people, but it turns out most of Ravenous's female staff members signed up to attend as well, and I had to bring my older brother and younger sister in to manage the group size.

As the thought of my younger sister enters my mind, I find her in the crowd, sitting at a table with some women. Kate meets my gaze and smiles before returning to her conversation.

Not everyone is comfortable around my brothers and me, so having Kate attend these types of meetings can be helpful. Most of the time, she listens and provides feedback on how we can be more approachable and "not so assholey," as she puts it.

"How are things looking?" Alexandra approaches our table, and Jax cuts me off before I can answer.

"They're looking really fine." He makes no move to hide his innuendo as he openly takes in Alexandra's person.

I'm not sure I've effectively hidden my smirk. My brother knows who Alexandra is. He's done his homework, and, judging from the many questions he's asked me about the club and its owner, he likes what he's seen.

Jax isn't normally a player, but he has a way of weeding people out. He always says the best way to learn everything you need to know about someone is to irritate them.

Judging by the look on Alexandra's face, he's about to learn a lot.

She props a hand on her hip, and her smile fades but doesn't entirely disappear. "Please tell me that doesn't work on the women in your circles."

I chuckle and cut in. "Everything is set up, and we can start any time. Alexandra, this is my brother, Jaxon Wolfe." I gesture to Jax, and he straightens, standing taller. It isn't often I witness my brother trying to present himself to a woman.

Women normally fall all over him, so this is refreshing. Out of the corner of my eye, I catch Kate looking our way with a hint of amusement in her expression.

Alexandra turns her attention to me and smiles. "Please,

Marcus, call me Lexa." Then she turns her attention to my brother and extends her hand to shake his.

Jax clears his throat before lowering his voice. "It's nice to meet you, Lexa."

I do a double take at whoever this is that took over my brother's body.

She isn't having it.

Tilting her head toward me, her smile doesn't falter, and she doesn't skip a beat when she looks him dead in the eyes and says, "He may call me Lexa. You're still stuck on Alexandra. Good luck with that, Romeo." Then she leaves us, walking over to the tables where the audience is seated.

It takes a minute for Jax to recover before he speaks under his breath while watching her walk away. "I like that one."

Lexa looks around the room, then glances at the entrance to the club before checking her watch. Her content expression slips for a moment.

"Don't start yet." I speak over my shoulder to Jax as I head to the front doors.

When Alexandra looks at me from across the room, I splay my fingers, telling her to give me five minutes.

I get the impression she's expecting there to be more people here—or she's waiting for someone. We've done presentations where some attendees are hesitant to join for one reason or another, and I slip outside to see if there is anyone else.

There is.

A woman stands on the curb.

I know it's a woman because I'm an ass man, and her yoga pants are doing her all kinds of favors from back here.

Normally, it would be harder to tell her intentions, but it is Sunday night, and no other businesses on the block are open.

Her back is to me. The hood on her sweatshirt covers her head, but her hesitation is visible in her body language. She waffles between straightening her spine to steel herself and taking a step farther away from the building.

I wonder for a moment what she's struggling with.

Maybe she thinks she won't learn anything, and this would be time wasted. Maybe there's something triggering about our information. Or maybe she's here out of some sense of obligation, and she doesn't want to disappoint someone.

Whatever it is, she isn't here because she *wants* to be.

As soon as she pulls her keys out of her pocket, I know she's made a decision, and it's the wrong one.

"You look like you're about to make a run for it." I take another step, my voice low.

She startles like I thought she would, and I take a half step back, raising my hands to show her I'm not a threat. Her wide eyes meet mine, and I nod my head toward the door to Ravenous. "I'm here for the presentation."

Her eyes bounce from me to the door and back. "Do you work *here?*"

Her word choice just gave her away. If she wasn't here to enter the sex club, she would have distanced herself and said "there."

"Something like that. The presentation is about to start."

A cab pulls up to the curb, and we pause our conversation as the door opens and three women step out, straightening their dresses before they walk between us and head into the club.

None of them pay the woman any attention. All eyes are on me as the women smile and saunter by. One of them greets me with a sultry "hey." My smile is curt but polite, and they keep moving.

Their voices are cut off abruptly when the front door closes, and I glance back at the woman standing near me.

She's looking down her front at her own clothing, and she mutters, "I'm underdressed."

I barely catch it.

I'm convinced she's trying to give her excuse a voice, to test it out in the hopes that it will be enough to get her out of entering those doors.

"The club isn't open for business. There's no dress code. I'd say you're dressed exactly as you should be."

I'm not enabling the excuse she's trying to manufacture, and that earns me a scowl, but she recovers quickly, which sends a surge through me.

"Really? Are you saying that this"—she points to her outfit—"is the same as that?" She points to the door to indicate the three women dressed in tight skirts that barely cover their asses.

A smirk spreads across my face.

There is always a time for *that*, but right now I'm more interested in what *this* is attempting to hide.

I shrug, lowering my chin and tilting my head in her direction. "It's no fun for the wolf if the bunny just covers itself in blood and wanders into the field shouting, 'Eat me, eat me!'"

She leans back, raising her eyebrows with a confident grin. "But the wolf will still eat the bunny, won't it?"

Touché.

This conversation just got interesting.

Sensing the hint of an invitation, I take a tentative step toward her.

She holds her place, but her shoulders drop just enough to draw my attention. My own predator instincts spark at her attempt to hold her ground.

I'm about to tell her that it will, but the wolf won't be completely satisfied if there is no chase, when the front door to Ravenous opens.

A relieved Lexa looks between us, her gaze landing on the woman. "There you are. I thought maybe you"—her eyes flicker over to me—"got caught in traffic."

It's Sunday night.

There is no traffic.

Whoever this woman is, Lexa was worried she wasn't going to show, but she's covered her doubt.

"No. I'm good." My little mystery easily pivots away from our conversation.

Alexandra gestures to me. "I see you've met one of our presenters." Then she meets my eyes. "Marcus, this is my friend Elle. Elle, this is Marcus Wolfe."

I turn my attention to catch Elle mouthing the word "wolf" before she gives her head a shake.

I'm quiet for a few seconds before lifting my hand to shake hers. For some reason, I want her complete attention on me when I touch her.

Then she looks at me, holding a pleasant expression on her face. Her hands are slender in my own, her cool fingers a welcome relief against my heated skin.

She attempts to pull her hand back.

I tighten my grip, and her expression cracks just a little—just enough that the thrill of a tiny victory rumbles through my chest.

I hold her hand in mine as I turn my attention to Alexandra. "I was just telling Elle that we should get inside before my brother starts the show without us."

I'm with Elle on the curb, and we have another ten feet before we reach Lexa at the door. Lexa nods and steps inside, and the door slowly closes behind her.

I carefully turn my attention back to Elle.

She's fixated on me.

Her expression has changed, and she's sizing me up.

Now she's cautious.

I extend my free hand toward Ravenous. When she attempts to walk inside, I tug her back. Leaning into her, I lower my voice. "Wolves crave the hunt. You would do well to remember that."

The rattled look that crosses her face as her step falters hits me like a sucker punch.

I hit a nerve.

What's more surprising is my reaction to her response.

She's an interesting combination of confidence and demurity, and it turns out it's a combination that piques my curiosity, which isn't easily done these days.

But I'm not here to sate my own cravings. Ravenous might be the place for it, but it certainly isn't the time.

I release her and wait for her to take a few more steps, putting some space between us before I follow her inside.

As I cross the room to join Jax at the display table, I watch from the corner of my eye as Elle joins Lexa at her couch. She reaches for a sealed water bottle that the staff placed on all of the tables beforehand.

Jax looks up from his task, asking if we're ready to begin. I take the opportunity to look just over his shoulder as I answer. Now I have a clear line to Elle. A waitress steps over, seemingly to ask if she wants anything to drink, and she smiles warmly when Elle shakes her head.

Then I catch Lexa looking straight at us. I recover quickly, nodding at her and telling her we can start.

Lexa stands to introduce us. She's immaculately dressed for business. She commands attention from the women and two men seated around her, and she exudes confidence.

We've given her some background on us, credentials she can share with the group. As she starts with a short history of our security company, I scan the crowd.

Most of the women in attendance have dressed up. Some have even gone so far as to wear their regular club outfits and high heels—which is going to be awkward if any of them want to try the self-defense moves we plan on showing them after our presentation tonight.

As she talks about Ravenous's commitment to a safe environment, many of the women size us up. I imagine some are trying to work out if we can help them; others smile back, angling their bodies to show off whatever they think is their best feature.

When Lexa is done, it's Jax who steps into the middle of the room to thank her for having us here tonight. He makes some small talk, then he starts to go into an overview of what we want to discuss.

When the attention has faded from me, I casually walk around the room in plain sight. Laughter builds when Jax says something funny, and I continue to slip among the audience as he distracts them.

Jax follows me as I walk, drawing everyone's attention off of me as he flirts and works the room.

I hit all of my marks.

By the time he's halfway done with his spiel, I have two cell phones and a wallet that I managed to lift from women around the room. And that isn't the worst of it.

The worst is yet to come.

I make my way over to Lexa's table, determined to make the club owner my last victim—yet again—but I slow in my step as I approach.

While Lexa is focused on Jax and listening to his every word, Elle is sitting quietly with her arms crossed. Her eyes are leveled on me.

She doesn't flinch when we enter our staring contest.

There's something about the haunted look on her face that sends a cold shiver down my spine, and I turn back to my brother, making my way to the front without the victory of my last victim as he finishes. "And here's my brother and business partner, Marcus, to prove my point. What do you have?"

I hold up the cell phones and wallet, and hushed voices fill the room. I hear a couple of gasps. I spend the next few minutes telling everyone how important protecting their property and their space is. This is also the time I need to make my point. While I only took a few items, I hit every table here.

Every table except one. My failure gnaws at me.

I steal a glance at Elle once more.

I consider myself an expert at reading people. Hell, Jax used to work as a profiler before we went into business together. I can tell who is here because they want to be and who is here because they have to be. I can even assess my chances with most of the women in the room, if I was interested in hooking up.

But I can't read her.

Elle remains still, observing me without any discernible expression. She's giving nothing of her thoughts or emotions away.

I clear my throat, and my head, and get back to my point.

"I'm going to ask everyone who has a drink to take a sip." I pause for a few seconds, and everyone lifts their glasses. Then I ask, "Whose drink tastes like salt? Don't worry; your drink is harmless, and it will be replaced, but please raise your hand."

Gasps and groans sound around the room as hands raise one by one. "Now look around." The room goes quiet as everyone realizes just how many drinks I could have drugged if I meant harm.

One woman's eyes bug out as she stares at her glass, no doubt remembering how I "accidentally" knocked her clutch off the table as I passed by. When she looked down to check that it was still closed, I slipped the dose into her cocktail.

Now, when I look over to Lexa's table, there's a hint of something in Elle's smirk.

A thrill runs through me when I recognize her expression.

I've exceeded her expectations of me.

Personal security is an in-depth topic with many facets, but we focus on the basics for the next hour. This session was designed for group participation, and most of the room is eager to play the guinea pig for demonstrations.

Elle observes the entire time.

She doesn't raise her hand to answer questions or ask any of her own, but I get the sense she's listened to every single thing we said tonight.

We touch on many subjects, but Elle remains unfazed, making it difficult to read her—which only makes me more determined as the minutes pass.

Alexandra, on the other hand, gives something away when we turn our attention to one particular subject: stalking.

It's one I usually don't spend much time on because there's only a small fraction of people who take behaviors like that too far. Most often, it ends at harassment.

But when I bring up the subject, I notice two things.

The first is how Lexa steals a glance at Elle with a sympathetic smile before quickly looking back at Jax and me.

If it wasn't for that, I might have missed it.

The second thing I notice is how Elle seems to close herself off even more than before. She tightens her arms, which are again crossed over her chest, and reclines further into her seat. Her eyes burn into my own when I look directly at her, but there is no warmth.

I get the message loud and clear: *move along.*

There are moments when I wish I couldn't read people. This feels like an intrusion.

I turn my attention away from their table for the rest of the presentation.

By the time we are wrapping up, Elle has relaxed. When I scan the room to ask if there are any group questions before we break, I find her and Lexa huddled forward in casual conversation.

We hold ongoing self-defense classes at one of our locations, and I step to our display table, inviting anyone with questions to come up.

I nod at Lexa, who stands to wrap it up and thank the group for coming out on a Sunday night. As she speaks, Elle stands as well, making her way to the exit without looking back.

She's leaving.

I'm about to excuse myself when a group of women surround the table, grabbing at pamphlets and asking questions.

There are too many people, and this topic is too important, and this isn't about me. Someone might learn something tonight that could save their life one day, and I owe it to the one I lost to be here for them.

My own need comes second to that.

I glance at Lexa, who is all smiles, as she gives me a thumbs-up. She's satisfied with our night.

I find it interesting that Elle watched me like a hawk all night, except for when she left. The moment she chose to scurry off, she didn't look back once, and I wonder if it was because she knew I'd be standing here, challenging her to stay.

It doesn't matter anyway.

I know how to find her when I'm ready.

And this Wolfe definitely prefers the hunt.

CHAPTER 4
ELLE

I look forward to Sunday afternoons, and a sunny, warm Sunday afternoon in May is as close to perfection as one can get.

Sundays belong to me. Or maybe I should say: I belong to Sundays.

Every other day of the week, I am tethered to something else. It's mostly my company and its responsibilities that claim my attention.

From Monday to Friday, I am Elle Sinclair, CEO of Swank Events.

Saturday during the day is spent running errands, cleaning, chores—all of those adult things we wish we were too rich to do but, alas, are not. And since I have the best accounts management staff in Chicago, my Friday and Saturday nights are filled with exclusive event after exclusive event.

It's all about rubbing elbows, growing our client list, and representing Swank. Our clients like to know that when they work with one of us, they work with all of us—even the owner.

It's hardly work, as I see it. I have an automatic ticket to the year's most exclusive events.

I usually stay in the background and enjoy the party, but I do show up. I smile for the camera, check in with my staff and their clients, then spend the rest of the night enjoying myself.

Tough life, I know.

Don't get me wrong: I am Elle Sinclair. She isn't a persona. She is who I am—most of the time.

Except Sundays.

On Sundays, I'm my whole self.

I'm the same person, but I get to shed that practiced smile that tells the world I have my shit together when sometimes I don't.

I release myself from the responsibilities of my company. I kick off my shoes, so to speak, and I get to turn my phone off, disconnect from the digital world, and reconnect with, well, me.

I focus on the things I would normally miss: the sound of my footsteps on the pavement, the birds singing in the mature trees that line my street, their branches growing into each other and forming a canopy over the road, someone practicing piano in one of the apartments in the four-story building across the street.

Wolves crave the hunt. You would do well to remember that.

Those words invade my thoughts, and my next step is off. My foot hits the sidewalk a fraction of a second before I expect it to, and I half trip but recover quickly.

Marcus's words impose on my me-time the way they have so often over the past week. The guy definitely knows how to make a lasting impression, because our interaction was brief, yet I'm still thinking about him.

The way his voice dropped into a low timbre when we seemed to cross some invisible threshold still sends a shiver through me, and those piercing eyes that held me in place even though my heart felt like cowering away...

The man is dangerous. I'm just not sure in what way.

When I take a deep breath to clear my head and return to my self-care, I catch a hint of cocoa on the wind. It's rare that the smell from the chocolate company reaches all of the way out here. I instinctively turn my head to take a second whiff, then realize I've walked a whole block without realizing it.

I switch my bag of groceries from one hand to the other when an ache starts in my shoulder. I wasn't expecting so much fresh produce at the outdoor market today since it's still early in the season, but I got everything I need to make a couple of quiches so I'll have leftovers for days.

If my main-floor tenant, Barb, were here, I could drop one down to her, but she won't be back from her cruise for another five weeks since she decided to tack on an extended visit with her kids and grandkids on her way back.

Maybe I'll share it with her cat, Allie, so named because she was found in our back alley, all skin and bone, hiding behind a garbage can as a kitten a few years ago. Now she's an indoor cat who hasn't gotten the message, as she always tries to run out when Barb opens the door. Allie doesn't make it far because there is a shared foyer, then a separate back door. Most times, the cat ends up meowing outside of my door at the top of the stairs. Regardless, I'm sure I'll be in for an escape attempt when I stop in later to spend some time with her and water the plants.

I reach my free hand out to my side, catching my fingers in each metal slat of the fence and letting them *thump, thump, thump* to the next. The steady, rhythmic sound matches the beating of my heart.

Nestled between two three-story walk-ups is my house and the little parcel of yard I call home. The small patch of tulips I planted last year are blooming, and they make me smile every time I see them. They were a gift that Daniel organized with my team last year, and it's a shame they don't last longer.

I follow the stepping-stone pathway around the side of the house to the back entrance, which is technically my front door, then remove my shoes, leaving them downstairs in our shared mudroom before taking the stairs up to my home on the second floor.

A breeze carries the fresh smell of cut grass into the room, and I lift the cloth bag to the island in my kitchen, careful not to break the eggs at the bottom.

A cat meows. The cry is out of place, and I pause, mid-step, between the counter and my fridge and swivel my head to listen.

I'm used to hearing Allie's odd meow through the vents, but this sounds—closer.

Four steps take me into my living room, and I freeze and wait for the sound to come again. When I hear nothing, I meow, mimicking the sound I just heard, and wait once more.

There it is.

A meow clearly registers from behind my couch.

I glance up to my open window. The screen is still intact, so it couldn't be a stray.

I close the distance to the wall and slide the couch forward, and Allie perks up as soon as she sees me.

"Wha—how on earth did you get all of the way up here?"

I reach down, scoop her up, and bounce on my feet to soothe her. As she tries to bury her face in my hair, she purrs like an engine.

Spinning slowly in a circle, I examine my windows, vents, then the door to my place, which was shut and locked when I came in.

This cat is resourceful, and she must be missing her owner.

I'll have to spend some time in Barb's place below me to see if there is a hole I'll need to fix. For now, I carry the cat to the kitchen. I search my cupboard for a tin of tuna while she nuzzles her face along my jawline, meowing passionately. I imagine she's trying to tell me how she got into my locked apartment, and it sounds like it's quite the story.

I set her down, then place a plate in front of her. As soon as I straighten to stand, a cool shiver runs over me, standing the little hairs along my arm on end.

The only way up here from the main floor is up the stairs and through my locked door—I know this.

When I look around my apartment again, it's with a sense of unease. I stand still, in complete silence, my attention bouncing from my books on the shelf to the remote on my coffee table, then over to the blanket tossed on the couch.

I question if I left my knit throw lying as it is or if the door to my bedroom was shut when I left earlier today.

I can't remember.

It isn't until a satisfied Allie rubs up against my calf that I snap out of my haze, telling myself that Greg is serving time for what he's done, and this is nothing more than me scaring myself over nothing.

Still, I dig my hand into the pocket of my jacket and pull out my phone, powering it on and opening my contacts.

If I'm not by myself in my home right now, I want someone on the other end of the line to hear me scream.

Lexa picks up on the second ring. "Elle?"

She knows about my alone time on Sundays, so I expect the worry in her tone.

"I'm fine—um, I'm just returning your calls. This week got away from me."

"But this is your—"

"It's fine." I wrap my free hand around a chef knife and

slide it out of the block. "I'm fine." Padding as softly as I can, I cross the room, heading toward my bedroom. "I'm sorry it took me so long to get back to you. What's up?"

"I was hoping we could chat about the personal safety event last weekend. I'm thinking about asking the guys if they would do something a couple of times a year, for our new members, and I wanted to know what you thought about it."

I keep my tone relaxed as I sidestep around the foot of my bed and check the empty space between the bed and the wall.

Nothing.

"I thought they had a lot of helpful information. It looked like the crowd sure ate them up." The memory of the hungry looks on some of the women's faces makes my stomach knot.

There's silence on the line before she speaks. "It didn't help that they were easy to look at."

She's waiting for me to bite.

It just so happens I need her on the line while I check the rest of my place, so: "What are you getting at, Lexa?"

I lower myself to my knees and lift the bed skirt with the tip of my knife. Logically, I know no one can crawl under my bed— there is only six inches of space between the floor and the frame—but I won't sleep tonight if I don't make sure.

Nothing.

The pitch in her voice starts off high as she pretends to be casual. "Oh, nothing. It's just that you and Marcus Wolfe seemed to be deep in conversation when I found you outside."

Ravenous is what it is because Lexa is extremely perceptive.

"And the way he watched you as you left..."

I pause in my kneeling position while that little nugget buries itself into my head.

I didn't look back when I walked out of Ravenous. I bowed out before the self-defense portion, like a chicken, because

Marcus knocked me down a peg, and I didn't look back for that exact reason.

Wolves crave the hunt.

I liked the way he looked at me, as though he had caught the scent of something he wanted to taste. He touched on a piece of me so secret that I don't even allow myself to entertain the fantasy anymore.

"Elle?"

I push myself up to standing, then face my closet.

Lexa's goading me, and we both know it. I gloss over her insinuation and return to her previous question. "Both him and his brother did an amazing job. You should ask them if they can offer those self-defense classes at Ravenous once a month. I bet they could charge whatever their full price is and still have a full house."

I reach out and tug the closet door open.

Only clothes.

"Very well." I get the impression Lexa's response is more about my poor evasion techniques than about my suggestion. "There's something else I wanted to talk about—this is business related. I'm thinking about hiring Swank for an event."

I stop mid-step toward my bathroom. "Really?"

"Yes. We've been doing our new-member nights for a while now, and interest has dwindled. I think I'm exhausting our current reach, and I want to hire Swank to help us find a new pool of members. With a second Ravenous opening soon, I think this would kill two birds with one stone. What do you think?"

I turn on the bathroom light and step back, looking into the empty room through a large glass pane in my barn-style door. I don't need to open it, and I turn my attention back to my living room.

The only other place is my second bathroom and the closet near the front door.

"I think that's a great idea. Swank would love to handle this for you. I already have a few ideas."

"Wonderful. Do you think we could set something up to discuss it this week?"

The little bathroom off of my living room is already open, and I peek in.

Empty.

"One moment." I open the front closet, and there's nothing out of place. The tension runs out of my shoulders, and I relax them away from my ears. "Just grabbing a pen," I fib.

With my home clear, I walk to the front door and lock myself in, then walk over to the couch and sit down. The breeze from the open window feels good against my heated skin. "I think we're pretty full this week. We have back-to-back events next Friday and Saturday, but next week opens up. How about midweek next week? Let's say either the twenty-second or twenty-third? Daniel is wrapping up with his client, so I'll have him join me for the presentation, then I'll hand you over to him, if that's okay?"

"Absolutely. I trust your judgment."

"Great. I'll message Nat to set it up. You'll probably hear from her in the morning. This'll be fun."

"I agree. I'm looking forward to watching you in action."

The line goes dead, and I'm left staring at the face of my phone with an unsettling feeling that Lexa's final words hold more than one meaning.

It's been a few months since I stepped through the front doors to our office. I was never a nine-to-five kind of guy.

Out of the three of us, Kate is here the most. She's a people person, and she enjoys the office banter and team-building bullshit. You know, those office meetings where everyone stands around playing trust games and catching each other, games that only prove you can follow directions. Then they serve doughnuts, and all the team-building goes out the window when there's only one cream-filled doughnut in the bunch and everyone scrambles to get it first.

Jaxon keeps a secondary office here, but he's rarely in. He does a lot of consulting work, and he jokes that his main office is his car.

Our rogue brother, Cillian, is a silent investor only.

I have an office here, but there's nothing in it. I think Kate is hoping I'll decide to join her like I used to, but I'm not ready to be here. We have a dedicated group of department heads that run our operations, so I'm free to handle my own business for the time being.

Except today.

It's rare that Jax calls a meeting and demands my presence, so my curiosity has been piqued.

I push through the doors to our conference room and find my brother placing a few notebooks and pens around the table. "Hey, man."

He looks up and smiles before pointing to the seat beside him. There's only one other seat with a pad of paper in front of it.

He unbuttons his jacket and sits in his chair. "Alexandra Loren from Ravenous called Kate and booked a meeting. She wants to speak with us about an opportunity to work together." My brows furrow, creasing my forehead, and I glare at him to give me more to go on. This sounds like a regular client intake meeting. There's no need to call me in for this. "I thought you'd be a good buffer. You two hit it off, and I may have come off a little strong at the—um—club."

He clears his throat.

Why would he care how he came off if—*oh*.

OH!

I suck the inside of my cheek between my teeth and bite down to stop myself from grinning as the doors open and Jax shoots to his feet.

"And here they are." Kate smiles at both of us as she steps in and clears the entrance so Lexa can join us.

"Alexandra, you remember Jaxon and Marcus. I'm going to leave you with them. It's nice to see you again."

Jax and I wait in silence while Kate excuses herself, closing the door behind her. Lexa approaches the table, taking the seat in front of the only other pad of paper.

I offer Lexa a drink, and she scans the table as she asks for some water. Jax slides his chair back to get it for her, but I interrupt him, telling him I'll grab it so they can get the meeting started.

I take my time, deciding to pour a cup of coffee for myself that I won't end up drinking. Then I casually add cream and sugar, which I don't usually add, and stir slowly as I listen in on Lexa and Jax talking about our presentation at Ravenous almost a couple of weeks ago.

Has it been that long?

When I think about that night, I think about Elle. She's been on my mind, and I was tempted—on more than one occasion—to call Lexa and ask about her.

I return to the table, handing Lexa a bottle of water then setting my coffee mug down.

Jax lifts his pen. "So tell us how we can help you."

"I'd like to hire security for an event in a few weeks. The evening is designed to draw new members to Ravenous. I've done them in the past on a smaller scale, and always at the club. Usually invitation is by word of mouth, but I am hoping to expand our community by reaching new members because we are opening a second club in a couple of months."

Jax finishes writing down his thoughts before asking, "Why do you feel you need security for this event?"

Lexa glances my way for a moment, and I catch a hint of camaraderie. She feels, between my brother and me, I would be the one to understand what she's trying to get at.

She would be right.

"The...dynamic and...*freedoms* Ravenous offers its members require them to place themselves into extremely vulnerable situations, and I take that responsibility very seriously. Any time we open our doors to new members, we run the risk of exposing our community to—"

"Predators," I offer.

Lexa nods. "Yes." Jax returns to his notepad to jot something down, and Lexa waits a few seconds longer before she continues, "So, having security at the event to make sure no one gets out of hand, and having your expertise in possibly weeding out any applicants who may not be...suitable for membership would be helpful."

I haven't written anything down yet. This is fairly straightforward to me. Also, I'm not a notetaker.

"Tell us more about this event."

"I've hired Swank, a promotions company, to handle the details, and I'm meeting with them next Thursday afternoon to lay out some initial plans. I'd like you to attend with me, to bring you in at the start." Lexa glances between the two of us, but her gaze lingers a little longer on mine.

I wonder if Elle will be attending Ravenous's upcoming event as well since she's Lexa's friend.

"Having security for something like this is a good idea."

The corner of Lexa's lip twitches up at my brother's compliment, but he doesn't notice, as his gaze is on the sentence he's writing. "I'm able to attend the meeting with you. I'm sure we'll have a list of questions of our own as well."

Jax writes "Thursday afternoon Swank" on his notepad and smiles at Lexa.

She returns the warm gesture, but I narrow in on her hand. Her wine-polished nails pick at the corner of the pad in front of her, and I sense there's something coming.

"Marcus, are you able to attend the meeting as well?"

I point at Jax. "My brother can bring everyone here up to speed when he gets back to the office."

"Or *you* could go to the meeting," Jax offers.

I sense the rejection he feels from here, and confusion sets in.

Lexa shakes her head. "No. What I mean to say is—I would like that very much, Jaxon. But I'd like both of you to attend, if it isn't asking too much."

"I'm not sure you need both of us at"—I glance for the name on Jax's sheet of paper—"Swank."

I'm really not a meeting kind of guy, and if this is something Jax is willing to take on, then I'm happy.

"Of course." Lexa reaches for the bottle of water, twists off the cap, and takes a sip.

Jax shifts his gaze from Lexa to me and back again before breaking the awkward silence. "I can ask Kate to join us. She can draw up a list of everything you require from us, and we can work out the financial part of it before you go today."

Lexa nods her head as she digs into her purse, pulling out a planner and opening it on the table.

That's my cue. It's time I bow out and give Jax some time alone to talk with Lexa. I slide my chair back and stand, nodding to my brother, and Lexa's eyes go wide when I announce I am excusing myself for the remainder of the meeting.

I'm five steps away from the door when she speaks. "Are you sure you won't reconsider meeting with me at Swank next week?"

I square myself on her.

I'm missing something.

"I have every faith that my brother can handle it on his own. But I appreciate the invitation." I nod, then turn, and my hand is almost on the door handle when Lexa speaks again.

"That's unfortunate. Elle will miss seeing you again. You two seemed to hit it off at Ravenous."

Hold up.

I'm so close to the door, I follow the pattern of the dark grain in the wood as I consider my next move.

Taking a deep breath, I turn back to the two at the table.

Jax looks puzzled.

Lexa won't meet my gaze. Instead, she takes a sip of her water and glances over her little day planner as though her words were inconsequential.

She knows they are not.

"And why would I see Elle at the meeting at Swank next week?" My careful smile hides my intentions.

"She owns the company," she answers matter-of-factly, then feigns ignorance as she looks between us. "Didn't I mention that earlier?"

Both she and I know damn well she didn't.

Jax, bless his stupid-ass heart, shakes his head as though her question wasn't rhetorical.

Have I wanted to see Elle again? Yes.

Have I stalked her to get more information on her? No.

That's not my style. I need to be invited in.

There is currently nothing between us that would warrant me invading her privacy, so I know nothing outside of her first name—yet.

Do I want to know more? I'm starting to believe I do.

Like an idiot, I'm still standing here when I excused myself minutes ago. I'm validating Lexa's assumptions just by breathing at this point.

Jaxon remains still; however, he's looking at me in a new light. He never noticed Elle or my reaction to her at Ravenous because Lexa consumed his attention.

I exhale my frustration in one long breath. "On second thought, having everyone there would avoid any—confusion."

Lexa nods, a sneaky smile stretching across her lips. "It would."

"Jax, text me the information when you have it." I smile once more at Lexa. "I'll see what I can do."

When I turn to leave, for real this time, I swear I hear Lexa say "I'm sure you will" under her breath.

Nat stands from her desk and matches my pace as I step off the elevator and head for my office.

I've been putting out fires since I arrived this morning. The most recent being the transportation of the rescue animals to the venue on Saturday night and three cancellations for our charity date auction that is taking place alongside them.

I had to cash in a favor to fill the auction spots. Daniel was able to secure me the quarterback from his client's team, and I just got back from pleading with the anchor of the six o'clock news, so we are only down to one, which shouldn't be too hard to fill.

"You haven't eaten yet—here." Nat grabs the files and my purse out of my hands, exchanging them for a deli sandwich. She opens the door for me as I inhale my first bite.

"I don't know what I'd do without you, Nat. I'd starve to death—that's for sure." Another bite. "What's on the calendar?" I ask as I lower to my seat behind my desk.

"Your three o'clock is here. I put them in the corner room. Daniel is with them to start. It's Ravenous."

It's three minutes after three.

Dammit.

I forgot.

Today has gotten away from me, and Lexa slipped my mind. I told her I would take the lead before handing them off.

My ass doesn't fully flatten against my chair before I'm standing again.

"Walk with me, Nat."

I take another big bite, estimating the time it takes for me to make it down the hall with a mouth full of food before I have to hand the rest of the sandwich over.

I swallow just as I reach the door and glance down my front, tugging at the edges of my blouse to straighten it out.

The lights at the back are already out when I enter, and Daniel glances over, smiling in my direction.

"Here she is. Ms. Loren tells me you already know each other, but we can turn the lights on to meet—"

I step into the path of the projector, blinded by the light. "It's alright, Daniel. Alexandra, I apologize for being late. It was —unavoidable. This is my assistant, Nat Wheeler. We'll continue."

Alexandra says hello from the shadows, and I catch the outline of more than one person, making a mental note to revisit introductions when our presentation is over.

"Great. We were just covering some of our tried-and-true event outlines, as well as a few of our newer ideas that have been gaining traction among social influencers. Would you like to speak to that?"

I had already discussed with Daniel that I would lead most of the meeting before handing it off to him since Lexa and I have a personal relationship. He steps to the side, takes a seat, and grants me the floor. Nat joins him.

"Thank you, Daniel. Yes. We have tried a few new tactics at our events this year that have been received well on social media." I fall into step as I present a couple new ideas that made our past events shine, then finish with, "But we recognize that Ravenous is a different beast. You don't want to go viral, because going viral draws everyone into your orbit. But you do want to be noticed by those who would be a fit for your members. It's for this reason that we recommend against a masquerade ball or any type of event that allows people to hide who they are. It is also our recommendation that you allot a certain number of tickets to your current members at a special discounted price, to reward your long-standing and committed core. But not just any members—these would be your elite community. Those who have a long and positive record and who speak highly and respectfully about Ravenous. This should hinder anyone who wants to lurk in the shadows or use the event for nefarious reasons, as it is harder to hide in the light."

I take a step to the side, grab a water bottle off the table, crack the seal, and take a sip before I keep going.

"We have a database of social media influencers we work with, and there are a couple on the list who focus on sex positivity. They are staunch supporters of the communities they speak to, and I would limit the invites to only them, under the agreement that this is an exclusive event and the location is not to be mentioned on social media until the day after the event. Stressing that this is a safety measure to protect those in attendance will go a long way in driving excitement for the evening, as well as portraying Ravenous as the safe environment we all know it is. The exclusivity will also drive a level of excitement, and it may encourage further interest even after the event is over."

The room remains silent as I list a few examples of places where we would promote the evening, then I finish with a list of three venues that fit their needs with dates I know are available.

I take a step back from the light to give my eyes a break and ask if there are any questions.

There's always that couple of seconds of awkward silence. I remain still, my smile on my face, waiting for everything I've covered to be absorbed and for the first question to come.

I'm about to add a couple of suggestions for catering when someone at the back of the room clears their throat.

I expect it to be Lexa, but it's a man who speaks.

"I think it would benefit Ms. Loren to work with an agency that understands the nature of the lifestyle that her company caters to. Is anyone here a member of Ravenous?"

What?

Our personal lives have no bearing on our professional lives.

If Lexa wasn't my closest friend, I would have drawn my lines right here and now. But she is, so I stall as Daniel turns on one of the overhead lights, illuminating the room. The blood drains from my head when one of the men with her leans forward in his seat with an oh-so-smug expression plastered all over his gorgeous face.

Dammit—not gorgeous. I mean infuriating.

Wolves crave the hunt.

A painful silence fills the room as the memory of Marcus's words burns through my psyche and kindles a fire I thought had long since extinguished.

Alexandra and Marcus's brother, who was with him a

couple of weeks ago at the club, sit in silence, waiting for my response.

"I assure you, Mr. Wolfe, that Swank is more than capable of managing this event for Ravenous regardless of our *private* lives." I hope my emphasis on that one word gets him off the subject.

"Please, call me Marcus, Elle."

The entire room swivels their heads toward Marcus.

He has an arrogant air of confidence in the way he leans back in his chair, making himself comfortable.

I smile sweetly. "Please, call me Ms. Sinclair, Mr. Wolfe."

Everyone in the room turns their attention back to me.

Another beat of quiet hangs between us, and it lasts one second too long before Nat perks up and tries to be helpful.

"One of us attends a different club. Swank is more than capable of representing Ravenous." She nods at me, grinning like she just did me a solid. I half expect her to give me a thumbs-up.

My eyes bug out, and her bright smile falters when she sees the look of horror on my face as I shake my head curtly.

I've lost control of the meeting.

I can't even remember the last time this happened.

Marcus is like a machine, and all at once his wheels start working. He shifts his attention between Daniel and Nat before deciding to narrow his gaze on Daniel, who quickly bows under the pressure, shaking his head and silently telling him he isn't a member of a sex club.

My face heats under Marcus's scrutiny as he holds my attention.

He's picking us off.

If it were anyone else, I'd be furious. But there is something about being noticed and challenged by this man that makes my skin feel too tight for my body.

While holding my stare, Marcus directs his question to my assistant. "Tell me, Nat. Which club do you belong to?"

A wolfish smirk tugs at the corner of his lips as she struggles to answer.

She chokes on a series of nonstarter responses, and I assume it's because she's just realized her response will out me. I'm the lone person left standing in the room.

Nat knows a lot about my past, but I never told her that I stopped going to that club after everything with Greg. My situation resolved itself, so there was no further point in bringing it up, and she respects my privacy—unlike the man sitting in front of me.

There's no point in waiting for my assistant to try to dig herself out of this.

"My personal life has no bearing on what Swank can do for Ravenous, Mr. Wolfe." I raise my eyebrow and loosely cross my arms.

My answer doesn't deter him in the slightest.

"It probably doesn't, but if you are the one who understands the nature of Ravenous better than anyone else in this room, why are you not the one who is overseeing this event?"

I meet Lexa's eyes. Her lips are pinched together to stifle her amusement.

She set me up for this...*for him.*

"I oversee all of Swank's events, Mr. Wolfe. Daniel has already started setting up the logistics for the evening, and I assure you, he's perfectly capable of handling anything Ravenous needs." I glance at Daniel, who nods once to back me up.

If I clenched my teeth together any tighter, they'd shatter.

I narrow my eyes at Lexa, who clears her throat before she

agrees with me and tells Daniel she is looking forward to working with him.

"That just leaves the two of us then, Ms. Sinclair."

"Pardon me?"

"Before you arrived, Lexa had just finished explaining to Daniel that Ravenous hired our security firm for the event. Having him handle all of the logistics will free up your time to work with me on the...finer details."

I've barely spoken to this man, and somehow he's already figured out how to knock me off my game.

I fist my hands at my sides.

"I—" Warning bells in my head give me pause when Marcus's smile slips into something sinister. This man is ready for whatever I'm about to say. I'm not even sure where this is going, but there's something in his expression that tells me he is, and he's one hundred percent ready for it. This isn't the fight I want to take on today, and I won't give Marcus what he is looking for: a willing opponent. "Of course. Let's move on. Daniel?"

I lower my gaze and take a step back, turning the floor over to Daniel, who steps up to review our next steps.

Just like the moment I decided to leave Ravenous before the night was over, I don't dare look at Marcus.

Daniel switches slides on the projector, and I turn my attention to the board, but I don't see the bullet points or the words. My mind revisits the night I met Marcus, conjuring the vulnerable emotions our conversation brought out in me. Heat travels up my spine when I remember the way his eyes bore into me, like he could see every depraved thought floating around in my head.

The remaining lights in the room come on, pulling me from my thoughts as Daniel wraps up our presentation.

The Wolfe brothers stand with Alexandra, and Daniel

circles the table to shake her hand. Nat joins me in my spot off to the side of the room.

She lowers her voice. "I am so sorry. I—you know me and conflict. I get nervous. That guy is intense. I'd sell out my grandma in a heartbeat if he looked at me like that for too long."

I chuckle under my breath. "Yeah. I know the feeling."

Lexa excuses herself from the group and walks in my direction, so I tell Nat she can head back to her desk. The look she flashes as she leaves is a grateful one.

Lexa takes her place. "That went well."

"You could have warned me you were bringing—*backup*."

"I didn't think it was necessary. I mean, it's not like you guys are interested in each other, and you are both professionals in your own fields."

I side-eye her, only to find her side-eyeing me right back.

"He can call my office if he has any questions. I won't see him again until the event in a few weeks. I can manage that." I smile, and Lexa winces.

"Oh, right. You were late to the meeting." She bites her lip, telling me I'm not going to like what she says next. "Daniel mentioned Swank still had some space left at a charity function this weekend, and—well, Marcus thought it would be a great idea to see how your team handles their events up close."

I look around the room, only to be captured in Marcus's leveled stare. He makes no effort to look away, even though I've clearly caught him staring. Those are the eyes of a predator who knows, without a doubt, what his next meal is.

"Lexa," I warn.

"We bought tickets. We'll see you on Saturday."

CHAPTER 7
ELLE

Fashionably off time is how I roll when it comes to our company events. I'm not late, I'm not on time, and I'm not the one in charge of the client, so I'm definitely not early.

I've learned that there are people who like to go over heads and right to the top of the food chain when every little thing goes wrong, and I've trained my staff well enough to know they can handle anything that pops up. If I show up to our company events too early, I undermine my team.

Julie worked tirelessly on this charity event, and this is her night to shine.

I time my arrival so I miss the first surge of people. There is no line, and almost everyone has found their seats.

The ballroom is alive with the hum of chatter mixed with the occasional yips from the dogs off to the side of the room. The music is low, as requested by our clients, so as not to upset the animals, which will only be here for the first portion of the night.

The event serves drinks and hors d'oeuvres, and the tables

are low, lounge-style, and surrounded by padded chairs instead of dining chairs to accommodate the evening's casual vibe. A few people look up from their spots as I scan the room. A couple of them wave to catch my attention, and I smile, making a note to circle the room later.

"Am I glad to see you." Julie joins me with a flute of champagne in each hand. She offers me one, and I take it.

"Is everything okay?" I glance over to where I know her clients are seated. She set them up with the best table in the room.

We had a small blip when I had to knock their event date back, but, judging by the smiles on their faces, everything seems fine.

"Yes—I mean no—I mean yes." She waves her hand, gesturing around the room. "This is all great. The rescue shelter is doing amazing. Two of the animals already have adoption applications. There's just one little problem, but I have a solution."

"What's the problem? Do you need my help?"

I catch sight of Lexa, who's seated at a table with Daniel. They are deep in conversation as Daniel points around the room, no doubt telling her about how we work and what he has prepared for Ravenous's event next month.

"Well, it's just that a couple of people for the auction have had to cancel at the last minute. It's no big deal, but I need to find one more person willing to put themselves up, or that part of the evening looks really light. Considering Daniel got a couple of guys from the football team to auction off their time, I would hate to cancel it, because I think that will be the big moneymaker tonight." She hesitates for a hot minute before turning her gaze to hold mine. "So, yes—I kind of think you can help me with that."

I scan the room, looking for potential candidates. It

shouldn't be hard with the group we have here tonight. My gaze lands on a woman standing with the dogs, taking a selfie. "I could ask one of the influencers."

Julie follows my gaze to the woman posing with a shih tzu. "Actually, I already asked her, and she's going to auction off a day in her life. We are short on women. I was thinking...maybe..."

Her eyes meet mine.

"What?" Now I understand what she's getting at. "Noooo! No, no, no, no, no." Now I take a larger sip of champagne.

"Please? You would totally go for a huge amount." I'm not sure if I should be offended by what she's trying to say, so I chuckle, and Julie keeps on pitching. "I'm serious. Look." She points around the room. "There are so many people here who would love a moment of your time. You could auction off a free planning or coaching session, or a business dinner. And I mean..." She scans the height of me, sizing me up. "Damn, look at you in that dress. You are looking fine. There are a ton of eligible men here. You could totally—"

"Are you seriously trying to sell my body to a roomful of philanthropists right now?"

"No. I mean—unless you're okay with that?" She catches an eyeful of the expression on my face, then shakes her head furiously. "I mean, NO!"

I sigh into my glass of champagne. "*Shih tzu*," I mutter under my breath before giving Julie my answer. "Fine. But keep it business-related. You are auctioning off my *professional* time."

Julie jolts with joy, tells me I'm the best, then hurries away before I change my mind.

Daniel and Lexa have stopped talking, and I leave my empty glass on a nearby tray, then make my way to their table.

He stands when I approach, drawing Lexa's attention to me.

"Daniel—Lexa. It's so good to see you here."

She stands, hugging me and kissing my cheek. "I was just telling Daniel that I can't believe I've never been to any of your events. The weekends are usually our busy times at the club, but now I'm starting to think maybe I should delegate more and get a life."

"I would love to help with that." A deep baritone voice at my back startles me, and I turn to find Jaxon Wolfe extending a glass of wine to Lexa with a smile. When he meets my stare, he winks, then takes a seat beside her, setting his own drink down and opening up enough space for Marcus to approach.

Marcus extends a glass of red wine to me. "Ms. Sinclair. You look—beautiful. I saw you come in, but I wasn't sure what you were drinking, so I took a chance."

"She likes white wine," Daniel interjects, then smiles at me when I glance over. He's no doubt trying to show his support after our last meeting with Marcus went off the rails.

Jaxon asks Daniel about the sports team he worked with last weekend, and the conversation picks up as I take the glass from Marcus. "Red is fine, Mr. Wolfe. Thank you."

His fingers brush along mine as he pulls away, and his touch caresses every nerve ending in my hand. My inhale comes a little faster than I expect it to. When I dare to look up at him, his smile is relaxed. "Please, call me Marcus."

I sense this is a do-over of sorts. "Thank you—Marcus."

He circles behind me, pulls out the chair beside Lexa, and gestures for me to take a seat. I would have most likely found Daniel or someone else from the office and sat with them anyway, so I accept, and he claims the open seat beside me, setting his glass on the table.

Julie joins us, pulling in a chair beside Daniel and setting her own glass on the table. "Okay. It's all set. Thank you so much, Elle. You're a lifesaver."

"Has everyone here met Julie?" I ask quickly, changing the topic.

Daniel tells me she was already by earlier, and he made the introductions.

"I expected a Swank event to be more formal. I was surprised to see 'semiformal' on the event details." Jaxon scans the room.

Julie is already standing to make her rounds again when she answers, "It was at the request of our client. With all of the adoptable animals present, we felt people would be more inclined to approach them if they weren't in danger of getting fur all over their designer clothes." She waves at someone over my shoulder and excuses herself from the table just as quickly as she arrived.

"So, what did you agree to do?" Daniel leans closer to the table.

I roll my eyes. "They were short on female auctionees for the fundraiser, and I let her add my name."

A male voice cuts into our conversation from behind me. "Well, if that isn't the best news I've heard all evening." I turn, craning my neck up to find Remy Larsen hovering above me.

I plaster on my smile and shift in my seat, leaning away from his gaze since it's clear he's looking right down the front of my dress.

Remy has walked a fine line over the years that I've known him. We run in the same professional circles, and I have no interest in anything beyond our business connections, so avoiding his advances always proves challenging.

"Mr. Larsen, it's a pleasure to see you out tonight. What brings you to our little charity event?"

As Remy tells me he just signed the quarterback who is up

for auction and he's here as his agent, I sense Marcus's eyes on me before I steal a glance at him out of my peripheral vision.

Sure enough, his attention is divided equally between Remy and myself as he sits quietly beside me.

I guide the conversation toward the table. "Everyone, this is Remy Larsen. He's a sports agent. Remy, you know Daniel. This is Alexandra Loren, and Jaxon and Marcus Wolfe with Wolfe Security."

I take a sip of my wine as everyone shakes hands and greets each other.

Remy is already leaning into my space when I set my glass on the table. "Now, tell me more about this auction."

"It's—um, it's just to raise money for the animal shelter."

"What animal shelter?" His eyes follow the curve of my neck down to my chest as I remind him it's the reason we are all here tonight.

He recovers quickly, then says, "I look forward to bidding on you tonight." His keen tone has me backpedaling.

"It's just for fun. I'm auctioning off my *professional* expertise. It's just a business meeting, really." I smile, attempting to brush him off.

All the while, Marcus watches me with rapt attention while he sips his drink, and my face heats under his scrutiny.

"I'm sure the donation I'm about to make will get me more than that." Remy seems to remember there are other people at the table who can hear him, and he corrects himself, adding, "I've been trying to get some time with you for a while now. I'm looking forward to cashing in." Then, with a wink that was nowhere near as innocent as Jaxon's earlier wink was, he straightens and excuses himself from our group.

I lock eyes with Lexa and shake my head, happy Remy has moved on, and she offers me a reassuring smile before turning her attention to Daniel and asking him about the venue we have secured for Ravenous.

Marcus gives me a minute of silence before leaning over. "I notice you're not enjoying your wine. I can get you a glass of white if you prefer." His words are carefully spoken.

He isn't asking about the wine, but I let it go and take his question at face value.

"Between you and me, your assumption was correct. I prefer red, and this is quite good. I order white at events because I drink it much slower."

My answer earns me a smile from Marcus. "Thank you for sharing that with me."

His close proximity to me scrambles my thoughts, and I slip into ramble mode. "It's also fun to have on hand. When someone spills red wine on themselves, I counteract it with white. That really works, you know?"

Marcus's gaze lowers from my eyes, landing on my mouth. Only then do I realize I've begun nibbling my lower lip to stifle a stupid grin.

A warm rush flows over me. I could easily get lost in a conversation with Marcus. He doles out the perfect amount of compliments and praise to make me forget myself and crave more of his attention.

A fork clinks against a glass from the front, and the room goes silent as Julie steps to the mic and starts talking about the rescue shelter and where the funds raised tonight will go. The audience chuckles and claps on cue. When she's done with her rehearsed speech, she announces that the animals are being moved to another room so we can continue our evening without disrupting them. This earns her a collective groan, and she recovers quickly, telling everyone that they can still visit them across the hall for the remainder of the evening.

Then she reviews the evening's schedule before calling

everyone who has volunteered for the auction to meet her at the back of the stage.

"I guess that's me." I smile, and Lexa wishes me good luck.

The men around the table stand when I rise. I catch sight of Remy watching me from his table, and a chill slithers down my spine.

I've politely turned him down more times than I can count.

Before I join the rest of my group at the stage, I circle the table to Daniel, unsnap my clutch, and pull out my credit card.

I hold the smile on my face as I square myself on him. To everyone around us, I'm just having a regular conversation. I reach down and slide my card into his palm. "There's a thousand on there. Do not let Mr. Larsen win his bid on me."

I've seen these types of auctions before. They are all lighthearted, and I've never seen the bidding go over five hundred dollars.

He glances down at my card in his hand, furrowing his brow before returning to my gaze with a firm smile. "You can count on me."

With that squared away, I turn and set my clutch on the table in front of Lexa so she can watch it while I'm on stage. Then I straighten my shoulders and make my way to the front of the room, all in good fun and knowing full well I just bought myself.

This would be funny if it wasn't so sad.

When Elle is a few steps away, Jax, Daniel, and I return to our seats. The conversation around the table resumes, but I'm too wrapped up in what's just happened to follow what everyone is talking about.

Instead, I take my drink and lean back in my seat to contemplate the goings-on around me.

Elle steps out of a waiter's way. She says something that makes him smile, but she's too far, and I can't hear what it is. Then she approaches the growing group at the side of the stage.

Jax catches my attention when he asks Lexa to switch seats with him so he can sit beside me. She accepts, then continues her conversation with Daniel.

"I don't like that guy" is the first thing I say when Jax sits down and looks at me.

"I imagine you don't." He sips his drink before setting the glass on the table and glancing over his shoulder at the person we're talking about.

Remy Larsen.

I have no right to Elle, and neither does he, but the difference between us is: I understand that.

The way this guy openly glared at Elle's chest, as though he had a right because he deemed it so, made me want to mark my territory, which is the dumbest thing that's gone through my head this year.

I've been able to think of little more than Elle for the past two days. There's something about her that affects me, and this level of need is new territory for me.

It's also precisely why I checked myself. I backed my tactic the fuck up to show her my better side tonight, but this Remy guy is pushing my buttons.

Elle's employee takes the stage, and a hush falls over the crowd as eight people file out behind her, standing in a row with Elle at one end. A fit man to her left turns and says something to her, and they chuckle together as Julie talks about the rules of the auction.

I listen to the basics: Bidding can be made in denominations of twenty-five dollars. This is a fun auction and in no way obligates anyone on stage from anything more than what they agree to, and at the time and place they agree to it. Payment is due when the proverbial gavel drops.

Julie calls the first person forward, and a woman steps out from the other side of the group to stand by her side. She pulls her phone out of her pocket, spins, and takes a selfie with the room as her backdrop. Julie introduces her as a social media sensation, and I check out shortly after that. I return my attention to Elle at the far end.

Elle looks around the room as hands go up and the bidding rises over one hundred dollars. She wears a smile on her face, but her body language betrays her. When the winning bid of three hundred and seventy-five dollars is announced, Elle squeezes one of her own hands with the other. It's a self-comforting move.

The person standing beside the influencer steps forward next, and the bidding is repeated over and over again, with different winning amounts as they make their way down the line.

"That's Rick Taylor. Quarterback." Jax offers, knowing I don't follow sports closely, as the man beside Elle is called to step forward. He ends up going for the highest amount of the evening, at six hundred and twenty-five dollars.

Elle smiles at him when he returns to her side, but when he looks away, I catch a glimpse of her unease. Then her name is called.

She steps forward, smiling at the room, and Julie introduces her as the owner of Swank. Then she says Elle has graciously offered her professional time in a personal setting before starting the bidding at fifty dollars, just like she did for everyone else.

The first bid comes from Remy Larsen at the base amount.

There's a second bid from the table right behind me, and I turn my head when I hear a woman's voice offer one hundred dollars. It's quickly followed up by another bid from Remy, for two hundred dollars, and a murmur goes around the room.

For everyone else on stage, the bidding increased by twenty-five-dollar increments.

Before I process what this means, Daniel raises his hand and bids two hundred and fifty dollars. Elle's shoulders relax as she looks out at him.

I look at him too. He's leaning forward in his chair, fiddling with a plastic card he holds between his fingers.

Remy's bid jumps aggressively again—this time to four hundred dollars—and Lexa sighs from her seat.

Daniel clears his throat. "F-five hundred dollars."

Julie looks at Daniel quizzically before opening her mouth to accept the bid, but before she says anything, Remy bids again.

"Seven hundred and fifty dollars."

"Uhhh." Julie forgets the microphone she's holding is on, but she recovers quickly. "We have sev—"

I catch Elle looking over at Daniel, who speaks up. "Eight hundred."

"Nine hundred." Now a hint of frustration laces Remy's bid, and Julie's jaw drops.

"Okay. We have—"

"One thousand dollars." Daniel bids to Julie but his eyes are on Elle, and she looks stunned.

When Remy bids eleven hundred dollars, Daniel breaks eye contact with Elle and reaches out, opening the clutch Elle set on the table and sliding the plastic card inside.

That was her card.

Elle must have been bidding on herself.

There's only one reason why she would ask Daniel to do that for her. Knowing she doesn't want any time alone with Remy Larsen does it for me.

"Twelve hundred dollars." I raise my hand for the first time tonight and catch both Lexa and Jax swiveling their heads hard in my direction.

When Jax's look turns accusatory I shrug my shoulders, saying, "What? I'm having fun."

"Th-thirteen hundred." Remy doesn't sound as confident as he did earlier, and I'm sure I can outbid him.

"One thousand four hundred dollars." I speak clearly, drawing the amount out so he can hear exactly how much is on the line.

The confused look on Elle's face alone is worth the money I'm putting up.

"I feel like I need to clarify that everyone here is bidding on a business meeting," Julie chimes in, to a chorus of laughter from the audience.

"Fifteen hundred," Remy bids.

"Sixteen hundred, " I counter.

"Seventeen hundred." Jax holds his hand up beside me, and my eyes bug out of my head.

"What the hell are *you* doing?" I round on him.

He shrugs and drains his drink. "You're right. This is fun." The bastard chuckles.

I raise my hand once more, accentuating every syllable. "Two thousand dollars."

Elle's jaw drops.

I don't look over at Remy's table. I know his type: He's ready to back down, but he won't want to lose face. If I make eye contact with him now, it will be taken as a direct challenge to his ego.

Julie looks in Remy's general direction and pauses for a beat before saying, "What a way to finish. This ends the auction at two thousand dollars. Congratulations to all of the lucky winners, and thank you for your donations."

The room erupts in applause, and Elle wastes no time stepping back into line with everyone else.

When I pull my gaze away from the stage, the whole table is gawking at me in surprise. "What?" I shrug. "Wolfe Security has some things coming up that Swank would be an excellent partner for."

Jax does a double take because he knows everything I just said is horseshit, but Lexa and Daniel look unsure, so I end the conversation quickly, saying, "I'm grabbing a drink."

Before anyone gets the funny idea to join me, I stand and hightail it to the bar.

What the hell has gotten into me?

Not what—who?

I ask for a whiskey sour when the bartender looks my way, then I slide a ten over.

"Congratulations on your bid. I wasn't expecting it to go so high." When I turn, following the woman's voice, it takes me a moment to remember that it belongs to the only woman who tried to bid on Elle.

"Oh. Yes. Thank you."

She looked a lot older when we were all seated, and I take another look at her. I'm about to introduce myself when I'm interrupted.

"Excuse me," Elle cuts in. Her voice is kind, and I steel myself for the barrage of questions that are, no doubt, going to come.

"Oh, sorry." The woman takes a step back to leave us alone, but Elle doesn't take advantage of the space.

Instead, she turns to face the woman.

"You tried to bid on me." Elle states it more than asks a question, and the woman blushes, tucking a strand of hair behind her ear.

"Yeah. Um, my friend works at the animal shelter, and I couldn't believe my luck. I'm in my second year of college. I'm a marketing major, and I thought I could ask you some questions and talk to you about your intern program. I had to try, but—the bidding went...out of my price range."

Now I recognize the expression on this woman's face: it's admiration.

"What's your name?" Elle speaks to the woman with us like she is the only one here. She doesn't look away; she isn't scanning the room for someone more important.

The woman beams. "I—I'm Tory. I mean—" Recognizing this is her shot, she straightens her spine and extends her hand. "I'm Victoria Windsor."

Elle's grin stretches across her face as she shakes Victoria's hand. "It's nice to meet you, Victoria Windsor." When their hands release, Elle lifts her purse, which she must have picked up from the table on her way over. "I have to make my rounds and chat to a few people here tonight, but"—she opens the top, fingering through a few things before she pulls out a business card—"I'd like to have that conversation if you are still interested—free of charge." She extends the card between two fingers.

Poor Victoria looks like she's going to combust. "Really?"

"Yes. Call this number on Monday morning, and we'll find a time that works. I look forward to hearing from you, Victoria."

"Thank you, Ms. Sinclair. I will. Thank you."

"Please, call me Elle." Elle nods at the card in Victoria's hand. "And see that you do. I'll be expecting your call."

Victoria thanks her again, forgets all about the conversation she was having with me, and runs off into the crowd, leaving me with Elle at the bar.

I point to the bartender. "Can I buy you a drink?"

"I'm not sure you can afford it after that stunt," she jokes before asking the bartender for a club soda and lime.

I glance into the crowd, in the general direction Victoria took off in. "That was nice of you to do that for her."

Elle shrugs, attempting to deflect her kindness. "I was her once. It was brave of her to put herself out there and bid in front of everyone for my time."

I'm just now realizing I've only seen the tip of the iceberg when it comes to Elle. I've seen what everyone else gets to see, but there is a lot she glosses over.

"Club soda, lime." The bartender sets it down and waves me off when I go for my wallet.

"Thank you." Elle looks from the bartender to me, and we

step out of the way, taking our drinks and heading back to the table.

It's in my nature to scan the room, and I instinctively land on Remy Larsen's table. His eyes are following Elle. When he sees me watching him, he stands and excuses himself from the table, then walks toward the exit.

"The auction was—interesting." Elle pauses her thought, taking a sip of her drink before continuing, "That was a lot of— you didn't need to do that."

I hook my hand around her upper arm and gently stop her in her tracks, turning her to me. "I didn't need to do it. I wanted to."

It's brief; if I wasn't looking directly at Elle, I would have missed it. For a moment she looks surprised, then she looks at me. She's looked at me before, but this is different. This is deeper than our banter and surface-level flirting.

This is me shooting my own shot.

I'm grateful the lights haven't dimmed, because her cheeks flush with the perfect amount of rosy pink as she breaks eye contact and lowers her gaze. "Thank you."

I can't help myself. After my financial pissing match with Remy earlier, I need a release. Just enough to entertain this thing that is brewing between us. Just enough to put her as on edge as I am.

I boldly lean into her, dropping my free hand to rest on her lower back and brushing the helix of her ear with my upper lip.

She shudders.

Then I lower my voice. "Don't thank me yet. You don't know what I have planned for you."

CHAPTER 9
ELLE

I should have asked.

I should have just asked what Marcus was hoping to get out of the business meeting he won with me.

I didn't ask because I became intoxicated by the anticipation. A surge of excitement consumed me like a shot of adrenaline to the heart. I've never felt that high. Every nerve ending begged me to prolong the weightless euphoria of the unknown, the raw exhilaration of the fantasy I've denied myself.

I've been attracted to Marcus ever since he warned me that wolves crave the hunt. With that simple sentence, he took aim at my resolve.

His name is fitting.

He is wolfish.

He is commanding, dominant, and, most dangerous of all: he is charming.

Or is it that he is a perfect fit for what I need?

I should have asked, and now I'm paying the price. Marcus booked two hours of my time with Nat for late Thursday morning, and he asked her to tell me to bring a change of active clothes.

Julie, Daniel, and close to the whole office have been asking about this two-thousand-dollar date all morning, and I have no idea what to tell them.

I decided to change at work. I packed my business clothes and my heels in a backpack that's now sitting on my lap in the back seat of a cab.

The morning is uncharacteristically cool, reminding me to follow up with the venue from last weekend to see if my full-length, double-breasted jacket has shown up yet. It went missing after the charity event on Saturday night.

The driver pulls up to the curb. "This is the address."

I check the numbers on the building against the address in my phone, then hand over two twenties, thanking the driver and stepping onto the curb.

The address points to the main floor of a twelve-story apartment building. There are no flashy signs, and the windows of the storefront are made of a dark mirrored reflection glass, making it difficult to see in. WOLFE SELF-DEFENSE: ADELAINE CENTER is written in capital letters on the door.

It's difficult to tell how big it is from the outside, but once I open the front door, I find it takes up the entire first floor, with the exception of a blocked off hall that leads to the building's elevators and mailboxes.

No one pays me any mind when I first walk in. There are a few people in the main area, standing outside of a closed door, and I imagine they are waiting for the room to open up. A woman glances up at me from behind the front counter and smiles, but she returns to her conversation when the man with her asks a question.

Raised voices drift from one of the rooms, piquing my curiosity, and I hoist my backpack higher on my shoulder before I cross the open space. The door is closed, but a glass panel off to the side gives me a good view inside. A group of four women and two men face the front of the room. They are all in the same pose, with their legs slightly bent at the knees and their arms tight against their bodies in a punching stance. Walking around the room and adjusting their positions is Marcus, and my hard swallow echoes in my ears at the sight of him.

The cut of his muscles is evident through his shirt, and his track pants wrap around his hips like they were painted on—and that ass.

He turns to point something out to the group and catches me openly staring at him through the window. The corner of his mouth ticks up with a smirk at the same time I'm startled from behind.

"Do you need help?"

YES! a voice screams in my head, and I spin around, my hand clutching my chest to settle my nerves.

The woman from behind the desk startles when she sees my face, and she steps back. "I'm so sorry. I didn't mean to startle you. I saw you when you came in. You looked—lost."

I half laugh and take a deep breath. "I'm fine. I'm here to—Marcus Wolfe told me to meet him here. We have an appointment."

"Elle Sinclair?" I nod, and she extends her hand. "I thought you looked familiar." I must be wearing my confusion on my face, because she clarifies, "I saw you at Ravenous—during the presentation. I was in the audience. I'm Kate, Kate Wolfe."

"Oh...OH! So Marcus is your—"

I'll be sick if she says "husband."

"Older brother. Well, one of them." She smiles.

"Oh—man—what's *that* like?" I ask, trying to imagine living with those two twenty-four hours a day growing up.

Kate doesn't skip a beat. "I know, right?" She laughs, then offers to store my bag behind the counter.

I follow her to the front desk and pass my backpack over. She opens a small cupboard behind her, setting it in before locking it away with a key she tucks in her pocket.

"I'm heading to the office in about fifteen minutes. Yelina will be in this afternoon, so just let her know I stored your bag in there, and she'll get it when you're ready."

"So this isn't Wolfe Security?" I gesture to the room around us.

"No. Our main office is in Lake Meadows. That's where we handle our accounts. Jax wanted this place so he could be closer to the center of things: universities, transit, and areas where people were more likely in need of the classes we offer."

A door opens behind me, and voices fill the main area, drawing our attention to the room Marcus was just in. Men and women file down the hall toward the back, breaking apart to go into their respective changing rooms.

Marcus exits, waves off one of the guys he's with, and heads right for us.

Now that I'm not holding my backpack, I have nothing to fidget with, and my stance feels off, so I shuffle my weight from one foot to the next to find a comfortable position.

"I see you got my message." Marcus's gaze drifts all of the way down to my running shoes before returning to my eyes.

I don't tell him I wasn't completely sure what to expect, that my backpack is filled with a few extra pieces of clothing just in case. Instead, I rock in my sneakers, pleased with myself. "I did."

"Very good."

In my head, I hear *girl* at the end of his sentence, and my face heats up.

Marcus smiles at me but doesn't say anything else. His gaze

is narrowed on my cheeks, and I lift my hand to my hair to ease the tension in the room around us.

The silence stretches on for a second too long when Kate clears her throat.

"So—I'm obviously not supposed to still be standing here, but now I don't know how to get myself out of this without being weird, so I'm just going to say, it is nice to finally meet you, Elle." Kate looks around the desk then takes a few steps to the side and heads toward one of the rooms at the back.

"It was nice meeting you too."

"Text me when you get to the office." Marcus keeps his eyes on me but raises his voice at Kate before she gets through the door, and she gives him a thumbs-up over her shoulder. He doesn't see it as he informs me, "I booked us a room."

"Should I be worried?"

"With me?" He drags his teeth over his lower lip. "Always, Ms. Sinclair."

I'm now convinced his smirk could melt panties, and if he keeps it up, I might have proof.

He steps to the side and extends one arm around my lower back, but he doesn't touch me. I take the hint and walk with him across the room.

"Thank you again for—bidding. That was a generous donation. Our clients are still raving about it."

My small talk sucks.

He doesn't respond.

I want him to though, and it's unnerving, so I keep talking. "So, what are we doing here?"

"That night at Ravenous, you left before we could demonstrate some easy self-defense maneuvers, and I thought we would revisit that."

"How is this a business meeting?"

Marcus rests his hand on the door handle and meets my

gaze. "I'm killing two birds with one stone. I'm using my time to pitch Wolfe Security, and I'm teaching you a valuable skill."

"Pitch Wolfe Security for what?"

Marcus opens the room and reaches along the wall for the light switch. "Swank handles many high-level events that require security." He crosses half of the room before he looks back at me. "I'm going to assume you've been using whatever security the venues provide for most of them."

It isn't a question, but I answer it anyway. "We do."

"I think offering your clients another option, even at an added price, will be beneficial to everyone involved. Most hotel and event staff, including those in security positions, have never had any relevant training for work like that. Not to mention proper background checks." He doesn't talk down to me or make me feel stupid. He just speaks matter-of-factly as he turns, walks across the room, and picks up a phallic-looking wooden stick. It's about six inches long and a couple of inches in diameter.

I open my mouth to respond, but then I snap my lips shut.

I never considered this. I assumed someone wearing a security uniform would have earned the position.

"You're right. It never hurts to have the option. Then it's up to our clients to turn it down." Marcus doesn't dwell on it. He closes the distance between us, holding up the wooden item as he does. He waits for me to ask, "What are you going to do with that?"

"This"—he glances at the stick, then back to me—"is the fun part. With your permission, I want to see what you know." He twirls the baton, then shrugs his shoulders. "It's simple, really. Just don't let me touch you with this or get you pinned down."

Marcus takes five steps back, giving me space to prepare myself.

"Okay. I'll bite." Darkness washes across his expression at my words, and I quickly steer him away from the gutter. "What are the rules? I mean, I don't want to hurt you."

That makes him laugh.

"Don't worry. You won't." His confidence is off the charts, but it doesn't matter.

I believe him.

"Fine. *I* don't want to get hurt."

He points to some thick mats on the ground. "We stay on those. If *one of us*"—he rolls his eyes at that; we both know full well he means me—"gets hurt or needs a moment, then say 'purple.'"

I nod in agreement, stepping to the edge of the mat, and he joins me, taking a spot on the opposite side.

"Say 'ready' when I can start." Marcus stands still, tapping the wooden item on his thigh and waiting patiently for my signal.

Now that I'm out of my heels, he's a few inches taller than I am, but his strength is far superior to my own. The muscles in his forearm tense with each tap of the object.

"Ready."

Marcus crosses the mat, coming straight toward me. With each step, his features harden into focused determination. It startles me, and I take a quick step back, barking, "Purple!"

His face contorts in surprise, and he changes course in an instant. "Are you okay?" He steps back.

I lower my eyes to the ground. "Um, yeah. Sorry. You just caught me off guard." I chuckle to lighten my reaction and shed my anxiety, but he doesn't soften. "Can we—um, try it again?"

"Sure." He nods once, then returns to his original spot, but his expression has changed. I'm not sure what's going on in his head.

I'm not sure what's going on in mine.

I wasn't expecting my reaction when Marcus stalked toward me. I've been afraid before, and this wasn't fear.

I felt...wild and elated.

Between one of his steps and the next, a sense of being hunted hit me. It aroused me, and that isn't what I'm here for.

"You will always be caught off guard." Marcus pulls me from my thoughts. "That's what your attacker will have going for them. Show me what you have going for you," he challenges me, and my depraved thoughts are replaced by a need to make him proud of me.

I step up to the mat. "Ready."

This time when he steps toward me, I raise my arms in front of my face, my hands fisted, and meet his gaze.

When he reaches out to touch me with the stick, I lunge back. He just misses me, but the move sends me off balance, and Marcus takes advantage of it by stepping into me and spinning my back to his front. He holds me close for a moment before letting me go and stepping back.

"Don't look at my eyes—I'm not going to stab you with those." His voice is brash as he slips into trainer mode, and I nod once, stepping back and steadying myself to try again.

This time when he comes at me, I wrap my hand around his wrist, pushing the stick up high. But with it goes my hand, and he pushes his body flat against mine when I open up my center. Then he kicks my leg out from under me, taking us both down to the mat.

"This was better, but the last thing you want to do in a fight is get close. Your attacker will probably be stronger than you, and they'll use their weight against you."

He drops the wooden stick onto the mat, then braces his palms on either side of me before raising himself up and offering me his hand so I can stand. When he picks up the stick, I lift my hands and say "ready" again.

He makes the same approach. This time, when I block his wrist, I pull my arm back, closing myself off, then I lunge.

I only know one move, and I try it out.

I aim the heel of my hand toward his nose and put all of my weight behind my punch.

I don't get anywhere near Marcus's face. He steps back and grabs my wrist hard, a look of surprise crossing his features.

My shoulders slump.

I suck at saving myself.

"That was your best move yet. I'm impressed."

"Please. I didn't even touch you."

"That's not the point. I'm trained differently than your average person. If someone came at you and you did that move, you would have most likely connected, and you could have used that time it would have given you to get away."

"I just wouldn't have been able to get away from you."

Marcus makes a point of holding my gaze. "I'm a different breed, Ms. Sinclair."

He doesn't look away until I break our stare. Then he walks to a table at the back of the room and sets the wooden stick down.

I'd be lying to myself if I denied my attraction to him. While his back is turned, I look around the room. Outside of that door, I have my shit together. At least, I give the impression that I do. But these four walls hide us away from that world. In here, it feels like an alternate reality where I'm not expected to have all of the answers.

The longer the room sits in silence, the more pressure I feel to say something.

"Could you train me to beat you?" I have no idea where that question comes from, but it gets his attention, and he joins me on the mat once more.

"I could train you." He closes the distance between us, and

the meeting feels like it has moved away from business. "But I don't think you'd ever be able to beat me."

I push back against his assessment by crossing my arms and tilting my head.

He chuckles.

"What I mean is: I know the way out of most moves. I could train you to hold your own against me though, and that is the point. When you are attacked, it isn't about winning. It's about survival. I can train you to fight long enough to send the message that you are more trouble than you are worth. But as for beating me"—what little distance we had between us disappears as he steps closer, tucking a strand of hair behind my ear—"I've been trained to keep getting up, and I won't relent. Especially when it comes to something I want."

His last words come out on a warm breath against my face.

"And—um. What is it you want, Mr. Wolfe?"

He plays with the ends of my hair just below my shoulder as he contemplates my question.

"I thought I was making myself clear, Ms. Sinclair." Marcus twirls a section around his fingers until they are tangled in my hair, then he tugs just enough to send a shiver over my skin. I set my palm against his shirt, my fingers trailing along the ridges in his chest. Then he leans close, his lips only inches away from my own. "I most definitely want you."

Elle's pupils blow out, swallowing up the hazel in her eyes, and her fingers curl in, fisting my shirt in her hand.

I got the reaction I wanted, but she's having her own effect on me.

I unravel my fingers from her hair, then clear my throat. "At the very least, I want the chance to get to know you better."

She blushes, dropping her gaze to her hands. When she notices what she's doing, she releases me and swipes her own fingers across her forehead before tucking them behind one ear. It's a nervous move more than anything; there was no hair in her eyes to move away.

I glance over her shoulder at the clock on the wall. "I'd like to take you to lunch for the other half of our...business meeting. Would you like to get dressed first, or..."

She looks down at herself. "I'm fine in this."

"There's a restaurant around the block, and their pierogi are legendary."

When she smiles, I lead her through the main area, stopping at the front desk to inform Yelina I'm on my way out.

When I tell Elle the restaurant is a five-minute walk, she asks me to share how we decided to start Wolfe Security on our way.

I search my memory for how long it's been. Since we went into business for ourselves seven years ago, the months have flown by, but at the same time I don't remember doing anything else.

At least until things went horribly wrong a couple of years ago, but I don't want to dwell on my darker days right now. Not when Elle is smiling at me like that.

"I think it was Jax's idea first. My family was sitting around the table at Thanksgiving, and Kate had graduated college earlier that year. I don't know how we got onto it, but she was telling us horror stories from her time away at school. Most of the stories weren't hers to tell—they were her friends'—but she wanted to get across how isolating and terrifying life can be for anyone who isn't trained to protect themselves."

Elle only nods her head. I wonder if she has her own version of experiences like these.

"My brothers and I followed our father into various fields of law enforcement, and she was trying to tell us our training afforded us a security that we took for granted. She told us one story about how someone had slipped something into her friend's drink at a party. No one saw a thing, but Kate's friend had become unusually incoherent after half a glass, and Kate recognized what was going on right away."

I still remember Jax's and my anger. We erupted into shouting matches as we demanded to know why Kate waited to tell us until then.

I already knew why. Being her big brothers, we would have

stormed onto campus throwing our weight around. We would have made everything worse and demanded she come home immediately.

"Brothers? I thought Jax was your only brother."

"Jax is the oldest. Then Cillian, and I'm the youngest of the boys. Then there is Kate."

She nods before getting back to the story. "So what happened?"

I shake my head. "To this day, she's never told us how the story ended. She has only ever said that her friend made it home safe, and she took care of it." When she doesn't ask for any more, I offer a bit extra. "In our family, 'I took care of it' is code for 'I did something that is most likely illegal, and you shouldn't push this or we're all liable.'"

Elle's step falters. She looks over at me with a shocked expression before tossing her head back and laughing.

I really like this one.

"Anyway, it opened up a conversation about how society is missing the 'in-between': the steps between when you are just a person living your life and the point where you are already a victim and need the law to step in. We wanted to fill that void, and it turns out it was a big void that needed filling."

As soon as I step inside, I make eye contact with the owner. I order the same thing every time I'm here: kielbasa and pierogi. I'm ruined for anything else they make. I hold up two fingers and look at Elle, and he nods as he turns to go into the kitchen.

I walk to the back of the little restaurant and sit at a table that is removed from the rest. Elle looks around the room and takes a seat.

My curiosity overrides my restraint. "May I ask you a question?"

She smiles so sweetly before shrugging. "Sure."

"Tell me about the membership at the club you belong to."

It's clear by the way she freezes for a second that Elle wasn't expecting that. She glances at the people closest to us, who are nowhere within earshot, before she braves a look at me.

"Um—I—I'm not a member there anymore. That was a while ago."

"Fair enough. I'd like to know more about it."

She sits up straight in her chair when Oleksiy approaches us with two plates full of food. Someone hollers a greeting at him from the front of the restaurant, so he quickly excuses himself.

"This looks amazing." Elle picks up her knife and fork, quickly cutting a pierogi and taking a bite, no doubt to avoid answering my question.

I can be a patient man, especially when it comes to her, and I wait until she swallows her bite before prompting her to answer me. "You were saying?"

She stabs her meat with her fork and goes to cut it when I place my hand on hers. When I release her, she sets her utensils down and folds her hands in her lap.

"Um, yeah. We went there one night, mostly for something new to try."

"We?"

"Nat, Daniel, Julie, and an old staff member. I can't remember whose idea it was. It was fun, but a couple of them bowed out quickly. I stayed behind with Nat and Daniel for a drink, and then I started talking to one of the—um—members." There's no mistaking the blush that starts at Elle's jawline and creeps its way up and over her cheeks.

Oleksiy leaves two bottles of water with us on his way back to the kitchen. I break the seal on mine and take a sip before asking, "A dominant?"

Elle nods before breaking eye contact. She picks up her fork and pokes at her food.

This is a side to Elle I haven't seen yet. Even when I called her out during Swank's presentation, she confessed from a hiding spot behind a wall she's built up. But now, I'm not backing down.

I caught a fleeting glimpse of this vulnerability the first night I met her outside of Ravenous, when she looked like she was a split second away from ditching our presentation.

"Tell me about him."

"H-he was nice, um, to me, but it didn't work out."

"Do you mind sharing wh—"

"Can we talk about something else? I don't want to—that's just not a great topic for a *business meeting*." Elle attempts to smile, but it doesn't light up her eyes.

"Sure."

In hindsight, I came on too strong.

I unknowingly touched on something incredibly personal right out of the gate, and I'm going to lose her for the rest of our time together if I don't put myself out there.

On the other hand, we've ventured into something real. She's shown me a glimpse of something I sense not many get to see, and I don't want to go back to casual flirting.

"Wolfe Security didn't always have a self-defense center under its umbrella. It was a couple of years ago that my brother came up with the idea."

Curiosity gets the better of her, and she comes back to our conversation. "What happened?"

"I did." I've never talked about this with anyone outside of my family and the authorities involved, and I don't know why it feels right to share it with her, but I inhale and give it a go.

"I made a mistake a little over two years ago, and it cost

someone their life. You don't like me much now, but if you met me a few years ago, you would have hated me, and it would have been deserved. I was arrogant, self-involved, and so sure of the world around me."

My mouth has suddenly gone dry, and I reach for my bottle, taking another sip. When I put it down on the table, I notice Elle is no longer eating. Her expressionless eyes are round as she waits for me to continue.

"I made a snap judgment about someone I'd never met before. A woman wearing a tight dress approached me in the bar of a hotel I was staying at. I took one look at her and filled in the rest of her blanks for her. I assumed she was a paid escort looking to pick me up, and I wasn't interested. I was waiting on a new client, and I brushed her off and sent her on her way. She turned up dead five hours later, stuffed into a dumpster, and it's my fault. The damn thing is, I couldn't be bothered to give her a few minutes of my time, and now I'm damned to carry the last moments of her life with me for the rest of mine."

I clear my throat and take another sip. "So many moving pieces failed that woman before she ended up dead, and I was probably the breaking point, her last chance. I didn't take it well. I became a silent partner at Wolfe Security and withdrew from everything. I felt like a fraud. How could I head a security firm and let something like that happen? Kate tried to talk to me; she tried to get me back to work, but I wouldn't have it. Jax let me be for a while. He gave me time to spiral, but he made sure I wasn't reckless about it. Then, one morning about three months later, he showed up, dragged my ass out of bed, and told me to get dressed. He and Kate had decided to expand to include a self-defense center. They'd hired a company to help them find some properties they could buy, and they needed my input. When I told him no, Jax snapped. He pushed me up against the wall and told me I could do something about

Adelaine's death so she didn't die for nothing, or I could crawl back into bed and let the world take me down with her. We signed on a new building later that day and opened Wolfe Self-Defense two months after that in her memory."

Suddenly, sharing the worst moment of my life doesn't feel like the best decision. I pick up my fork, stabbing at a pierogi and shoving it into my mouth. It doesn't taste as good as it did just moments ago.

"Why are you telling me this?"

That is a good question.

"You strike me as someone who prefers the ugly truth to pretty lies. And this"—I tap the table between us with my forefinger—"isn't a business meeting, and we both know it."

We sit in silence, staring at each other. My observation hangs between us for a long minute before I reach for my bottle of water. Then I return to my meal and eat a few bites in silence, more than happy for her to change the subject.

The ball is in her court.

She can discuss business, and I'll talk shop. Or she can keep the conversation focused on the two of us.

When she clears her throat, I realize I really want her to keep it personal.

"He was a dominant—Greg, the man from the club—but I wasn't his submissive. I—um, I wanted something else. We saw each other for a few months while I tried to figure things out, but then things went really wrong. I'm not sure how far it went back, but I started to notice odd things maybe a few weeks into our relationship. At first, I thought I was misplacing things. There was always some kind of an explanation, like I would take a load of laundry down the hall to the shared machine, and when I went to get my clothes out of the dryer, I could have sworn I had washed a certain piece of clothing—but socks and underwear go missing all the time, right? Then I noticed scratches around the lock on my front door, but maybe they were always there, and I just never noticed until that moment. There were some disconnected phone calls late at night, but people misdial all the time. The list went on. Everything could be explained away, except I felt it in my bones. I didn't say anything for the longest time, until—"

Elle lifts her hand to her forehead, propping her elbow on the table. She rubs her fingers over her skin until her palm is stretched wide, placing her thumb and middle finger on each temple.

"I was out of town at a meeting, and I had the chance to catch an earlier flight home. I took advantage of it, because then I could get a good night's sleep and work the next day instead of spending it on an airplane. Anyway, when I got to my place, it was late, and someone was there. It was dark. Before I could turn on the lamp in my living room, someone pushed me hard from behind, and I went flying into the wall. I'm lucky they ran out. I went down like a sad sack of potatoes. The cops who responded said it was a break-in and I surprised them. They said I was lucky to get away with a split lip, but it didn't feel right. If I was being robbed, they would have taken something. My expensive camera was sitting on the table near my front door. After that, I couldn't shake the feeling that I was being watched, but I couldn't prove it either."

"What happened?" It isn't until I voice the question that I realize I've stopped doing everything but breathing.

"I told a friend—it was Alexandra—how I felt, and she convinced me to go to the police. When the officer found out that I belonged to—um, a club...well, let's just say I knew I wasn't going to get any help. I don't know if they thought I was into it, or if I was making things up, but I felt more alone than before. At least before I went in, I had the stupid notion that someone would help me. Knowing for sure that I was alone was the worst feeling."

I wince. That officer treated Elle the same way I treated Adelaine. The only difference between them is Elle's pursuer didn't want to kill her, or she'd be dead. The thought makes my lunch sit heavy in my stomach.

"I ended up telling my assistant and Daniel what was going on, but I asked them to keep it between us. I think maybe telling a few close friends was the best thing, because I didn't feel so targeted after that. The creepy stuff kind of thinned out. Then, three weeks later, Greg was arrested and charged with human trafficking."

My eyes must have bugged out at that nugget of information, because they sting with a shot of cool air.

"I thought about coming forward and sharing my experience at his trial, but I decided against it. I was sure I wouldn't be a credible witness for the prosecution as soon as their lawyers got wind that I knew Greg from a sex club. I had no contact with Greg when I found out. I blocked his number, and I left the club. I bought a place of my own, and at the end of the month, I canceled my lease and moved out. I walked away from that part of my life and didn't look back."

"Where is he now? Greg?"

"He was sentenced to two years, and that was about a year ago now. I don't know anything beyond that." She looks sheepishly down at the table. "I just wanted to move on."

I'm shocked by her forthright honesty.

I ask her the same question she asked earlier. "Why are you telling me this?"

"You were wrong earlier when you said I don't like you much, and I don't want this to be just a *business meeting* either."

Elle's vague confession of interest intrigues me. She strikes me as a woman who is determined, who doesn't mince words when there is something she wants to get across, yet she offers just enough to show interest while still challenging me to be the pursuer. I like this about her. I enjoy being the aggressor.

I entertain the possibilities between us. "Have dinner with me tonight."

My mind has been on one thing all afternoon.

Have dinner with me tonight.

It wasn't a question. It was more like a confident command, but with no arrogant intent, and I keep coming back to it. The excitement it stirred in me coiled deep in my belly and refused to let me concentrate on anything else.

I said yes. Well, inside my head, it sounded more like *HELL YES!* But I think I came off a bit more composed than that.

Now I'm sitting at my desk, staring at some company reports but not processing a thing. Over the last twenty minutes, I've gone from scanning our social media—which is not my job—to glancing at our company email inbox—which is not my job—to searching for Wolfe Security online—which is most definitely not my job. I'm too chicken to do an internet search on Marcus directly. A little piece of me is sure that he'll know if I do.

Now it's three thirty, and the phone on my desk rings,

pulling me from my daze as someone knocks on the door right before they open it.

"I told him to wait," Nat whisper-hisses into the phone as I look up to find Remy Larsen smiling at me.

"Thank you, Nat. Can you ask Daniel to see me about the Ravenous account?" I wait for her to confirm before I hang up and greet my unexpected guest. "Remy, always a pleasure. What brings you by today?" I stand to circle my desk, hoping to meet him closer to the door so I can guide him back out, but he takes quick steps to one of the chairs in front of my desk.

"One of my clients made an appearance across the street to promote his new sports shoes, and I thought I'd drop by before I make the drive back to my office." He glances out the window before his gaze returns to slither over my body. Suddenly, standing in front of him doesn't feel like a great idea. "You have a much better view than I do."

With that, I round my desk and take a seat, threading my fingers together and placing my forearms on my desk. "I apologize that I don't have much time to speak with you today. If you schedule an appointment with Nat, I can give you my undivided attention for whatever *business* you wish to discuss."

"There's no business between us, Elle. I want to steal you away for an afternoon drink."

Remy has always hinted at the two of us getting together, but it's never going to happen. He's a player who uses his position representing the city's athletic elite to sleep his way around.

"I'm sorry, Remy. I have too much on my plate and—"

He doesn't make eye contact. Instead, he busies himself with the pen holder on my desk. "Who was the guy who bid on you last weekend? I think you said he was a security guard."

His abrupt change in topic catches me by surprise, but I don't show it.

"Mr. Wolfe—of Wolfe Security," I correct.

"Is he just *business* as well?"

His direct line of questioning throws me again. In the past, it's always been sleazy innuendos and suggestive remarks.

"He used his time to discuss a partnership with Swank. Now, Mr. Larsen, I think you should—"

"Oh, come on, Elle. I should be back in the office by now, getting work done. I stopped in just to see you. The least you could do is grab a quick drink. It would be good for you to work with me on this. I represent a lot of big names that would look pretty nice on Swank's client list."

My back stiffens at his unspoken suggestion that I give him what he wants in exchange for access to his A-listers.

I know for a fact that the people he represents are clamoring to get into the events that Swank holds, and it isn't the other way around. However, I am a professional.

I stand, reaching a hand out toward the door. "As I said, Mr. Larsen, kindly make an appointment with Nat on your way out, and I will gladly meet with you another time to consider adding your clients to our list."

He stands but makes no move to walk toward the door, and I'm saved from cutting all professional ties with him when someone knocks, interrupting us.

"Come in." I don't care who it is on the other side of the door.

"Nat said you wanted to talk about Ravenous." Daniel pokes his head in. When he sees Remy, he steps further into the room saying, "I have all of my notes right here, and there are a few urgent things we need to discuss."

"Of course." I point at the chair Remy was just sitting in, and Daniel walks to it, greeting Remy as he passes him.

"Thank you for dropping in, Mr. Larsen. Please see Nat on your way out to schedule a better time."

Remy buttons his jacket and glances at Daniel before deciding to give up his pursuit. An eerie shiver makes the fine hairs on my arm stand on end, a sense that this won't be the last time he tries for something he's not going to get.

Once Remy is out of the room, Daniel lowers his voice and relaxes. "I got here as fast as I could." He angles his knees so he is facing me in the chair.

"I appreciate it. Did you say there's something wrong with Ravenous?"

"No. Well, I did, but there's nothing wrong. I got the sense you wanted him to leave." He points at the door.

"Right. Thank you, Daniel."

As I take my seat behind my desk, Nat joins us. "I am so sorry, Elle. I told him to wait, but he just walked right past me. Are you okay?"

I shake my head. "It's nothing, really. I handled it."

In truth, I'm not sure I really did, but if I can minimize the situation, everyone will move on.

"Did Mr. Larsen book a future meeting?" A long mental list of excuses to cancel on him forms in my head.

"No. He just walked out without saying a word." Nat turns to leave, then spins around. "I almost forgot. How did your auction lunch go today?"

"Was that today?" Daniel looks from Nat—who nods—to me.

I pick up a pen and underline a section at the bottom of a page on my desk. I will never need that information—I just want to occupy my attention so I don't have to look at either of them.

"It went well. I think we might be working with Wolfe Security on some events in the future."

"Is that all?" When I glance up at Nat, she doubles down on her stink eye. "I'm just saying—it's the guy from the meeting last week, right? Mister tall, intense, and sexy—muscles for miles? And he really bid two thousand dollars just to pitch his company to you? That's sus."

"Fine. It wasn't just that. We're having dinner tonight, but I don't wish to discuss it."

"Is that—that isn't like a conflict of interest or anything, is it?" Daniel asks, and Nat shrugs him off.

"I'd be *interested* in his *conflict* any day."

"Okay. That's enough. It's just dinner, and we are not discussing anyone's"—I glare at Nat—"conflict."

"Fine. I've got to get some filing done before I go."

Nat leaves the door open on her way out, and I check the time. A rush of nervous energy surges through me. It's almost time to go.

"Are you sure this is a good idea?" Daniel asks. "I mean, do you know him that well?"

I know what he's getting at by how he carefully chooses his words. He's asking if I know enough about him, because I apparently didn't know anything about Greg.

"I appreciate your concern, but it's just dinner."

This is not just dinner.

A giant plastic bowling pin sits angled on the wall on top of a plaque that states: BOWLERS NEVER DIE, THEY JUST END UP IN THE GUTTER.

Marcus sits up from tying his bowling shoes. "What do you think?"

I still have mine sitting on my lap as I pick at the knot in the laces to separate them. "I'm glad you gave me a heads-up. I wouldn't have nailed the dress code otherwise."

He returns my smile, then slips from his seat beside me to

kneel at my feet. He takes the shoes from me before twisting the laces to loosen them. "I wanted to make it very clear that this is not a business meeting."

One of the shoes falls to the ground, and I reach for the one he's left holding. He pulls it away, admonishing me with a look. "You'll allow me this."

His tone is playful, confident, but it dances close to a firm command.

Wolves crave the hunt.

I acquiesce, withdrawing my hands and placing them on my lap.

He holds my stare, but he smiles in appreciation before wrapping his fingers around my calf. He lifts my foot off the floor and into the shoe before resting it on his thigh as he tightens the laces.

I don't remember the last time someone tied my shoes for me. The act renders me speechless, and I sit with the foreign feeling.

When he's done, he taps my ankle to let me know I can remove it. Then he wraps his hand around my other leg and repeats the process.

This time, when he finishes tying my laces, he cups his palm around the back of my calf but leaves my leg in his lap.

He trails his fingers along the back of my leg and lowers his tone. "Have you bowled before?"

I remember that I have, but I'm not sure exactly when it was. Since it was most likely at a birthday party when I was a teenager, I simply nod. Then I ask, "Have you?"

His cheek ticks with the hint of a smile, and I imagine he's recalling a memory. "Kate went through a phase for a few years where she insisted we all go bowling for her birthday. Jax calls it the dark ages. He hates the game because he always ends up in the gutter. I think it's the only thing he hasn't mastered."

I laugh at that. "I've seen him with Lexa. Bowling isn't the only thing he hasn't mastered." Then I cover my mouth with my hand as my eyes go wide.

I can't believe I said that out loud.

Marcus chuckles, unfazed. "You noticed that too?" He stands, extending his hand to help me up, and changes the subject. "Ready?"

"As I'll ever be."

It takes a few tries to get away from the gutter and into the swing of the game. I'm tempted to try tossing it using two hands between my legs, but I get better as the game goes on.

It helps that Marcus's attention isn't really on keeping score so much as getting to know each other.

At the end of the first game, I'm ahead by one spare. I'm not sure if I've earned it or if Marcus is taking it easy on me. The pizza we ordered comes just as I'm taking my victory lap, and Marcus orders us some drinks and suggests we move to a table to open up the lane for someone else.

I wiggle into the tall seat to get comfortable, and Marcus hands me a plate before pointing to the pizza.

He waits until I've taken a piece before he serves himself, and the waitress stops by with two beers.

"Tell me what you want, Elle." Marcus's tone is casual as he takes a bite of his pizza.

It's a vague question, designed to lure me into the conversation, and I bite.

"What I want?"

"You mentioned earlier today that you weren't Greg's submissive because you wanted something else. What are you looking for?"

"At the time, I didn't know. He borrowed some kind of form from the club. It had a long list of limits and different types of play, and he went through it with me, asking me questions to see where I might land."

"And did you—land?" Marcus is still enjoying his beer and pizza, but he hasn't taken his eyes off me since we started talking about this.

"I—uh, yes. There were some things I was interested in, but he wasn't as much."

Marcus stares at me for half a minute before he starts talking again. "You're stalling."

I sit in silence a little longer, because, yes—I am stalling.

"I want to know more about you, and I very much want to know about what you like. And you're going to tell me everything."

A chill rolls across my heated skin. I shift nervously in my seat as I reach for my beer to break this hold Marcus has on my senses. I want to tell him everything, and that scares me.

"I—I'm not sure. Um, I mean..." I fade away from my thought when Marcus stands, then circles the round table to take the seat beside me, sliding it nice and close to my side. Then he angles my seat toward him and turns his body so his spread legs brace each side of my knees.

Leaning in close, he grips the side of my seat, caging me in, lowering his voice so I have to strain to hear him. "Tell me why you aren't answering my question, Elle."

CHAPTER 12
MARCUS

Elle's gaze drops to her lap when I lift one of my hands to draw slow circles on her thigh.

"I like you." Her voice is a whisper.

She stiffens as soon as she says the words, and I wonder if she meant to confess that out loud.

I place my free hand on her other thigh and massage my way up.

I wasn't lying when I told her I craved the hunt.

Every time she gives me a little piece of herself, I tuck it away and go in search of more, and I won't stop, even after I have all of her.

"Like?" I clarify, letting the word linger between us and challenging her to consider her feelings.

She breaks eye contact to scan the room over my shoulder, and I'm not willing to let her run away this time. Tilting my head, I insert myself into her line of sight and pull her back to me, silently demanding an answer.

"I mean—it's hard to just say it."

Elle is a unique creature. She's guarded yet vulnerable, strong yet fragile.

I lean forward, snaking my hand around her throat to the back of her neck, and slowly draw her into me. The closer I get, the wider her eyes become, and her chest rises as her breathing deepens.

I flex my hand, which is still on her thigh, massaging my fingers into her leg through her jeans.

"You'll find it's not hard at all." I brush my lips against the shell of her ear, and my breath makes her shudder in my hold as I whisper, "Just tell me what you found out about yourself when you were a member of the club."

"What if—it's something that..." She lowers her voice below a whisper, so the words come out on her breath. "It's not normal."

I release her neck and regroup, returning my palm to her thigh.

She's worried about my perception of her. If she tells me what she needs, she fears that not only will I reject her, but I'll also know this *thing* about her.

She's already told me this dominant from the club helped her discover certain things about herself, but she said he didn't share those same kinks. Shining a light on your darkest desires requires an insane amount of strength.

I'm betting the figurative farm that we both want what the other so willingly wants to give. So I lean in, brushing my lips against hers before I pull back and stare her down.

"Do you want to know what I want?"

She nibbles her lower lip and nods as she reaches for her beer, her nails picking at the label on the bottle.

Her expression is light.

It won't be in a minute.

"I don't want to be nice right now." I reach up, twirling

some strands of her hair between my thumb and forefinger before returning my hand to her thigh. "I don't want to play fair. I want to hunt you down. I want to break you apart and consume you. I want you to show me every delicious morsel. Open yourself up to me, and expose that soft underbelly of yours. I want you to surrender everything, all of you, to me; I want to prey upon it. Then I want to gorge myself on your offering."

Elle's eyes turn glassy as she hangs on every word. The gentle smile is long gone from the mouth I want to kiss, which is now slightly rounded in a daze. "I hope I made myself clear when I told you that wolves crave the hunt, because I'm the darkest wolf of them all, little one." I lean in close, sliding my hands up over her jeans and digging my fingers into the softer fleshy part at the apex of her thighs, causing her to exhale a depraved whimper. "And it's already too late for you."

I sit in silence with her while she slips into the mental images brought on by my confession. Her swallow is forced as she absentmindedly peels another small piece of the label off, and the paper joins a growing pile between us.

Slowly, painstakingly slowly, I lean back, giving us both space because we are still in public. Right now, we look like two people deep in conversation, but if she keeps biting her lips like she is, things will escalate quickly.

"Now, tell me what you want, Elle. I won't ask again."

"P-predator—prey. That's, um, what Greg called it." Elle breaks our connection, lowering her eyes to my lips. "I like to be stalked, and—um, taken, and handled...roughly."

A muscle in my cheek twitches.

"And you'd like it if I handled you—roughly?" A low, gruff tone accompanies that last word. "If I dropped all pretenses and went after you with the sole goal of owning you and binding you to me, making you my beautiful possession? If I hunted you, learned everything about you—things no one knows, things I could use against you to make you powerless to resist our connection?"

Elle stares me down for a long minute. It reminds me of when I challenged her during Swank's presentation in their office. She backed down then, and I wonder if she's going to back down now.

"But it's not that simple." She tries to backpedal.

I know what she's trying to say. Having a kink like this walks a fine line, and fantasizing about it is far removed from wanting it as a reality.

It's similar to our business. I plot and plan ways to attack, break in, and take over, and I do it all the time, as a way of preventing it from happening to our clients.

In truth, taking on the headspace of a predator gives me a rush. When I consider doing something like this for Elle, it fills a void inside of me, one I've been neglecting to entertain for a long time. But it doesn't mean that I am a threat to her. It isn't something I would do without negotiating.

"Our particular interest never is."

"Our?"

I lean back, reaching for my beer and taking a sip. It's gone warm. "Yes. I think we're very suited for each other. However, something like this requires a lot of open communication and trust, and that isn't something we just decide to do. It's something we work toward."

She's stopped picking at the label on her bottle, and she clears her throat. "H-how would we do that?"

The hopeful look in her eyes hits me square in the chest, but I don't show it. I haven't been instantly drawn to someone for a long time, and to find someone who shares so many of the same kinks is like hitting the lottery.

I only wish I'd been at this club she went to on a whim.

That I was the one who sat down and talked to her, because I would have never let such a treasure go. I would have nurtured her beyond her wildest expectations and opened her eyes to more than she could ever imagine.

I will still do that for her.

I stay still until she meets my gaze, then I smile. "We've already begun."

We've only eaten a piece of pizza each, but I'm no longer hungry for food. Catching the server's attention, I ask for a box. As soon as the waitress walks away, I glance at Elle, who's been sitting subdued beside me.

I don't hide my covetous inspection of her body. Thoughts of every way I want to have her manifest in my expression, and I revel in the voracious proclivities rising inside of me.

"I'm taking you home."

What little expression she holds on her face falls away as she considers my directive. Her eyes dance between my own, unwilling to look away.

Then she licks her lips and nods.

I wish I could say Elle's home was exactly as I pictured it, but in truth I had no idea what to expect. If I only knew her as a client, then I would have expected it to be extremely clean and uncluttered.

When she opens the door, I'm hit with a personal intimacy that I wasn't expecting.

The dominant side of her personality is one she openly shares around the office.

This space is warm, inviting, and comfortable. The furniture is retro, yet recovered to look updated. The area rug in the living room is plush, as are the couple of knit blankets on the chairs in the room.

Elle removes her coat and hangs it in a small closet near the entrance, then reaches out for mine.

"Do you rent out the other floor?" I take a few steps into her space.

The room smells sweet with a hint of grapefruit and orange.

It smells like she did when I managed to get close during our sparring match. The scent goes straight to my cock, igniting my base need to smell her on me always and return the favor by having her carry my own scent around with her.

"I wasn't going to, but the woman who sold it to me didn't want to move." When I tilt my head in confusion, she continues, "It's not like that. Her son owned the house, and he was worried about her. He lives in another state and wanted to put her into a home. She and I got to talking when I dropped in for a final walk-through, and I offered her the main level. The house is big for just one person, and this way we both get what we want. Her son is happy because she only pays for her groceries and half the utilities. She travels a lot with a group of women, so she has a familiar place until she's ready to go into a home. She's been talking about giving it another year on her own. And I like having someone around who keeps to themself. Can I get you something to drink?"

I want to ask for a glass of water, but it can wait.

"Show me your bedroom, Elle."

The atmosphere in the room compresses into a pinpoint of anticipation, and Elle shifts her weight between her feet before pointing at a closed door off her living room.

I tilt my head toward the door, holding my leveled gaze on her. I won't cross the room until she leads me there.

She takes my unspoken hint and pads across the room, her

attention now on the door, and I slip into step, quietly stalking behind her.

The door opens without a sound, and she steps in before inviting me to join her. There's a bathroom off to the side, closed off by a large glass door, and a flash of watching Elle naked in the shower hits me hard.

I turn toward her and close the distance between us, gripping her hip with one hand while wrapping my other over her shoulder, near her neck. Then I step her into the wall at her back.

Her eyes go wide as her own hands brace against my forearms.

I lean in, sniffing her neck. The soft scent of coconut fills my nostrils. I'm at a new level of closeness with her.

I whisper low against her ear, "Is your tenant home, Elle?"

Her small body shivers in my hold. "No. She's away."

"Good," I growl. "Because I'm going to make you enjoy some very dirty things, and these walls aren't thick enough to hide how much you're going to love them." I crash my lips against hers in a kiss I've thought about since I saw her outside of Ravenous, and she turns pliable in my hands.

I step forward, wedging my leg between hers and grinding my hip into her core. She opens for me, and I thrust once more, capturing her moan in my mouth. My hand slides from her shoulder to close around her throat, and I hold her head in place for me while I pin her arm against the wall. She rolls her hips forward, riding my upper thigh in response.

There is no planning for tonight.

I've seen the way she looks at me.

We've been dancing toward this since the first night we met, and the song is done playing.

I drop my head to smell her neck again, then nip at the

juncture between her neck and shoulder before tightening my hold on her throat.

"We're going to talk about everything else later. Right now is about us fucking. It's about me taking what I want and giving you what you need. Am I understood?"

Round eyes stare back at me in muted awe, then she nods.

"Say it."

"I understand."

"Good. If anything isn't working out for you, just tell me to stop. Do you understand?"

She nods, and I double down on my glare before she uses her words. "I understand."

"Good girl." I'm not kind when I say it. I'm demanding, basking in her depravity, and she bites her lip one time too many. "Get your pants off and get on your knees."

Up until this moment, I would have told you I was a methodical person. I considered situations and my responses to them. It's a great skill to have when you own your own business.

But something changed somewhere between Marcus telling me what he wanted to do to me while we sat casually at dinner and when he ordered me down to the floor of my bedroom.

Wolves crave the hunt.

And this prey craves to be consumed, that moment when you surrender, allow yourself to float freely in someone else's chaos.

I unbutton my jeans and slide them down as I lower myself to the floor, fully aware that I'm not being graceful about it.

Marcus has tapped into whatever this is that turns me on, and I tuck my legs under me, settling on my knees and sinking my bottom into the heels of my bare feet.

The moment I stop shifting, he steps closer, drawing two fingers along my hairline, down the side of my face, and outward over my jawbone. His expression has changed once again, and my nipples pebble under my shirt at the look of appreciation in his smile.

"Stay kneeled; spread your knees."

When I open myself, his exhale is heavier than before, and he takes a half step, placing himself between my legs.

"Such an obedient little thing." He traces his fingers along my lower lip. "Aren't you?"

I answer him by sliding my tongue out and licking the salty tips of his fingers, and Marcus swears under his breath as he slips them between my teeth and deeper into my mouth.

Gone is the person who concerns herself with appearance, and I go to work unbuttoning his pants. He covers both of my hands as he brushes them away. Then he finishes my work for me, releasing his cock to bob at my eye level.

"You keep biting that lip of yours, and you won't be able to walk for a week." Marcus hooks his fingers under my chin before cradling my jaw in one hand and fisting his erection with the other. "Open."

When Greg spoke about domination, I wasn't interested. But now I'm starting to wonder if it was submission or the vessel that offered it, because I open my mouth willingly and wait in a content state.

Moving closer, he offers the tip of his cock to me. I reach up, only to be chastised and told to keep my palms on either my thighs or his. I acquiesce to a degree and glide my fingers along his muscular thighs as I lick his cock head.

I relax and open to take more of him down, and he feeds himself into my mouth, groaning with every inch he claims. His hand on my jaw angles my head until he pushes against the back of my throat, and I gurgle around him, my gag reflex kicking in. He backs off just enough that I calm myself before he glides back in, and his hands go to either side of my head.

His fingers gently comb through my hair as he vigorously fucks my throat, and the contradicting sensations send my mind reeling.

"Open your eyes, Elle."

The room filters in through my haze, along with the rest of my reality, and shame floods my cheeks with warmth as I remain on my knees in my bedroom, sucking Marcus off on our first date.

This is both nothing like me and everything I've wanted.

"Touch yourself." There's a long pause before, "That's it. Settle that needy pussy of yours down. I'll soothe you soon enough."

I whimper around his girth as he holds my head still around him. His eyes bore into my own, and it takes everything in me not to flutter my eyes shut as I circle the most sensitive spot on my clit.

Spittle covers my chin when he pulls his length out of my mouth and leans over, claiming my lips in an aggressive kiss before lifting me to a standing position.

"Keep your fingers where they are." He leans into me, kissing up my neck before whispering in my ear, "Slow it down, but don't stop touching yourself, Elle. You're being so good for me."

Dammit, his words are lighting me up from deep inside my belly.

Marcus turns his attention to the buttons on my shirt. He undoes the first one, then, once he realizes the buttons open with little effort, he tears open my shirt in one go, leaving it hanging off the wrist of the hand that is shoved down my panties.

Embracing me, he walks us back to the bed and helps me to lie on my back before standing over me.

"Spread your legs wide open. I want to watch you get yourself off."

His eyes dance between mine and the movement of my hand under my panties. Then he climbs onto the bed and slowly peels my underwear away from my body and down my trembling legs.

My mind swirls with pent-up need. A desire that's gone unchecked for too long is rearing its deprived head, and I groan when my legs are released and I'm free to offer him everything.

Holding his attention on my writhing body, Marcus stands slowly and removes his clothes. His face is a mask of stone determination. He moves to the foot of the bed and climbs up between my legs, his face only inches away from my fingers as I play with myself.

I'm close—too close to tipping over the edge.

"You are a work of art. My fucking masterpiece." Marcus pushes my hands out to the side and lowers his head, licking his tongue flat along my pussy before latching on to my clit, and my vision goes blindingly bright.

I arch my back to a painful angle to battle the onslaught of sensation barreling toward me. The first wave of my orgasm crashes into me without warning, and I jerk in his hold.

Strong arms slide over my abdomen and settle me back against the bed. I feel his chuckle in vibrations against my body that combine with the aftershocks.

When I open my eyes, I find Marcus tossing a wrapper to the side. He rolls a condom down the length of his shaft before he pulls up and settles himself between my legs.

"We good?" he asks, searching my face.

"We're goo—"

Everything else is pushed away when he thrusts inside of me until he bottoms out, and I moan along with him as he groans into my ear, carrying his desire deep into my bones.

I drop my head back to the bed as Marcus pulls out in one fluid motion, only to drive back in.

"That's it. Give yourself to me. Let go and drop your hands to the bed. Let me take you." His deep command sinks into my soul, and I let go of his arms and let myself float away.

Marcus takes over, hooking his arms around my legs and spreading me open as he angles himself into me, seemingly deeper and deeper each time. My body bobs and lulls as he claims every piece of me in this moment, and for a short while, I don't want to be my own person.

When I look at him again, my heart cracks.

I want to be his. At his mercy and for his pleasure. Because, right now, his will is my purpose.

In this moment between the chase and the connection, I'm just as wild as he is. I want to be taken, ravaged, consumed, and I want to be freed.

I clench around Marcus as my second orgasm builds, and he continues to pound into me. The weightlessness of my body under him makes my head spin. I moan as his hand finds my throat, and he squeezes just enough for a pressure to build and my pussy to clench again.

"Fuck. I love how your body reacts to me like that. Are you going to come, little one?" The question is more of a taunt, and it sparks my defiance.

I'm about to open my mouth to tell him no, but that would be a lie. My body betrays the words I won't dare say when my legs shake uncontrollably in his hold. I seize up tight before I break wide open and scream his name.

Marcus cuts off all sound when he grips my throat once more. I spasm around him as he draws out my euphoria, and he throws his head back with a roar and follows me over the edge.

Dropping his weight onto my body, Marcus releases my legs, and I wrap them around his midsection as we come back from the abyss. He kisses my forehead a few times before shifting his weight and pulling himself out of me.

He works the condom off, then rolls to the side of the bed and quickly tosses it in the trash bin. Then he returns, wraps an arm around my midsection, and slides me into him before drawing lines along my abdomen and circling my nipple.

I roll on my side, tucking my head under his chin. I'm thankful we aren't staring at each other, because I don't know what to say. I mean, let's gloss over the fact that we just had sex on our first date, but what do you say to the guy who's just given you the single best orgasm of your life?

"I like you too, Elle." Marcus speaks against my hair before kissing my head.

My name sounds off somehow, and I lie in silence, trying to make sense of it. Then I realize it isn't the name I want him to have.

"Elora."

He shifts, angling his body away from mine to look at my face. "My full first name is Elora. Only Lexa knows that, and—um, I want you to know it too."

I don't know where this came from. I've never felt the need to share it with anyone. Lexa knows it because she overheard my mother use my full name once when I was in trouble.

This makes me feel even more vulnerable than sharing my darkest fantasy did, but I can't take it back now. A cold sweat washes over the warm bliss that covered my body moments ago, but Marcus stills my thoughts.

"Elora." He tries my name out, and it sounds seductive coming from his lips. "It suits you. Thank you for giving it to me."

We stay wrapped up in each other until the room grows dark, and I finally stand to turn on the light and grab a robe.

Greg and I kept our arrangement in the club and we never

saw each other outside of those doors. I'm painfully aware of how long it's been since I've progressed beyond the first date with anyone when I fail to remember the protocol for staying overnight.

"You look like you're struggling with something." Marcus stands and gathers his clothes.

"Well, I—it's getting late. Would you like to—" I point at the bed, and Marcus smiles as understanding dawns.

"I can't. Trust me, I will. But I have an early morning staff meeting, and I need to get going."

His answer is bittersweet. I wonder what it would be like to wake up next to him in the morning, but at the same time, I want to be alone with my feelings tonight.

"I'll walk you out then. Would you like to take the pizza home?"

I turn my back on him and wince. What a way to cool the vibe. Send him home with pizza, like it's a gift with purchase.

"Actually, why don't you bring it to work tomorrow. I'll meet you at your office for lunch. I'd like to go over some security details for the Ravenous event." He closes in on me quicker than I realize, and I jump when his fingers pull the hair away from my neck. He brushes his lips against my throat, trailing kisses along my skin. "Plus, I'm not sure I can go much longer than that without seeing you again."

His answer makes me sigh. I literally sigh, then it turns into a choked cough to hide my mortification.

"Sure. Yes, I'd like that." I pull my pants up under my robe and grab a hoodie out of my closet before leading him back to our shoes and down the stairs.

We talk about the yard, and Marcus asks who planted all of the beautiful flowers. When we round the path to the front of the house, I stop short.

It takes a moment for my disappointment to set in as I stare at a spot in the garden, and I sense Marcus turning to look in the same direction as me.

"My tulips."

At least, they *were* my tulips.

Now they are just a pile of petals and hacked stems lying in the dirt. At least the bulbs are still in the ground. They should come up again next year, but I hate that they were snuffed out so soon.

"Does that always happen around here?" Marcus steps to the edge of my garden.

"No. Maybe a dog got loose." I look out toward the street, as though the little culprit will present themselves, but it's quiet.

"Well, I'm going to say good night now, but I won't pull away until you text me that you are locked upstairs safe and sound." He turns, squaring himself on me and closing the distance between us.

When he tips my chin up, I capitulate into him.

His soft lips brush against my own. Then he leans in, nudging at me to open for him, and I do. His kiss blocks out the world around us and demands my surrender.

When he breaks away, his grin holds a hint of confidence.

"Get your rest, Ms. Sinclair. Next time, I won't go so easy on you."

If that was him going easy, I'm not sure I can handle what comes next.

The street is quiet when I pull up to the front of my building.

I'm so lost in my thoughts about earlier and fumbling for my swipe card to the front door that I'm oblivious to the world around me.

"Hey, stranger." I spin in place, startling Noah and Hazel. Noah quickly recovers. "Sorry, man. I thought you heard me calling your name back there."

"Oh. Sorry. I was looking for my card."

Noah pulls his out of his pocket but doesn't use it. "We were just talking about you. We haven't seen you around for a couple of weeks. Everything good?"

Noah's realty company helped us secure some of the buildings we operate out of, so I reached out to him when I was looking for a place of my own. It turned out he was looking for an occasional driver and someone to help around this building, which he owns. So I moved in.

I stopped driving for them when I went back to my own business. That was shortly after he and Hazel had a run-in with a stalker of their own, last year, and I still keep an eye on their security.

"Things are good. Actually, I haven't had the chance to thank you and Joshua for connecting me with Alexandra Loren. We have some projects with Ravenous because of you."

"I'm glad it worked out." Noah swipes his card against the reader, and the door clicks open.

"Speaking of which, have you received any invitations from Ravenous lately?"

Hazel defers to Noah, and he holds up his phone. "I have something here about an upcoming event. A new-member thing. Are you working on that?"

When I tell him I am, Hazel tugs on his arm and asks if they can go. Noah tells her they'll take a closer look at the invitation when they get upstairs.

Then she looks at me. "I'll make sure Emilia and Joshua know about it too. It would be fun to get out together."

Noah rolls his eyes behind her. "Fine. Just let me tell Joshua about it first. You know he likes to think he's the one making the decisions." He reaches for Hazel's arm and guides her toward the elevator. "Let's make plans for a game night or something. Beers at our place. Soon."

Noah looks over his shoulder to make sure I heard him, and I nod and wave before stepping into my apartment.

I instantly miss the atmosphere of Elle's place.

Not Elle—*Elora*.

The name is as special as she is, because not everyone gets that part of her, but she wanted me to have it.

I enjoy the hunt, but I'm starting to think it's the possession I crave beyond all else. Having pieces of Elle no one else has. Her full name, her screams when she releases herself to me, and her vulnerability—those are treasures I covet.

But *Elora*, that part of her is extremely personal, and I will reserve it for special moments, tucking it away in my mind for later.

I've never noticed the empty echo my keys make when I drop them on my counter, but tonight the sound is amplified, and the room feels colder than normal.

Morning meeting be damned, I should have stayed over. I could have been wrapped tightly around her—or in her.

My phone rings, and I waste no time glancing at the screen, hoping it's Elle, but it isn't. I have her number saved in my phone. This is a blocked number.

"Hello." I wait for a few seconds before repeating myself. I pull the phone away and glance at the screen. The seconds on the call continue counting up. I'm about to tell whoever it is that I can't hear them when the line goes dead. I set my phone on the counter beside my keys, opting for a cool shower before bed. Otherwise, I might decide to drive back and crawl under the sheets with Elle.

My meeting went longer than I thought it would, and everything got pushed back. So when it was finally time to leave for lunch, I tore out of our office, leaving Jax to wrap things up.

He'll no doubt have questions for me later, but I don't care.

The elevator doors open to Elle's floor, and I turn away from the conference room and head toward the offices along the back wall.

Her assistant looks up and smiles as she lifts her phone to her ear. "Yes. Elle, your lunch—um, meeting is here. Sure thing." Then she hangs up and points to a closed door. "She's just wrapping up; she said you can go right in."

"Thank you." I step to the door and knock twice before entering, even though she knows I'm on my way in.

A woman I haven't met before is sitting in a chair in front of Elle, who is sitting behind her desk with Daniel standing over her, pointing to something on the paper in her hands. They break apart when I enter, and Elle smiles.

"Ms. Sinclair. Your receptionist told me to come in. Is now a good time?"

"Absolutely. Daniel, how about the two of you work on the catering issue this afternoon, and we'll meet again in the morning?" She glances up at him, but he doesn't notice because he's looking at me.

"Of course." He tilts his head in my direction. "Mr. Wolfe." He doesn't wait for me to answer. He motions for the woman with them to follow him out, and I close the door behind them.

Elle stands and circles her desk before leaning back against it and angling her body seductively. "What time is it, Mr. Wolfe?"

I wonder how long she's been saving that one as I step back to the door and turn the lock, securing us inside.

"Well, it is lunchtime." I close the distance between us until I'm leaning against her, and she has no choice but to arch her back, jutting her perfect tits out as I hover her over the desk. "And I am so, so hungry"—I lower my voice into a deep growl as I whisper into her ear—"Elora."

She sets her arms on the surface of the desk behind her to brace her body. As she shudders underneath me, I lower my head further to kiss her exposed neck.

When she doesn't make a move to break away, I push, placing one hand on her hip and sliding it up her waist, then her rib cage.

I glance over her shoulder at the desk behind her to make sure there is nothing in my way. "On second thought, lunch can wait. I want a taste of you—unless you have an objection."

I don't yet know what I can get away with in public with Elle—and at her work, no less—so for now, we need to communicate.

Her eyes flit from mine to the door over my shoulder. "Is it locked?" She licks her lips.

"Yes."

Her response is breathy. "Lunch can wait."

I cup the back of her head in one hand and wrap my other around her throat, holding her face inches away from my own. "I'm going to lay you back on your desk, take down your panties, and have my fill of your pretty little cunt while your staff works just outside that door. Do you like the thought of that? Having your pussy eaten while they all think you're in here being a good little CEO? We both know better, don't we?"

As she says yes, I rock my hands, controlling her head and nodding it for her before sucking that bottom lips she loves to bite between my own teeth.

"Good girl."

I release her and hook my hands under her skirt, wrenching it up and dragging her dark pink panties down to the floor, but not before I notice the start of a wet spot on the fabric. The sight goes straight to my cock, and I stand, guiding her back onto the desk and tugging her skirt the rest of the way up to her waist.

I leave her heels on. Those nude shoes that show off her calves when she walks are a symbol of her control and the power she holds in this office, and she'll come on my tongue while she wears them.

"Unbutton your top." She works the fabric as I trace my fingers along her slippery folds before I push two inside of her, and she fumbles with her task. Her back arches off the table.

I slide a chair closer to the front of the desk and wrap my hands around her hips, pulling her into me. "Get that top wide open," I command as I replace my fingers with my tongue and groan into her. The vibrations cause her to wriggle, but my hold on her is tight.

I'm so lost in the taste of her and how her body moves in reaction to my touch that the sight of her splayed across her desk with her top open for me pulls a groan from my throat.

Sitting up, I slide my fingers through her pussy lips as her chest rises and falls under her bra with her sharp breaths.

"Fuck. Look at you, little one. Are you going to be quiet for me? Let me lick this sweet pussy and take anything I want, right here? Or are you going to be loud and let them all hear how dirty their boss is?"

Elle's body bows, trying to delay the start of her orgasm as she whimpers. I adjust her and bear down, telling her how good she tastes when she opens herself up to me, and she stretches her arms away from her body.

"There's my good girl, Elora." I speak her name against a sensitive spot on her clit, and her hands shoot to my head. She tangles her fingers in my short hair, and her movements become frenzied as she pulls me into her and grinds her hips as much as she can in my hold.

"That's it. Show me how you like it."

She's moaning, but there's no sound. Instead, it comes out with each breath. She still knows where we are.

The muscles in her thighs tremble before her grip around my head tightens, and I pry open her thighs as I latch on to her clit and press my tongue against a sensitive spot.

Elle seizes. Her muscles tighten at once as her orgasm consumes her, and she spasms around my tongue as I shove it deep inside her. She tenses in waves as she rides out her release, and I replace my tongue with my fingers. My cock grows stiff with each thrust of my fingers into her slick channel.

Her eyes flit down, taking in my erection, and she lifts enough to tug at my pants.

"I don't have anything with me."

"I'm on birth control. Please. I want to—here."

Her eyes flit to the locked door before returning to plead with me, and I unzip my pants and slide into her in the next breath, returning my hand to her throat.

"Drop your hands to your desk." Grabbing her thigh with my free hand, I hold her open as I pull out and drive in, burying myself to my balls. "That's it, Elora. Let this happen. Lie there and let me fuck you while the rest of the world goes on just outside that door. Fuck. You feel so good milking my cock. There's my good girl."

She shudders at the picture I'm painting with my words, and an audible moan slips from her lips without warning.

"Shh, princess. You don't want your staff to hear you taking it like a whore. You be my quiet little mouse and come for me, or I'm going to work you up and make you scream my name."

She tries to tighten her thighs around my hips. But I hold one open as I pound into her, and they start to shake as she arches and wriggles against me.

I release her neck and move my fingers to her clit to pinch then rub along her slickened skin, and she sits up, wrapping her arms around me and pulling me close as she bucks against me with her orgasm. I rest my chin on her shoulder as I push deep a few more times and follow her over as I finish.

When she takes a cleansing breath, I pull myself out, then lift her from the desk and set her across my lap, sitting back in her chair and stroking her hair as she rests her head on my chest.

"I'm not going to be able to concentrate on a damn thing all day," I chuckle, and she laughs with me.

I could sit like this with her for the rest of the day, but eventually someone will come knocking. After a few minutes, Elle stands. She pulls her skirt down but leaves her underwear in their spot on the floor. Then she kicks off her heels and pads across her office to a small room off to the side.

A toilet flushes, then she returns, walking to a kitchenette off to the side of the room. She opens the bar fridge, removes a familiar pizza box, and returns, opening it and setting it on her desk.

"Now I'm really hungry." Elle takes a piece, hands it to me, then returns for one of her own.

We get dressed as we eat and end up on the couch at the back of the room. The conversation turns to business when I ask if Alexandra sent her a list of anyone we should watch out for during Ravenous's upcoming event.

"She sent it this morning, and I noticed she copied Kate, so Wolfe Security should have it soon. It's a short list. She said they've only had a few members become an issue." She reaches for a napkin, then stands and retrieves her phone, tapping the screen before handing it to me. "This is the whole list."

It makes our job easy when there are only six names on the list. I notice one of the last names from when Hazel had an issue with Paul Davenfield last year. I hand the phone back and go over what will happen in the background while the event is going on.

I confirm a few procedures that might be different than what Swank is used to, such as all phones being left at the door, or, better yet, at home, to protect the privacy of everyone attending.

There's no easy segue into my next topic, so I just toss it out there.

"You mentioned predator/prey as something that might interest you. I have a proposal for you."

Elle finishes her last bite. "A—proposal?"

"Yes. I want to make sure you're safe in your home, test your current security. And at the same time, I'd like to explore *that* with you a little more. I want your permission to stalk you and try to break into your home. It's what I did for Alexandra." When Elle straightens, I realize how it sounds. "What I mean is, an acquaintance of hers hired me to test her security, and I broke into her office, then gave her a list of things she could fix."

"Oh. And that's how you came to teach the defense class at Ravenous?"

I nod. "And I'd like to do that for you. I want to make sure you're safe, Elle."

She reaches for her napkin and wipes her greasy fingers. "How would that work?"

"Well, it would take some time to set up. I'd need your permission to look into you, to obtain what I would need to get close, and you wouldn't know ahead of time when I'd show up, but I can promise to do my best not to scare you when it happens." I speak slowly, making sure she understands this next part. "Unless you *want* me to scare you and make it real enough for you."

She sits in contemplative silence before speaking again. "I think I would want it to feel real, uh, I mean, with you." She tears at the napkin in her hands.

"Understood. In that case, I'm going to ask you to come up with a word you can say if you ever become overwhelmed or if anything starts to feel too real for you. Something easy that you don't say every day."

I give her a moment to search for one.

"Bowling?" she offers.

"Bowling," I confirm. "If you say that, I shut it down. Do you understand?"

"Yes. When are you—um, going to break in?"

I almost laugh out loud at the question, but one look at her wide eyes tells me she is honestly asking.

"That, you don't get to know. But it won't be in the next couple of days. I have some homework to do."

When the phone on Elle's desk rings, I check my watch to find that lunchtime—and playtime—is over, but I find myself not wanting to leave Elle once more.

CHAPTER 15
ELLE

I will never look at my desk the same way again—ever. I may have to burn it and get a new one if I ever hope to get any work done.

Every now and then, I still catch a hint of Marcus's smell, even though it's fading now that others have been in and out of my office this afternoon.

The door handle clicks. There's only one person who enters without being announced, and that's Nat.

At least I think it's her, but I can't tell yet, because whoever it is is hidden behind the biggest bouquet of flowers I've ever seen in my life.

"Where's the table? I can't see a damn thing under all of this bullshit."

Yup, it's Nat.

I jump to my feet. "Here. Let me help you."

I guide her to my little meeting table, then help her set it down.

We both step back to take in the mountain of roses in front of us.

"Who are these from?" I ask, and she glances down at the piece of paper in her hand.

"It doesn't say on here. Let me check for a card."

"Maybe it's a happy client." I take a second look at the flowers. "A really happy client."

"Or a secret admirer," Nat says, but half her words are muffled by the sheer number of roses in her face. She keeps digging around before she jolts. "Ouch! Stupid thorns."

She stands up straight, sucking on her forefinger, and I take over looking around the stems.

"There it is." Nat points to a rectangular card nestled between the cellophane and the vase, and I slide my fingers down and grab it.

I turn it over. There are only four words on the front of the card:

The time has come

"That's weird." Nat reads the card over my shoulder. "Where's the rest of the message? Does that make sense to you?"

I look back at the flowers, wondering if this is part of Marcus's process.

"No idea. Maybe the card is meant for someone else. I mean, it was kind of just stuck in there."

"Maybe," Nat mutters, then sighs. "Well, this was anticlimactic. I'm going to go and photocopy something."

When she opens the door, Daniel is on the other side. He jumps, his hand already raised in the air as though he was ready to knock. "Sorry, Nat. There was no one out here."

I call around her, "Did you need to see me?" He nods. "Come in, I have some time."

It's hard not to notice the massive amount of flowers sitting on my table. Their scent is so strong that it's wiped away all traces of Marcus from the room.

"Thanks. Nice flowers. Who are they from?" Daniel asks.

"No idea," I lie. I have a pretty good idea.

"Well, you obviously mean a lot to someone."

I'm about to point at the seat in front of my desk when the sight of Marcus between my thighs slips into my mind, and I blush hard.

The flowers are taking over my table, and the couch is too personal. I have no other choice but to return to the scene of the crime.

"Have a seat." I gesture to the chair in front, circle my desk, and sit down. "What's up?"

"I think we sorted out the catering. I ended up asking Julie, and she knew of a caterer who was able to meet all of our client's requirements. We have a call in to them now."

"Wonderful. Thank you for stepping up to help our new intern, Daniel. I knew I could count on you."

Daniel smiles and looks over his notes, saying, "Thank you for saying that, Elle."

I open the middle drawer on my desk and pull out a file folder. "Where are we at for the Ravenous event?"

"It's going well. All of the main vendors are booked, and the contracts are signed. I have a few meetings left to go over our client request sheet. I'm heading out to one in an hour, and I'll finish the other two up tomorrow."

"Great. Are you waiting on anything?"

"Ms. Loren was going to send over a ban list, so we don't accidentally include anyone we shouldn't."

I click my mouse and open my email. "She sent it to me this morning. One second—here it is. I'll forward it to you. Done."

"She also mentioned a questionnaire, if anyone wants to participate? Do you have more details on that?"

I open my file folder. "Yes. It's similar to the one they hand out in their club, for anyone who would like to learn more about themselves or find people with similar interests. We need to be very clear that this is optional, and that by filling it out, they may be matched with certain interests, so it is important that they are completely truthful—and it is one hundred percent private. She is working on getting a final questionnaire ready, but this should give you an idea."

I glance at the sample form that Lexa sent over. Memories of sitting with Greg and going through something similar float to the surface.

I moved quickly with Greg. We weren't an exact fit for each other, but both of us were willing to look beyond our differences. It's hard to find someone who is perfect, so we settled for close enough.

It turned out my instincts about him were way off.

Arrested for human trafficking? And I wonder how close I came to being next. What would have happened to me if he wasn't caught?

A chill slithers down my spine when the question floats into my head: *Am I moving too fast with Marcus?*

We had half a date before I ended up in bed with him, not to mention what happened right in front of me on this desk only two hours ago.

This is unlike me, but I'm happy when I'm with him, and he makes me feel comfortable in my own skin. And now I've asked him to stalk me and break into my house. The thought alone should have me ending things with him, but each time I think about backing away, my heart aches.

"Hey, Elle? Are you okay?"

I snap out of my thoughts to meet Daniel's eyes. He's holding the paper I removed from the file, but I don't remember handing it to him.

"Yes. Sorry. Lots on my plate."

"Is there anything I can do for you?"

I smile, then shake my head. "No. I'm good. Thank you though."

Daniel stares at me for a long moment before sliding to the edge of his seat. "Hey, listen, it's probably none of my business, but are you sure seeing Mr. Wolfe is a good idea?" My questions must be written all over my face, because Daniel backtracks. "I mean, they are vendors now and—I just don't want to see you get hurt. Like with Greg. That really caught you off guard, and, well, it wasn't good for—you."

Daniel was one of the two people I confided in when everything fell apart, and he saw me at my rock bottom when I thought I was being stalked.

"I appreciate your concern, Daniel, but I'm okay. We should schedule one last meeting with Alexandra to go over the final details. Let's make it a lunch meeting. She likes those. Can you ask Nat to set it up for us?"

There's a beat before Daniel answers where he looks like he wants to continue the conversation we were having, but he ignores it.

"Sure thing." He gathers his papers and adds the questionnaire to his pile, then stands. "Also, remember we have our yearly audits coming up. I'll make sure Nat schedules a night together for us."

"Oh, right. Thank you." I'm slipping. It should be me reminding him of this.

Daniel takes a few steps, then turns to look at the bouquet on my table once more before looking back at me. "Just think about what I said."

He leaves before I respond, and I wait until the door closes behind him before I exhale. The force of my breath lifts the corner of a paper on the desk in front of me.

I glance at the flowers.

Maybe I am moving too fast, and I'm missing some red flags I'd see if I slowed down a bit.

But the thought doesn't sit right in my stomach.

If I start questioning Marcus now, I could lose a chance at happiness with someone who, so far, accepts all of me. But Daniel is right. I screwed up with Greg. Maybe my radar is broken.

These thoughts play over and over in my mind, chipping away at my confidence over the rest of my afternoon. By the time Marcus calls and Nat asks if she can put him through, I tell her to let him know I'm in a meeting.

Then, when he texts suggesting we get together this weekend, I tell him Fridays and Saturdays are always booked, that we have a couple of big-ticket events happening both nights, and I'm busy.

It doesn't feel right. None of this feels good, and by the time I'm done with work, I'm ready to go home and sit in my quiet house all by myself.

Swank has nothing planned for tonight, and it's the first time in a long time I'm actually free on a Friday. My guilt sits heavy on my shoulders and follows me all of the way to my empty home.

I was looking forward to seeing Elle at some point this past weekend, but Sunday night came, then went, and I had barely heard from her.

Many of my texts on Saturday went unanswered, except for the ones about the Ravenous event coming up. Those, she answered in short sentences.

With the extra free time on my hands, I decided to start looking for a way into her home as we had discussed.

One of the first things I found out was that Swank didn't have an event on Friday night like she told me they did.

I chalked it up to her just wanting a night to herself and being unsure of how to communicate it to me. I planned to talk to her about it, but then Saturday went by, followed quickly by Sunday, and now a new week has begun.

Alexandra texted first thing this morning, asking if Wolfe Security was attending the Ravenous business lunch that Swank set up for today. It was clear to me she thought we were invited.

We weren't, but I told her I would be there.

I don't want things to end with Elle—not before they've even started—but avoidance will only make matters worse, so she will face me.

I stroll into the restaurant five minutes late. It's not on purpose. A three-car accident in the middle of an intersection made getting here difficult.

Elle is seated with her back to me. She talks and laughs with Lexa as I round the table, coming into view of both her and Daniel.

It's clear they are both surprised to see me.

I don't look over at Daniel. My attention is reserved for my special girl, who's looking guilty in front of me.

There's a hint of her fire in her gaze, but her demeanor shifts instantly, and she shuts down before reaching for her glass of water as Lexa points to the chair beside her.

"Marcus, I'm glad you could join us."

"Thank you for inviting me—Alexandra." I make my point: that Elle did not extend the invitation.

"You're just on time. We haven't ordered yet."

Daniel clears his throat, and I glance over at him. "Mr. Wolfe. It's nice to see you."

"Please, call me Marcus." I slide my attention to his right. "Elle. How are you?"

She reaches for her napkin, unfolds it, and sets it on her lap. "I'm well, thank you."

Lexa fills me in on the few minutes of conversation I missed. As I listen, I hold my attention on Alexandra, but I look around the table in my peripheral. Daniel steals glances at Elle and me out of the corner of his eye, but Elle remains somber and unable to look over at me.

Something is definitely up.

The waiter breaks the tension when he arrives to take our

order. The women order first. Elle orders a chicken club with cheese, then the waiter looks at me.

"I'm interested in the same thing she is." I gesture to Elle, hoping to capture her gaze. It works for a fleeting moment.

When our eyes lock, my stomach sinks with a sense of helplessness. Elle is struggling with something deep, and she has chosen to keep it to herself. We're still new. So new that I'm not sure how to approach this without pushing her away.

So when she looks down, I back off and lean into my seat as Daniel orders the same.

For a business meeting, lunch is fairly quiet. Alexandra looks around the table curiously on more than one occasion, and I second-guess coming to the meeting at all.

Daniel and Lexa spend the entire meal giving up on Elle and ironing out all of the final details between themselves, with the occasional agreement and nod coming from the CEO of Swank.

By the time the bill is paid, my uncertainty turns to frustration and anger.

"So, everything is pretty much ready to go then, and we're on for Saturday? I look forward to seeing you all there." Lexa slides her chair back and stands. "I can't thank you enough for all of the work you put into this."

Elle and Daniel stand to say goodbye, and it's clear to me they are just going to leave along with her.

I deserve better.

"Elle, I'd like you to stay so I can speak with you."

She doesn't look surprised, but she is hesitant.

"I was just going to walk Alexandra to the door."

"I'll see myself out. We'll talk soon." Lexa levels her with a glare, silently telling her to deal with her shit before she attempts a smile and tells Elle she loves her. Then she dismisses herself from the table.

Elle turns back to the table, and we both look at Daniel, who isn't sure what to do.

"I'll meet you back at the office." Elle steps between her chair and the table and sits down.

Daniel looks at me before lowering his voice. "Are you sure? I can wait over there by the bar."

My patience is almost gone, and I'm close to telling the guy to just leave when Elle smiles up at him and says, "I'm sure."

Daniel looks to me and nods, backing away from us and heading toward the exit.

Now that we're alone, Elle finally looks directly at me. The weight of whatever is on her mind breaks through her expression.

She's exhausted. Her usually bright eyes are puffy.

"You're going to tell me exactly what has changed since the last time I saw you."

She breaks our eye contact, her eyes lazily lowering as she considers her answer. "I—I don't know." When Elle forces her eyes back up to mine, her forehead creases. She looks like I feel.

Helpless.

There is something, and I sense she's just as confused as I am.

"Then start at the beginning. I left you in your office after lunch on Friday." The corner of her mouth twitches up in a smile as she nods. "Then what happened?"

Elle starts telling me about her afternoon. Nothing stands out, and she smiles recalling how she couldn't stop thinking about what we did on her desk.

"And then your flowers showed up, and—"

"Flowers? I didn't send flowers." The hairs on the back of my neck stand up.

She snaps into place at that, pinching her eyebrows together in confusion.

Finally, Elle takes a deep breath, deeper than should be physically possible. Relief washes over her body, and she releases her shoulders for the first time since lunch started.

"Really? I—oh—"

She tilts her head in thought, and I imagine she's asking herself the same question I am:

If I didn't send her flowers, who did?

"There was no card?" I prompt.

She takes a little longer to answer this time. "There was, but I thought maybe it was just a mistake."

"What did it say?"

"*The time has come.* That's it. It didn't make sense." She returns to her thoughts, and I'm not willing to leave her there—not alone, at least.

"So you thought I sent you flowers and—"

Her lips round in mortification. "It's not like—no. I mean, I started to think, and—ugh. It's just that there were at least five dozen roses in there, and I panicked because we barely got through our first date before we..." She motions between us to indicate our rapid escalation to sex. "You know."

"Before we fucked." Shame flushes into her cheeks. She nods, and I keep going. "You think we're moving too fast?"

"Yes." Then she shakes her head, and her shoulders slump forward. "No. I wanted every minute of it, and I don't think we moved too fast, but that's what scared me." Then she leans in, her eyes pleading. "I'm worried that I'm not being rational. I've never been a part of anything so—intense before. I wasn't this close to Greg, and I still missed so much I should have seen. And with you, I feel like I could just lose myself sometimes."

I slide my seat closer to the table when she hits on her real issue, and I clarify, "You don't trust yourself to make good decisions because of what happened in the past."

Her chin trembles before she sniffles, holding in her

emotions. "I don't want to screw this up. But I think I already have."

I stand and circle the table, claiming the seat beside her and sliding my chair close to hers. Then I brace my arm around the back of her chair, lean in, and take her hand.

"Hey. Unfortunately, no one's doing any screwing right now." My sad attempt at lightening the mood breaks her misery, and she chuckles. "We're going to talk more about all of this soon, but nothing is damaged between us. This is your past experience talking to you. Learn from it, but don't entertain it. You need to talk to me when these thoughts come to you. Will you do that for me?"

"I'll do that."

I cup the back of her neck and pull her into me for a kiss. I'm not as aggressive as I have been in the past, and she tugs at my jacket, pulling me closer.

All of the tension around us dissipates as we break apart, and I tell her I'll escort her back to her building.

Once we're outside, I offer her my elbow, and she hooks her arm through and falls into step beside me.

"I'm going to continue my security check on your place, but I'm delaying my break-in. I'd like to make sure you're safe, but I think we need to work through a few things first."

Her step falters, but she recovers, and she sounds disappointed when she says, "I understand."

I also want to look into who sent her those flowers, but I don't share that part with her.

I stop on the sidewalk outside of Swank's offices and turn Elle to face me. "What is Greg's last name?" When Elle looks like she wants to challenge me, I furrow my brows and stare her down.

We really need to have a discussion about discipline soon.

She seems to know better than to question me.

"I think he went by Gregory Pasternak when he was on trial."

Even though the question is written all over her face, she doesn't ask me why I want to know, and I thank her before stepping into her and kissing her forehead. I want more, but we're in front of her place of business. While I have no problem defiling her behind closed doors, I won't do that to her in public unless it's something she explicitly asks for.

When we break apart, I hook two fingers under her chin and lift her eyes to mine. "I'm not going anywhere, Elora." Her eyes flit around quickly, looking for who else could have heard me say her full name. No one is close enough, and the din of the traffic is too loud. "I want to make you dinner tomorrow night—at my place, and at your pace."

"I'd like that."

"Good. I'll text you my address." She releases my hand and enters her building, looking one hundred times better than she did earlier.

I wait with my thoughts for a minute.

I don't like that she got close to sixty roses with a cryptic message attached to them. It doesn't sit well with me, and I wonder if it is my security background talking, or if I'm quickly becoming possessive of her.

"Mr. Wolfe." Daniel's voice pulls me out of my thoughts, and I turn to find him approaching from the same direction we came.

"Daniel, please, call me Marcus. I thought you would have beat us back."

Daniel looks at the door just beyond us. "I stopped to grab a coffee for the walk back. Did you sort everything out—with Elle?" He says her name slowly.

"I did. I'll see you on Saturday at the event."

"Sure." He steps around me to the door, then thinks better

of it and turns back to me. He points his thumb over his shoulder at the building that's now at his back. "We are all kind of protective of Elle. A few of us are close enough that we know what happened last year, and, well, we don't want it to happen again."

I sense he doesn't want to come right out and talk about Elle behind her back, and I don't push it. "I understand."

"No. I'm not sure you do. She doesn't need a repeat of what she went through, and guys like you and Remy are all the same."

"Remy—Larsen?" I interject in confusion.

"Yeah. The guy pretty much showed up at her office last week and demanded Elle join him for a drink. I had to step in to make him leave her office."

I mentally add this to my list of things that Elle isn't sharing with me. "I assure you, I am not like Remy Larsen."

Daniel takes a step backward before muttering, "We'll see." It's just loud enough that I catch it before a horn blares behind me. Then he turns and leaves me standing by myself.

Judging by the looks on everyone's faces, I should probably up my presence around the office.

Kate glances up as I near her desk, then does a double take before shuffling papers around her desk as she greets me. I pass her, and she grabs a notepad before chasing me to catch up as I head down the hall toward the office I never use.

"What are you doing?" I stop abruptly, and she barrels into my back before righting herself.

"I—uh—I'm not sure." She glances down at the pen and pad in her hands, then back up. "Did I forget about a meeting?"

I chuckle. "No. I just need to set up a place to work. Can you send IT over to my office?"

Her eyes go wide. "Are you—are you coming back?"

She looks so hopeful, and I consider her question.

I never really left the company, I just haven't been here. I've used these past couple of years to pull my ass out of the mental pit I fell into.

When Jax gave me the chance to work at the defense

center, it was what I needed to start climbing out. I immersed myself in hands-on training, and I strengthened myself by strengthening others. But it wasn't until our class at Ravenous that the thought of returning to the office started to take hold. I'd be lying if I said Elle had nothing to do with it.

Now seems like a good time to come back. I've missed working with Kate—and even Jax—and the fact that I need to look into Elle is also a deciding factor.

"I think I am."

A grin stretches wide across my sister's face. "Wow. Okay." Then it breaks into disappointment. "I told Jax you had two more months, then I was turning your office into a game room." She takes a long look at me, as if weighing both options before saying, "I'm glad I get you back instead." She opens her notepad and starts writing while she talks. "Okay. I'll get everything set up. Does Jax know?"

"He doesn't. I just decided today was the day. Is he busy?"

"He's on his way back from the academy. He should be here anytime now." We have a contract with our local law enforcement to provide sessions on profiling as part of their curriculum.

"Great. Can you tell him I'd like to see him in my office when he's back? He'll get a kick out of that."

"Are you kidding? He won't believe me."

I open the door to my empty office. "Not my problem, little sis." I wink at her.

Kate stays in her spot in the hall, staring at me while she plays with the corners of the pages in her notepad. "It's—really good to have you back."

It's in the way her voice breaks on the last word that tells me she means that in more ways than one.

"It's good to be back, Kate."

This would normally be the part where she leaves, but she

stays rooted in place, staring at me and grinning for a beat longer before snapping out of her thoughts. "Right! I'll give you some space to get settled, and I'll send Lewis over to hook up your computer."

I leave my door open a crack and take in the office I left a couple of years ago. It's weird standing here. When I left it for good, I never came back. I've been in the building for meetings, but this just seemed like a door I was never ready to walk through. Until now.

I circle the desk to take a seat. My chair is gone, replaced by some generic office seat that will probably put my back out by Friday. I'm pretty sure I saw my fancy ergonomic chair in Jax's office.

The desk drawers have been emptied, with the exception of a few pens. A cardboard box with my name on it sits on top of a bookshelf. Above my name, it reads DO NOT TOUCH in Kate's handwriting.

When I open the box, I see why she left it here and didn't send it to my place. An old award with my name etched into a glass plate stares up at me. It was recognition for all of my years at my old job. There are also some commemorative items from my time with Wolfe Security. All the things I didn't think I deserved over the last two years and have been shunning ever since Adelaine died.

I'm still not ready to display them on the shelf behind me, but I do find a picture of the three of us with our parents at their cabin. It was taken a few years ago, when we were celebrating my parents' fortieth wedding anniversary.

That, I dig out and set on my desk.

Along the side of the box is an old pad of paper, and I pull that out too, then return to my hard chair and take a pen from my drawer, drawing little circles on the paper to get the ink flowing.

I start by writing two names on the top of the page: Gregory Pasternak and Remy Larsen.

"Hey, Kate told me you need a hookup." A gangly kid hangs on to the door as he looks into the room, and I stand, waving him in.

He's short on social skills and makes a beeline for the computer on my desk, picking at the wires hanging from it and taking inventory of what he's working with. He shoves his phone into his pocket and kneels out of my line of sight, leaving me with only the sound of his shuffling as he plugs things in.

His head occasionally pops up when he follows the wires back to the monitor and keyboard. Then, a few minutes later, he stands and circles the desk to my side, powers the monitor on, and types away.

"Can I get a pen and paper?" He points to my desk, and I tear off my two names and slide the rest over to him.

My brother's voice resonates down the hall. "I'm telling you, Kate. I don't have time for this. What's really in his office?"

Kate's voice is filled with amusement when she swears it's me in the office, and my brother steps into the room with a sigh before stopping mid-step with a look of actual shock on his face.

"Holy shit—Marcus. What the hell? I mean—it's great to have you back, but—what the hell?"

Now Kate follows him into my office and glances between us like she's trying to commit this moment to memory.

Jax took on a lot of the company when I checked out, and I owe him more than I will ever be able to repay. The guy went into overdrive, running our operation and handling most of our clients.

I stand and take one look around my empty office. My eyes land on our family photo, then glance up to my siblings. "It's time, Jax. It probably should have been sooner, and for that I apologize, but it's time. I'd like to meet with you to discuss taking back some of the workload."

"Of course. I have time open this afternoon." He glances at Kate, silently confirming his schedule, and she nods.

The IT guy raises his hand to interject. "I have you set up and ready to go." He slides the notepad across the desk. "Here are your passwords to get into the system and your email, and my number is on the bottom. Text if anything doesn't work."

As he speaks, I take stock of the passwords and the phone number, which is written under the name *Lewis*.

"Thank you." I answer in unison with Kate, and Lewis takes that as his cue to leave.

"I'll give you some time to get settled." Jax looks around my office. "Come see me when you're ready." Then he looks at Kate. "We'll need to order some furniture for this room. Can I leave the design with you?"

Kate's face lights right up. We both know one of the things she takes great joy in is design.

"Actually, can I talk to you right now—for a minute?" I point to a metal chair in the corner of the room. "About Ravenous and a couple of things."

"Sure." Jax props his briefcase against the wall and slides the chair over to my desk. Kate backs out, closing the door behind her.

"I was at a lunch meeting with Swank and Alexandra today." Jax's expression lifts when I say Lexa's name. "They are all ready to go for Saturday, and you may want to touch base with both Ravenous and Swank to confirm any last-minute details. I didn't think we had any issues."

"We don't. I'll check in with Alexandra later today. Thanks for letting me know." He lowers his gaze to my desk and reaches for the paper I tore off the pad, turning it to face him and reading the names. "Anything else?"

"I'm just looking into a couple of things for Elle Sinclair."

"Uh-huh. And this is in a business capacity?"

There's no point in lying to him. Not only was he a profiler, but his experience makes him a damn good human lie detector as well. "No. It's personal. Elle and I have been seeing each other, outside of work."

He leans back in his seat and attempts to cross his arms, but the old chair creaks, and he corrects his position, losing the older brother glare he was going for.

"And why do you need to look into a couple of things for her?"

"She had an issue with an old relationship that didn't end well, and something just feels off—not with her, but around her."

He glances at the names again. "And you're going to look into this Gregory and Remy? Isn't that the guy who was bidding against you at the charity event?"

"It is. I was wondering what your initial impression was—of him."

"You're looking for a profile on the guy? You know these things take time. I can tell you that the guy comes on strong, but so do you around *her*. I've known you all your life, so I know you aren't a threat to Elle. As a matter of fact, I think you are good for each other. I'm convinced she's great for you. But I don't know Remy. I don't know his status or his past. I don't know what drives him, so I can't give you an accurate assessment. But, if you want me to..."

That would exhaust my brother and take Jax away from too many clients.

I shake my head. "Not right now. We have other things to focus on, but I appreciate the offer. I'll let you know if anything changes. I'm going to dig a bit and see what I come up with first. I'll have Kill find out more about Gregory's incarceration."

"He's in jail?" Now Jax's curiosity is piqued.

The profiler in him eats the criminal mind up.

"For human trafficking. Sentenced to two years." Concern etches across Jax's face. "What?"

"Is it a first-time offense? The system is strained. The guy might be released early—depending."

That should have been a thought of mine, but it wasn't. "You're right. I'll call Cillian right now. Can I meet you in your office in an hour?"

Jax stands, and the chair groans its thanks for the reprieve. It's on its last legs, literally. "Sure thing." He walks to the wall and picks up his briefcase before turning and looking around my empty space. "It is good to have you here, but you're not getting your fancy chair back. It took me months to break it in. Order a new one."

I double-check the address on my phone against his building before I approach it and search the panel beside the door for Marcus's name. There aren't many names listed, and I find Wolfe right below Wilde. Apartment 104.

I press the button, and Marcus's voice echoes when he answers. "I'm just before the elevator." Then the door clicks with a jarring buzz.

His door opens as I reach it, and Marcus steps into the hall.

"I brought wine." I hold up the bottle in my hands. It's one of my favorites from Argentina.

He takes it and closes the small space between us, angling his head and kissing me. He's gentle, and it's a contrast to some of his more passionate moments. I instantly like this side of him too.

Breaking our connection, he cups the back of my neck in his palm and kisses my forehead.

"I wanted to tell you that I invited some friends over. They are both members of Ravenous, and they'll be at your event on Saturday. I thought it would be nice to know some people there, but you don't need to tell them anything about yourself if you don't want to. They don't know anything about you."

Against my will, a smile spreads across my face at the knowledge that Marcus wants his friends to know me.

"I don't mind. Thanks for the heads-up."

When he opens his door and ushers me in, a man and woman stand from their place on the couch and turn to face us.

"Elle, this is Noah and Hazel. They live upstairs."

"Hi, Elle. It's nice to meet you." Hazel reaches over the back of the couch, extending her hand, and I shake it.

"You as well, Hazel."

Marcus helps me out of my jacket, and I step closer to them, shaking Noah's hand.

"Can I get you a glass?" Marcus holds up the wine I brought.

"I would love a glass. Thank you."

Marcus offers it to everyone else on his way out of the room. "Why don't you take your seats around the table? The lasagna is already there, and you can get started while I pour."

Noah steps back, gesturing for Hazel and me to go first, and I take a seat along the side, leaving the heads open. Hazel watches me, then claims the seat across from me.

"How do you and Marcus know each other?" She reaches for a pitcher of water and fills a glass.

"We're working together on an event. I work at Swank Events."

"You're being modest." Marcus joins us with the corked bottle of wine and fills our glasses. "Elle owns Swank."

My cheeks heat at the pride in his tone.

Noah perks up in his seat. "Really? We were just talking about your company at my work. Our staff events have become too big to manage in-house. Isn't Swank doing the Ravenous thing this weekend?"

Noah passes me a basket with garlic bread, and I take a slice and hand the rest to Marcus.

"Yes. That's us. We're working with Wolfe Security on it."

"I'll have to introduce you to Joshua and Emilia. They own Connor Realty, and they'll be there too."

"We're looking forward to Saturday." Hazel takes a sip of her wine and makes a satisfied hum before looking at Noah. "Emilia said Lexa won't stop talking about it."

I perk up at Alexandra's name and glance at Marcus. He answers the question I didn't voice when he chuckles. "Yes." Then he speaks to Noah and Hazel. "Elle and Lexa are really good friends."

"Are you a member of Ravenous?" She points between herself and Noah. "We are. Although we haven't been there much lately. It's been so busy." She looks to Noah when she says her last sentence, and he nods in agreement.

"I'm not a member." I scoop a piece of lasagna onto my plate, then slide it over to Marcus. Hazel nods in awkward understanding. I get the impression she regrets confiding that she goes to Ravenous if I don't. "I was a member of a different club a while ago though."

I feel the need to settle her worries. It's probably because I know how she feels. This isn't usually something that anyone leads with.

"Oh. I can see that. Especially if your good friend owns it. I mean, I talk with my friend Nina about some stuff, but talking about it and watching your best friend actually do it are two different things. Are you considering joining the second location when it opens next month?"

"I'm not sure if that's—" Marcus attempts to change the subject for me, but I'm oddly comfortable around his friends.

"You know, I hadn't thought about that. It might be worth

considering." I smile at Hazel, who looks relieved to have someone to talk to.

"Really?" Marcus sounds surprised, and when I meet his gaze, I realize he has his own silent question.

"I mean. I wouldn't join alone. It's just that—if there was—what I'm trying to say is—if there was someone—I don't know what I'm trying to say." I reach for my wine, glancing up from underneath my lashes as I take a big sip.

Hazel's lips are pinched together, holding back her humor, and Noah is nodding with a big grin on his face as he looks between me and Marcus. I don't know the guy at all, but I'm sure he's seconds away from saying something along the lines of *Awww, yeah.*

The little hairs on my arm prickle against my shirt, sending chills across my skin as we all dig in.

After a few minutes of utensils clanking on plates, I ask Hazel what she does, and she tells me about the animal rescue center she works at.

"Swank did a charity event for a shelter a couple of weeks ago. Was that yours?"

"No, but we should do something like that. I know a ton of people who would be all over it."

When there's a break in the conversation, Marcus fills it when he tells me he used to work as a driver for Noah, but they both play it down. Noah tells me having a security expert around the building is worth its weight in gold, and that's when I find out that Noah also owns the building we're in.

Marcus stands and tells everyone to move to the living room as he clears the plates, and I offer to help him when my phone rings in my pocket.

"I'm so sorry. I thought I turned it off." I pull my phone out to power it down when the call display flashes the name of my alarm company. "I think I need to take this. Hello?" I step to a corner of the dining area. I answer my security questions, then the guy on the line tells me my back door was opened two minutes ago.

Marcus enters the room to hear me say, "You mean my door was actually opened? Someone didn't just try the handle?"

He slows his movements and doesn't leave with the handful of cutlery he has in his hands.

"No, ma'am. The alarm only trips when the door swings inward to alert the motion detector inside of movement. Either the door opened, or someone walked in front of the sensor."

I glance at Marcus, and he's staring right at me. "Okay. Thank you for letting me know. Are you able to reset the alarm and tell me if there's still movement? I'll check on it."

The operator disconnects the call, and Marcus wastes no time.

"Is that your house alarm?"

"Yes. They said it went off. I think I should go check it out."

"We'll check it out together. I'm following you over."

"I feel bad though. You'll miss dessert."

Marcus looks over his shoulder at the kitchen, and when he turns back to me there's a hint of wickedness in his eyes. "You're right. The three of us will stay here and have dessert while you go home and get murdered." He says it convincingly, without missing a beat, and I pause for a moment before he drops his expression, shakes his head, and says, "Get your ass ready to go before I spank it so hard you won't sit for days."

He leaves me briefly at the table before telling Noah and Hazel something has come up and we need to go. When I join him, Marcus is wearing his jacket. He has mine in his hands, and Noah and Hazel are already on their way to the door.

Marcus reminds them we'll have more time to talk on Saturday as he ushers them into the hall.

"On second thought, I'm going to drive your car over, and

I'll call a ride back." He holds his hand out, palm up, asking for my keys.

I parked close to the building, and he opens my door before hopping in and pulling into traffic.

"Does your alarm normally go off?" He keeps his eyes on the road.

"I don't usually set it." I wince. This is hard for me to admit, and I earn myself an admonishing side-eye from Marcus.

"Why not?"

"Mostly it's because my tenant lives with me, and she's older and forgets the passcode. I set it when she isn't home, and when I do, it has never gone off."

"Is there any chance your tenant is home now?"

"No. I got an email from her yesterday. She's still in Florida."

I don't want to admit that this sets me on edge, at least not until I know for sure what caused it. As we drive, I try to remember my routine today. I went home from work to change, got ready, popped in to feed Allie, then locked up.

Did I close the door properly?

Did I lock it?

Why is it I can remember irrelevant details about my day, but the most important stuff just won't come to me?

Worrying won't get me anywhere right now.

"So you used to be Noah's driver?"

"I was looking for a place to stay back when I was having a rough go. I don't think he really needed a driver, but he offered the work and a place to live. I owe him a lot."

"It sounds like it's mutual for him."

"There was—an incident, about a year ago, I was able to help him with."

I take that as my sign to not push him on it, and it's just as well, because he pulls up in front of my house.

I get out of the passenger side and start walking through the yard when he wraps his hand around my upper arm and pulls me back to his side. "Let me go first."

His offer surprises me, mostly because I felt so safe with him that I was about to go wandering right into a house that might have an intruder. "Right."

He climbs the two steps to the back door, reaches out, and tries the handle.

"It's locked." He straightens and looks over the outside of my house, muttering, "That doesn't mean someone didn't break in another way. Can you unlock the door?"

He hands me my keys, and I find the right one, first clicking a button on my key ring, then unlocking the door.

It takes us twenty minutes to search the whole house, and nothing is out of place. I lock the main floor behind us as we make our way up to my floor.

"Make sure you call your security company and report that there are no open doors or any points of access that are disturbed. They should send someone out to evaluate their system."

"Can I call while you're here?" I don't want to miss anything important, and security is kind of Marcus's thing.

He looks pleased that I asked, and I hit redial on my phone.

After a quick conversation, the alarm company offers to send a technician out first thing in the morning. I send a text to Nat, letting her know I'll be in to work late and to push my meetings back or hand them off to Julie and Daniel.

When I finally look up from my phone, I'm standing in the middle of my living room, facing my open bedroom door. Memories of Marcus in that room dance vividly into my head, and I spin to find him sitting on the couch and watching me. He makes no move to fill the silence for half a minute, then he stands.

"From now on, you need to set your alarm—always."

"It doesn't seem to do any good," I mutter, and Marcus raises his eyebrows. "It's just that, sometimes when I set the alarm, it still feels like something is off. Maybe it's just me."

There's a tick in Marcus's jaw, a sign he doesn't like what I just said, but he drops it.

"It's getting late. I'd like to stay over—to make sure you're okay. I can sleep on the couch."

I know why he's offering the distance. It's because of my little meltdown over the flowers.

"And if I ask you to sleep in my bed?" I shake my head. "That couch only looks comfortable, and I appreciate you wanting to watch over me."

He examines my face for a long time before he agrees. "Fine. But this"—he circles his flat hand in front of his junk—"stays in its package. I don't care how much you beg, Ms. Sinclair. I will not be lured into temptation."

We stand in silence, staring at each other for a long minute before he chuckles. Then he says, "I'm just messing with you. You even so much as bite your lip in my direction, and I'm going to fuck you six ways to Sunday."

CHAPTER 19
MARCUS

All of the meetings, presentations, and walk-throughs before Ravenous's event have done nothing to prepare me for walking through the front doors for the first time after the lights have dimmed. It's an inviting atmosphere.

We arrived two hours early, to set up our equipment and circle the room, scouting out all the spaces we would be responsible for protecting.

We posted a call for security among our teams at the office, and we had an overwhelming number of sign-ups once word got out what Ravenous was. Many of the men showed up out of curiosity.

As long as they do their jobs, I don't care why they're here.

In all honesty, I'm here for an ulterior reason as well—and my reason just walked through the front doors dressed in a gorgeous black dress that hugs her body in all of the right places.

"This place is amazing." Kate sidles up to me as I watch Elle check in with her staff from my spot across the room.

I roll my eyes when I break my gaze to look down at my sister, who seems way too happy. "Do you *have* to be here?"

She hits my arm and laughs. "You know I do. And there is nothing you can do about it."

She's got me there.

Our office employs mostly men, and that's only because security is a male-dominated field. Every application we get from a woman is pushed to the top of the pile because we are hurting for female representation. Still, everyone who signed up for tonight's job was male, with one exception: Kate.

Jax and I went back and forth. Hanging out with your sister at a sex-club event is not ideal, but she can get into some places we can't. In the end, the safety of the guests overrode our comfort level.

"Do we have any concerns?" I track Elle as she crosses the room to talk to Alexandra, Jax, and one other woman I haven't met yet.

I watch as Jax greets Elle, then breaks away, doing his own circle of the room before casually heading toward us as Kate answers me.

"There's only one issue. There's an emergency exit near the women's bathroom that isn't alarmed, but it locks as soon as it shuts. No one can get in, but someone could pull someone out and trap them in the stairwell. I'm going to talk to the hotel staff about what we can do to either unlock it for the night or see if we can close it off and reroute to another exit. If worse comes to worst, we may have to post someone on door duty."

"Let me know what you find out."

As soon as Jax is within earshot, I catch a wicked grin slip across my sister's face, and she speaks loud enough for both of us to hear. "Okay then, I'm off the clock. I'm going to go get my kink on."

I roll my eyes again as Jax scowls at her. She giggles and

practically skips away, satisfied she got the intended reaction from her oldest brother.

"Does she *have* to be here?" he groans as he takes her spot beside me.

"You know she does." I echo her earlier response.

He shakes his head, then tips his chin toward Lexa. "The woman standing with Alexandra."

"I see her."

"Her name is Reva. Alexandra is training her to run the second Ravenous location once it's open. If you need anything and can't find Alexandra, you can go to her."

I check my watch, and it's five minutes past when the doors should open, but they are still closed.

Lexa and Elle cross the room toward us with smiles on their faces. I glance over their shoulders to see Daniel and Reva walking toward the doors.

"It's time," Elle says as soon as they reach us.

One of Elle's employees approaches us, handing Lexa and Elle a glass of wine each.

They accept with smiles before Lexa turns to us. "Before I get busy, I just want to say thank you to all of you for your work in putting this together. Everything is gorgeous, and I'm looking forward to tonight." Then she turns to Elle and smiles. "I'm so proud of you."

It's a touching moment. Jax turns away, giving them a minute, and I follow suit, calling in a head count through my comms.

One by one, everyone answers their all clears, and I repeat an overall all clear and the time. We'll check in like this every half hour unless something comes up.

"Hey, Marcus. You clean up nice." Noah steps up with his arm around Hazel.

"Thanks. It's good to see you. Hazel, you look lovely."

She looks down at her dress. "I got this at a thrift store for a ridiculous deal." Noah clears his throat, and she amends, "Thank you, Marcus. It's good to see you too."

"This is my brother, Jax. Jax, this is Noah and Hazel." They shake hands, and Jax tells me he'll cover things for a while so I can talk.

He steps away, opening up a space and revealing Elle, and Hazel excuses herself to talk to her.

"You guys are here early."

"Lexa asked a bunch of us to be here from the start. You know, to help fill the room."

It makes sense, and it was smart of Alexandra to consider that. Stepping out of your comfort zone is never easy, and it's even harder when you have to do it alone. Having a full room makes it easier to blend in.

"Are Joshua and Emilia coming early as well?"

"I saw them pull into the parking garage just as we were getting in the elevator. They should be here any minute." He glances over his shoulder. "Speak of the devil."

Joshua looks around the room before leaning over to speak into Emilia's ear, and she looks in our direction and smiles as he leads her across the room.

"Hey, man. What do you have there?" Noah points at the paper in Joshua's hand, and he glances down at it.

"Hey." He looks between us, then lifts the paper. "It's the matchmaker questionnaire Ravenous is handing out at the front. It's for Emilia."

Emilia blushes and excuses herself quickly, heading toward Hazel.

"Are you really going to let Emilia fill it in? What if Ravenous matches her with someone else?" Noah gawks at him, and I match his confusion.

Joshua looks at Noah like he has two heads and scoffs.

"Fuck no! Emilia is mine. We're not handing it in. I want to go over it with her, to see if there's anything on there she's interested in exploring that we haven't—yet."

I laugh along with Noah. That makes more sense.

"So who is the one who owns Swank?" Joshua looks around the room while he addresses us.

Noah points over at Elle. "The woman standing beside Lexa." Then he shifts his attention to me, looking unsure if he should share my situation.

I answer for him. "Her name is Elle Sinclair. She's —with me."

That catches Joshua's attention, and he levels me with a grin. "Is she now? Good" is all he says before returning his gaze to the women. "Well, I'm sure Emilia has already found that out. This is a good setup. I can't wait to enjoy the evening. Will you both join us if we grab a table?"

"I'll drop by later. I have some work to do first."

I sense movement at my back and turn to welcome Lexa, Elle, Hazel, and Emilia to our group. Noah and Joshua commend Lexa on the event so far, and Lexa pulls Elle forward and introduces her, gushing about everything Swank has done.

I back away to let Elle enjoy the spotlight and make my way toward the back of the room.

People file in consistently, and I watch as Reva circles the room. Her body language gives her away. I can easily tell who she knows and who is new by how she approaches each group. With some, she moves confidently, but those who are new, she approaches slowly.

Daniel isn't as focused on the attendees. He checks in with the table at the front, circles toward the coat check, then heads toward the DJ at the back of the room. The music is a combination of light jazz, R&B, and classical. Then Daniel walks to a grand piano off to the side. A few people stand from their surrounding seats when he approaches, some holding string instruments. I assume the evening's entertainment will be split between recorded and live music.

Joshua and Noah have escorted Emilia and Hazel away to a comfortable sitting area, and they are all talking intently, but Elle is not with them.

I start walking my circle, listening in on conversations as I pass tables and watching body language for red flags, all while keeping an eye out for her.

No one is talking on our lines, but I don't expect it this early in the evening. It usually isn't until the drinks have been flowing for a bit that we need to make our presence known.

A couple of women come in as I pass the entrance. I size them up because it's my job tonight, and I hang close to see if I'm right. I think they are new. One of the women looks excited to get inside. The other hangs back, pausing before she steps past the front area, as though invisible doors will close behind her and trap her inside forever.

When Reva greets them, I have my answer. She approaches with hesitation, introducing herself as a member of Ravenous and asking if they've had a chance to visit their new-member area yet. The girls giggle together before following her to a table.

I move on, scanning the room until I find Elle. She's smiling as she enters the room from the hall that leads to the bathrooms. Stepping out from behind her is Alexandra, followed by my sister, and they talk with each other, all smiling, as they head toward one of the bars.

I meet up with them at the same time Jax does. I hold my hand over Elle's lower back, gently touching her through her silky dress and testing the waters. She inches into my side.

"So what were you talking about?" I ask casually.

Kate accepts three bottles of water from the bartender and hands one to each of the women before answering, "Oh, I was asking Alexandra how hard it is to clean up a room after an aggressive round of bukkake."

Elle coughs on her sip of water as Lexa bursts out laughing.

Jax shakes his head. "Fucking hell." He turns to walk away, and Kate runs after him with a satisfied grin on her face as she hooks her arm in his. There is nothing that one enjoys more than pushing her brothers' buttons.

"She's fun." Lexa smirks at me, and I chuckle and glance over my shoulder.

The smile falls from my lips as Remy Larsen enters the room.

It hadn't occurred to me that Remy might be a member of Ravenous.

How else could he have gotten a ticket?

He doesn't seem to notice us right away, but he walks in our direction, and it's probably because we're standing right in front of the bar.

As he gets closer, we fall into his line of sight, and he takes a slight detour over to us. I can tell the moment Elle sees him, as her back tenses under my hand.

"Mr. Larsen."

"Elle." Then he looks at me briefly before he lowers his gaze to my hand, which is still wrapped around Elle's back. The muscles along his jaw tense. "Mr. Wolfe."

"Mr. Larsen, let me introduce you to Alexandra Loren. She is the owner of Ravenous." He plasters on a charming smile and greets her. Then he turns his attention back to Elle.

"This is a lovely event, Elle. We'll have to get together soon, to discuss some of my clients'...needs." He doesn't wait for a response before excusing himself and turning toward the bar.

Elle releases a deep breath. She doesn't look up at me or give any sign that the conversation put her on edge, but I know it did.

When Daniel joins us, Elle excuses herself and takes a half step back from our group, asking him how Remy got an invitation. Daniel looks mortified and tells her that one of the invited guests was a client of his and the invitation must have gone through him. He apologizes and tells her everything will be okay, and he'll handle it for her. Then he leaves.

I suggest Elle escort Lexa over to Joshua's table and hang out there while I take care of a few things. She looks all too happy to put distance between herself and our newest guest.

Elle's dress washes over her curves as she walks away, and I'm looking forward to getting her alone and out of it later.

"It's amazing what two thousand dollars will buy you these days."

I turn to find Remy standing beside me, taking in the same sight I am like he's entitled to it.

"What did you say?" I square myself on the guy, and he has the sense to back down.

"Hey." He holds his hands up in mock surrender. "Don't get me wrong. If I knew that was what I'd be getting for my money, I would have bid higher."

I stare at him until he flinches. "I'm going to say this once: This is not the place, and that is not the woman for you. Say one more word about her, and I will drag your sorry ass out of here in front of everyone."

"You'll cause a scene?" He challenges me.

"What do you think people will be talking about in the morning? The fact that I dragged you out of here like the alpha possessive man that I am, or that you got thrown out of a sex-club event like some kind of pervert?"

When he sizes me up to see if I'm bluffing, I stand my ground.

He seems to find his answer, and he backs down and walks away without another word.

Then I turn my attention to what's important and go in search of Elle.

While Lexa talks to Joshua and Emilia, Hazel tugs at Noah's arm, then points to a section across the room. I follow her forefinger to a group of people setting up an area.

"Is that the rope demonstration?"

Noah sits up straight and cranes his neck to look past Joshua before telling her it is, and she asks him if they can take a walk around.

"Save a couple of seats. We'll be back," Noah tells Joshua, who tips his head in response.

No sooner do they leave than Marcus joins me on the couch where Hazel just sat, setting a glass of white wine in front of me.

Instead of reclining, he leans into me, hooking his forefinger under the strap of my dress at my collarbone and trailing it along my skin while he whispers, "I have a nice bottle of red to enjoy with you later—as I peel this off of you." Then he places a kiss on my neck that sends a shiver across my skin.

"I'd like that," I whisper.

He reaches into his coat pocket and pulls out a piece of paper. Handing it to me, he takes a sip of his own drink as I unfold it.

"This is Ravenous's questionnaire."

"Yes. I'd like you to fill it out. Not here—when you are alone. I'd like to know you better."

"Am I the only one filling it out?"

"I'm not handing it in to match you up with someone else, if that's what you're asking."

"No. I'm asking if you'd fill one out—for me." I play with the corner of the paper.

A look of surprise flashes across Marcus's face before he grins. "I'll fill one out for you."

"We can go over it now." I'm not sure where my little brazen streak has come from.

Marcus takes a quick look around the room before sliding closer, erasing all of the space between us on the couch.

When he leans over to point at the place we should start, his scent hits me, and my regular breath turns into a deep inhalation.

I follow his finger down to the first list of kinks. They start off tame and escalate to more particular tastes the further down the page I look.

Marcus lowers his voice. "Lexa tells me this isn't as exhaustive as the list they have at Ravenous. I'd like to look at that one with you someday."

I point to spanking and bondage. Both seem simple enough, and I've fantasized about them. They seem to go hand in hand with what I like. I hold my finger over one of the options, and Marcus leans over to glance at it.

"Public sex. Hmm."

"It's not—I might like it, but not, like, if anyone can actually see us."

He sets his hand on my thigh as he leans close. "You want to be taken in a public place, but you don't want anyone to witness it?"

I nod, unsure if I can use my voice to outright tell him what I want, because I feel like we're getting close to it. When I glance up to see if anyone is listening in, I find we're alone. Lexa must have gone to visit with some club members, and Joshua and Emilia are looking at their own piece of paper as he brushes his fingers through her hair.

I take a sip of my wine.

I tap my finger beside another item, and Marcus whispers into my ear. "CNC. That stands for consensual non-consent." I sense his eyes on me. "Are you asking me what that means? Or are you telling me that's what you'd like?"

He's not moving. If it's possible, I sense he's stilled even more than he already was as he waits for my answer.

Marcus wants me to be open with him, and if I'm ever going to have the courage to admit to this, it's going to be in a roomful of like-minded people.

"That's what I want."

Marcus tightens his grip on my thigh. "I see." He lifts his head and looks around before returning to our conversation. "Tell me what you imagine it would be like."

I take another sip before clearing my throat. "It's—about power and feeling helpless. I don't want to submit on my own, but I want—"

"To be made to submit." His hot breath tickles along my neck, and my nipples pebble against my bra as I clench my thighs together. "You don't want to hand over your power. You want someone who will show you how strong they are by taking it, but only so much as you agree to and allow."

"I want to feel—subdued, entirely possessed. But I want to know I'm safe." I'm not sure I have all of the words to tell him that I want him to hold me down and fuck me while protecting me.

"Tell me, do you want that from me?"

When I lift the wine to my lips again, Marcus stops me, takes the glass from my hand, and sets it on the table. Then he wraps his fingers around mine and kisses the pads of my fingers.

"Yes."

"Do you want me to hunt you, collect you—piece by piece, until I have everything?" He pauses only to scan our immediate area to make sure we are not overheard. "Do you want me to learn all of your dirty little secrets and use any means necessary to own you? Because when I do set my trap for you, little one, there will be no escape. Do you want me to be rough? Because I'm not sure I could be gentle if we went that far."

My head spins with need. Marcus nailed every single one of my fantasies, and I answer all of his questions at once. "Yes."

When I lean back to look at Marcus, his darkened eyes stare back at me. He blinks a couple of times, trying to compose himself, and a rush of urgency rolls through me.

"I want—" His eyes snap to mine as I continue, "I think we should—be alone." I have no idea where my neediness is coming from. I just know that there is something building inside of me, and I am unable to stop it. No matter how tight I squeeze my legs or how much wine I drink, I won't be able to douse this fire.

Without a word, Marcus stands, takes my hand, and leads me across the room toward the women's bathroom. When he nears a man standing off to the side, he steps close to him. "You're off the door for fifteen minutes." When the guy looks him over, Marcus simply says, "Tell no one. Take a break."

The guy takes one look at me over Marcus's shoulder, and I avert my eyes. Then he walks away. Marcus continues down the hall and through a door, and just like that, we're in a secluded stairwell.

I gape down at the staircase, unsure of what to say. Then Marcus tugs my arm once, and we descend two floors until we're in a basement, with no more stairs below us. I can only assume the door at the end leads into either an alley or the parking lot below the building.

Marcus turns me to face him, lifting his fingers to my face and gently touching my cheek before his hand falls to my collarbone. His other hand slides up the back of my neck into my hair before he fists his fingers into my strands, and he steps me up to the wall behind me.

"Tell me right now if you want me to stop."

My answer is immediate. "I want this." With every cell inside of my body. I can't walk away now.

"Bowling. That's still your word. Say it." He presses the length of his body along mine, not bothering to hide his reaction to me.

"Bowling."

He leans in, and his expression breaks for only a second when he claims a gentle kiss before pulling away.

I watch him, transfixed as his features harden.

"Good. Now don't say it again unless you want me to stop."

Keeping his fingers in my hair, he spins me, then pushes my upper body against the wall. The cold cement seeps through the thin fabric covering my chest.

He slides his hand under the hem of my dress, roughly tugging my panties to the side.

Sliding his fingers along my labia and circling my clit, he growls against the side of my face. "Jesus, just fucking look at you. I can't wait to get this tight little body stretched wide around my cock." He grinds his length into me through our clothes, pushing me into the unforgiving wall, and I tremble as I attempt to dig my nails into the concrete.

Marcus tightens his grip in my hair. The strain on my scalp releases some built-up tension.

Then his lips brush the shell of my ear. His voice is deep and raw. "I imagine I'd catch you off guard in a dark stairwell like this. You wouldn't see me coming, and when I made my presence known, it would be when I was sure you had no escape." Marcus paints a picture while he rubs his fingers back and forth, pushing when he nears my pussy, and I shuffle my legs wider, bucking my hips at his touch.

He chuckles low in my ear. "You like that, little one. Knowing there is no escape, no reprieve"—his tongue on my neck, just below my ear, makes me shiver—"no salvation."

He pushes his fingers inside of me, agonizingly slow at first as he continues, "I imagine you would fight me; you might even be able to break free, but any small victory would soon end in your defeat. You'd try to run up those stairs, back to your friends, but you'd only make it to the next landing before I was on you, pushing you down against the cold ground, wrenching up your skirt and tearing your panties off. Of course, by then, you will have proven you won't be quiet, so I'd have to take away your voice."

Marcus releases my hair, wrapping his palm over my mouth while he picks up his pace between my legs, fingering in and out of my core at an increasing pressure. My eyes roll up into my head, and I rock my hips as the sound of his voice and the fantasy he's weaving consume all rational thought.

"I'd push your stomach hard against the landing, those beautiful legs dangling down the stairs. Then I'd mount you and fuck into you without warning, taking everything you don't want to give me and possessing you like no one else ever has."

My whimper dies in my throat, held back by his palm over

my mouth. He braces me against the wall, taking the brunt of my weight by sliding his thigh between my spread legs and holding me up while he fucks me with his fingers.

When I murmur a plea against his hand, he loosens his hold, allowing me to speak.

"Please, I'm going to come. Fu—"

His palm goes back to my mouth.

"And the best part would be your forced surrender as I rode your broken body against the cold, dirty floor while you came hard against your will, giving me everything I want to own. Show me how badly you want that. Come for me—Elora."

That does it.

My vision flashes white as I seize tight in his hold, then shatter free an instant later, oblivious of time and space and drifting away to him.

I'm vaguely aware of Marcus turning me to face him as I shudder between him and the cement wall that's now at my back.

With his eyes focused on mine, Marcus lifts his hand to his mouth. "If I have to watch Remy Larsen leer at you any more tonight, I'm going to do it with the taste of your sweet surrender on my tongue." He holds his eyes on mine as he licks his slick fingers, then slowly slides them between his lips and sucks my release off of them before crashing his mouth against mine and pulling me close.

My knees go weak, and his grip tightens, holding me upright.

When we break apart, his expression has softened as his eyes roam around my face. "Are you okay?"

The question renders me speechless. I'm better than okay. I feel like I'm flying. But he's asking the question, so there's a chance that maybe I'm not.

"I—uh, I think so. Yes." It's then I consider everything that happened—and everything that didn't. "Um, we didn't—you didn't get to—"

Marcus's smile turns wicked. "Don't you worry about me. I'm going to desecrate everything that's good about you when I get you home."

My face heats from my jaw all the way up to my forehead. Marcus has to notice, but he doesn't mention it. Instead, he kisses along my hairline, straightens out my dress, and tells me he better get me back to the party.

When we reach the top of the stairs, Marcus pulls out his phone, telling me he's going to text the guy he sent away to let us in. He runs his fingers through my hair, and I glance down, brushing some of the wall off the front of my dress. Then the door clicks and opens.

It isn't his buddy.

It's someone I've never seen before.

The guy looks from Marcus to me. His lips stretch wide in a wolfish grin that feels oddly familiar, but I can't place where I would know him from.

Then he looks back at Marcus. "It's been a while."

CHAPTER 21
MARCUS

It takes a split second for my brother's face to register.

Not Jaxon's, but Cillian's.

"Kill. What are you doing here?"

My question isn't accusatory.

I'm surprised to see him.

It's rare we ever get to see each other outside of private family functions because of his job working deep undercover.

"Can't a guy visit his little brother at a sex-club event and it not be weird?" Kill pulls me into a hug, then whispers in my ear before breaking apart, "I saw where you two just came from. You better introduce me to her before I introduce myself."

The shock of seeing my brother for the first time in a year wears off fast as I turn to a wide-eyed Elle, who's looking between us.

"This is my brother, Cillian Wolfe. Kill, this is Elle Sinclair."

I hate the word "girlfriend."

Ever since I turned twenty-one, that word has made me feel

like a kid. Like Elle is a girl I just stole a kiss from behind the bleachers, and I'm going to pass her a note in class asking her to tick a box if she likes me.

Fuck that bullshit.

No.

Elle is the woman I just got off in a stairwell while telling her all of the ways I wanted to violate her until she came all over my fingers. And she doesn't want me to ask her how she feels; she wants me to tell her.

So, instead of giving her a label that comes nowhere near describing how I feel and my intentions with her, I step to her side, circle my hand around her waist, and pull her to me. I tangle my fingers in hers and bring her hand to my mouth to kiss it before letting go so she can shake my brother's hand.

It's as close as I can get to dragging my tongue down her face and telling Kill I licked her, so she's mine.

"It's like that then?" He chuckles before taking her hand and telling her it's nice to meet her.

As they make small talk, I glance into the room and catch Remy standing with Daniel, and their eyes are on our group. It's better he sees she's with me now than waste time showing up in Elle's office again.

Elle looks to her left, and I follow her gaze to the women's bathroom. There's no doubt in my mind she needs to sort herself out after what I just did to her. I pat my brother on the back, asking Elle if she minds if we talk, and she excuses herself and heads toward the women's room.

"Is it serious?" Kill points in Elle's general direction as soon as we start walking, and I decide to lead him toward the bar.

"It will be." Two women clear one of the bars in front of us just as we arrive, and I order two bottles of water.

"Actually, make mine a whiskey, straight." When I look at him, he shrugs. "I'm off the clock."

"Not that I'm complaining, but why are you here?" I look around as I talk and meet Jax's eyes across the room. When he recognizes Kill, he starts walking over. Then a bad feeling settles into my bones. "Did you find out something about Gregory Pasternak?"

"Not yet. Settle down. You know suits don't work weekends."

Jax reaches us in record time. "What the hell are you doing here?"

"Way to make me feel wanted, assholes." Kill lifts his drink from the bar and holds it up in cheers.

Jax looks around the room. We all know the risks my brother is taking, both for himself and our family. His lifestyle is entirely undercover, and he rarely makes an appearance. None of us take offense to that; it's safer for him if he stays away.

Kill doesn't get a chance to answer. Kate shoves Jax and me out of the way and lunges into his arms.

"I don't believe it, Kill. When I told you what we were doing tonight, I never thought you would actually show up." She keeps her hold on him, as though he's going to run away if she lets go. "It's been years since I've seen all of you together."

"It has. We're all happy to see you—really happy—but what's going on? Are you in trouble?"

"You know me, I'm always in trouble." Kill attempts to brush off our concern, but we aren't having it. We stare him down until, "Fine. I've been thinking about making a career change. Something went down, and my alias is dead. I either need to book it to the other side of the world, if I want to keep working like this, or get out, and I'm thinking about settling down. You know, going into partial retirement and living the quiet life. I may be interested in being a not-so-silent partner at Wolfe Security. But maybe we can talk about that later. Can't a guy just enjoy hanging out with his family at a meet and greet for kinksters?"

Kate's face lights up. "Hell yeah! Come with me. I want to show you some of their displays. I'm thinking about adding one of the butt plugs to my collection. They call it The Donkey Kong." She holds her hands out to indicate it must be the size of her head, and Kill immediately looks to Jax for his reaction.

He knows what she's doing.

"Kate, I swear to God," Jax mumbles under his breath.

They both laugh as she leads him away.

Once they're halfway across the room, I clear my throat. "What do you think?"

"I think I need a stiffer drink." Jax holds up his water bottle. Then he considers my question as he looks in the direction they walked in. "It's got to be pretty bad if he's out. We should ask him to come to the office this week. His background is valuable, but we'd have to be cautious if we assign him so he's never discovered."

"I agree. I'm not gonna lie, I'd be happier having him around."

Over the years, I've mentally had to prepare myself for the fact that my brother might just not come home one day. In his line of work, it isn't unheard of for people to go missing, especially undercover informants.

My brother takes a sip of his water. "Yeah, me too. Listen, we've got things under control here. The guys are getting restless. Why don't you bow out for the night? It'll give them more area to cover. It looks like someone could use your attention."

Everyone has returned to Joshua's table, including Elle. She steals a glance in our general direction before returning to Lexa and nodding at something she's saying. If Elle wasn't here, I'd probably offer to go walk the outside perimeter, but I pushed her a little further than I was expecting to a few minutes ago, and I'm anxious to be by her side.

"You know where I'll be." I break away from Jax and walk over to take the open seat beside Elle.

The questionnaire sits on the table in the same spot I left it in earlier, and I fold it before tucking it away in my jacket pocket. I'll have Elle complete it another time. Going through it with her is what set both of us off to begin with.

Alexandra stands, telling us she's going to spend some time talking with new-member hopefuls, and Elle swivels in her seat, casually slipping her hand in mine.

"How late do you have to stick around?" I rub my thumb in circles on her palm.

She looks around the room, taking stock of where everyone is. "Let me check in with Daniel, then I'll say my goodbyes. How about fifteen more minutes?"

I tug her hand in mine, pulling her into me, then wrap my free hand around her head and kiss along her jaw before whispering in her ear, "Not a minute more."

I'm aware of everyone's eyes on us when we break apart, and Elle leaves our table. Emilia and Hazel have the biggest smiles.

Noah sets his drink on the table. His eyes stay on me, but he talks to everyone. "So, I'm thinking we should get together. Like really get together. Do this right. How about we plan dinner at our place?"

"Or ours," Emilia offers, and the women exchange glances. "Maybe we can do a once-a-month thing and change the place each time."

Hazel backs her up. "Oh, I love that idea."

"Look what you started," Joshua grumbles at Noah.

I've gotten to know him more over the last year, and I can tell when he's joking around and when he is actually moody.

Jax walks up and asks if I've seen Lexa, and I point over near the kitchen before telling him I'm taking Elle home shortly.

I catch his attention before he walks away. "You'll make sure Kill visits the office this week?"

"I already talked to him. He's coming in on Monday. I'll see you there this week too?"

"I'm back, Jax. I'll be in, and we'll talk about a schedule."

"That's what I want to hear. Have a good night."

When I stand to say good night, Emilia and Hazel have moved on to menu ideas for this dinner none of us have agreed to yet, and I chuckle, telling Joshua and Noah they are on their own.

I spot Elle making her way back to us, so I meet her halfway. She shakes her head as she approaches.

"Ready?"

"Yes. Daniel had a mini panic attack when he found out I was going to leave him to handle this on his own, but Lexa convinced him they could manage anything that came up." Amusement sparkles in her eyes. "Get me out of here. Please."

I wrap my arm around her, pulling her to my side, and escort her toward the coat check at the exit. I take her ticket and hand hers over with mine, and she smiles when the woman returns with our jackets.

I hold hers open for her, and she turns, sliding an arm into her sleeve. "Oh, good. I was running out of jackets to lose."

"Is that a regular occurrence for you?"

"Not really, but my favorite coat went missing at the rescue charity auction. It still hasn't turned up."

She spins and looks at me, shoving her hands into her

pockets as I get my jacket on. Her expression turns curious as she pulls a piece of paper out of her pocket.

As she unfolds it, it breaks apart into two torn pieces.

"Huh!" She looks up and around the room behind us.

"Everything okay?"

"I—don't know how this got in here."

I reach out my hand, and she drops it into my palm.

I fit the two pieces together along the tear line and read the words.

The time has come

"Is this the card that was with the flowers you thought I sent?"

As soon as she says yes, I mentally chastise myself. Making a mental note of where I touched it, I slide the pieces into my pocket. If I'm lucky, I'll be able to pull a print off of the card later, but it's such a small piece of paper, and both Elle and I have put our own prints all over it.

"And you didn't put it in your pocket?"

Elle pinches her lips together in a wince. "I can't say for sure." When I don't respond, she elaborates, "I threw the flowers out a few days ago. I went by the office briefly on my way here. Maybe I found the card, picked it up, and stuffed it in my pocket?"

"Was anyone with you at the office?"

"No. Everyone was here setting up."

I don't want to rattle her, and that could very well be what happened, but she strikes me as someone who would remember picking up a torn card and sticking it in her pocket.

I wrap my arm around Elle to lead her out. "Come on. Let's get you home. I want to continue our conversation from earlier." I take one last look over my shoulder as I lead Elle away from the party. The room has thinned out, but other than that, nothing looks off.

As the doors to the elevator close, a cool gust of air hits me, and a chill runs through me, making the hairs along the back of my neck rise as if I should heed the warning.

All of my training tells me to prepare for danger.

The last thing I remember is Marcus carrying me to my bed last night.

I had amassed a record amount of tension between meeting Marcus's friends, making sure Lexa's event went well, and what happened in the stairwell.

Marcus settled me into the passenger seat and held out his hand for my keys. As soon as he shut the door, started my car up, and the interior lights dimmed, my muscles relaxed.

As he drove me home, he handed me the questionnaire and told me he still wanted me to fill it out when I had time. He said it's even more important now because of what I shared with him. He told me that consensual non-consent requires open communication because the risk of crossing a line is greater.

By the time we stepped over the threshold of my front door, I had a surge of energy. But it turned out to be the last little bit of my adrenaline leaving me, and I faded fast.

Now, the sun has just risen above the building across the

street, and it's blinding to the point where everything behind my closed eyes is bright orange.

I never sleep this long.

Noise from outside my door catches my attention. It has to be Marcus. I don't think the guy would leave me all alone here without at least saying goodbye.

I sniff the air.

Whoever it is has coffee with them.

I swing my legs out of bed and am three small steps to my bedroom door when I catch a glimpse of myself in my full-length mirror. The sight makes me squeal, and I double over and take two large steps backward.

I'm naked from head to toe.

Before I decide on what to cover myself with, Marcus bursts through the door brandishing a doughnut.

We stare at each other for a few moments before I break the silence. "I'm naked."

He does a cautious scan of the room. Once he's convinced I'm not in danger and only embarrassed, his look of surprise is replaced by a smirk as he raises his eyebrow at me. "You're also observant." He winks. "I noticed a coffee shop on the corner when I drove you home last night. I picked up breakfast." He steps out of the room, allowing me some privacy to cover myself. I pull my robe on, tie it at my waist, and follow him out.

"That's not breakfast. It's a feast." I pull out a barstool from my kitchen island and climb up. Marcus leans over his side of the counter.

"I wasn't sure what kind of doughnut was your favorite, and I didn't want to wake you up. I'll take what's left over to work in the morning. Jax won't know the difference if they're a day old."

I settle on a chocolate dipped doughnut, and Marcus hands me a coffee along with a handful of cream and sugar packets.

"Thank you." I tear at the packets and load myself up before stirring and testing the taste. "Speaking of brothers, you haven't talked much about your other brother—Cillian. Is he like the outcast of the family?"

Marcus takes a sip of his coffee and shakes his head. "No. Actually, it's the opposite. We're all really proud of him. His line of work takes him away from us for longer than we would like, but it looks like he might be interested in a change of pace. I should know more this week. Do you have any brothers or sisters?"

"I don't. My mom calls me her little miracle. They had trouble conceiving; they were told that my mom had an issue with her ovaries that would prevent her from ever having kids. I was a surprise a couple of years later, and they weren't able to have any after me. I grew up with a lot of cousins though."

"You're my little miracle too, Elle. I think I'm lucky I found you."

The moment lingers between us. There's something in the way Marcus says those words that makes my heart warm.

Emotion bubbles upward from my chest, making it difficult for me to swallow the bite of doughnut I just took, and I reach for my coffee.

Marcus uses the silence to circle the island, step to my side, and swing my legs around so I'm facing him. Placing one hand on my knee, he draws little lines across my skin before pushing my knees open and circling my legs around him. Then he caresses along my jawline before angling my head up to him for a kiss.

I'm only partially aware of my robe opening as the silky fabric slides down my arms, exposing me to him.

When I drop my doughnut on the counter, he bends down, hooks his hands under my ass, and lifts me, urging me to wrap my legs around his midsection.

We're back in the bedroom in a few steps, my robe discarded somewhere between here and the kitchen.

Marcus is out of his shirt and pants before I sit up, and he nudges me onto my back.

"This isn't about anything other than exploring each other."

Lying on his side beside me, he examines my body, trailing his fingers and palm in circles over my nipples, then down along the ticklish spot on my tummy. He chuckles under his breath when I wriggle, then continues lower, and I shift my leg open for him, reaching between us to stroke his cock as it hardens.

Every motion is done with slow, purposeful intent. It's agonizing yet divine. He slides his fingers, massaging from my pussy all the way up and around my clit as I stroke his length. We watch each other in rapt silence, making note of every single touch that brings pleasure until we're writhing in each other's hands. Then he shifts his weight and settles himself between my legs, his cock ready and pushing against my pussy.

Marcus looks over at his discarded clothes and braces his palm against the bed when I wrap my hands around him. "I don't want you to use anything."

My head lolls back to the bed as Marcus cages me in with his arms at my sides, and he slides inside of me without resistance.

My body was ready for him the moment he walked me back into the bedroom.

"Open your eyes. Look at me."

The moment I lock eyes with him, my body reacts. Every body part comes to life; every sense amplifies.

I've never had sex with my eyes open. This is both terrifying and liberating. I always closed my eyes, often picturing a fantasy to push me over the edge, but this is different. Marcus is different because he *is* my fantasy.

His weight pins me to the bed as he presses his lips to mine. When he breaks away and makes eye contact again, he shoves me toward my end.

"M-Marcus, I'm going to—"

The rest of my sentence is carried away on a flagrant moan. Marcus swears under his breath before he comes with a roar that vibrates in my bones, and we shatter together.

I'm vaguely aware of him kissing my neck as I recover. Then he pinches my nipple, sending a delicious shock through my body and down to my sated sex. I've never experienced a connection like this, and I get the feeling Marcus is only getting started with me.

"—so lucky," he murmurs to himself as he rolls to my side, but he holds me close with his arm around my midsection. "Are you busy today? I'd like to spend some time with you if you aren't."

"Sundays are all mine." I stretch my body. Every delicious ache from our fucking settles into my muscles, and I feel amazing. "I would love that."

After I ran to the basement and threw in a load of laundry, we finished our breakfast and enjoyed our coffee on the front steps of my house.

I always love sitting out here, but I don't usually do it alone. When my tenant is home, I wait until I hear the front door open and her shuffling around on the doorstep before I make my way down.

Sitting out here with Marcus just hits different, especially after what I got to wake up to.

"Can we talk more about the list of items on the

questionnaire from Ravenous?" Marcus asks as two kids on bikes go by.

"Sure."

He takes a sip before setting his cup down beside him. The hollow sound it makes tells me it's now empty.

"There is no easy way to ask this, so I'm just going to ask it, because we need to talk—about everything—if you are interested in exploring consensual non-consent."

"Okay. I'm ready." I take a deep breath, unsure of where he's going but happy he understands enough to take the lead.

"Do you have any history of sexual assault, or have you witnessed abuse of any kind?"

I gawk at him. I hadn't expected him to come out swinging. Then I wonder if his questions are going to get tougher or easier from here. I must be wearing my thoughts on my face, because he keeps talking.

"There's no wrong answer, but there is miscommunication. If you trust me to explore this with you, I need to trust that you will tell me if there is something wrong."

That makes sense. "Okay. No. I have no history of sexual assault—of any kind."

He nods, deep in thought before asking, "Did your interests come after you were stalked, or have you always had an interest in being preyed upon?"

"I've always fantasized about it. But I should tell you that when all those weird things started happening, when I was really stalked, it drove them away. I felt like he ruined it for me. Like I wasn't free to have those thoughts anymore."

"You felt like there was no one to protect you while you entertained them."

That's exactly it. I pushed my fantasies down because, before Marcus, there was no one I trusted to watch out for me, to catch me. "Yes, and because it would kind of be like accepting I was okay with what was really happening to me. But you made me feel safe. Like I could let go and you would watch over me—without judgment."

"And I always will. We will always have a safe word. I want to make sure you always understand that this is normal and healthy. And if you ever feel otherwise, if you don't feel safe in any way, you need to tell me immediately. Do you understand?"

"I understand. Thank you—just for everything."

Marcus reaches out for my hand. He tugs me out of my chair and onto his lap as he hugs his arms around me. "I will take care of you, Elle."

I shift my weight, drape my arm around his neck, and kiss him.

I don't know how I got so lucky, but for the first time in a long time, I'm in a calm space.

I just hope it isn't the calm before the storm.

I'd almost forgotten how much I hate rush hour when I'm on a schedule. Scratch that—I forgot how much I hate schedules. But here I am, walking into our office with a box full of day-old doughnuts.

For the first time in a long time, though, I haven't dreaded being here.

Kate stands from her desk and steps in front of me, walking toward my office as she talks over her shoulder. "I had them do a rush order, and we spent yesterday setting this place up for you." She opens the door and steps in, extending her arm into the room. "SURPRISE!"

The place looks completely different. It's a sharp contrast to her area out front, which consists of bright fabric and simple yet practical furniture.

My generic desk has been replaced by one made of real wood. I run my hand over the grain. The thing is solid.

"It's mahogany." Kate beams and steps to the side, in front of what looks like a real leather sofa.

I circle the desk and pull out the new ergonomic chair.

"Nice job, Kate. Thank you."

She crosses the room to the shelf behind me. "I'm happy you like it." Picking up a picture frame, she shows me a picture of the four of us as kids. "I brought these from my place. If you want to use the frames and change out the images, feel free. Just give me back the photos, okay?"

I join her in front of the shelf, scanning all of the photographs. She has our parents in some, as well as pictures of Jax, her, and me when we first got this office for Wolfe Security. There aren't many of Kill, but we all know why. These will do for now. I'll keep most of them, and I'll hopefully add a couple of Elle when we get to the point where we're taking photos of each other. "I will."

I wrap my arm around my sister and tug her to me in a hug. I know being together makes her happy, and she confirms it when she talks into my chest. "I can't believe Cillian might be working here too. I can't wait to set up an office for him."

Then, as if saying that has reminded her, she breaks away. "Right. He's scheduled for a meeting in an hour. Jax should be in any minute now. Can I put these in the break room?" She sets her hand on the box of doughnuts.

I nod, and she carries them out, telling me to let her know if I need any help.

When I'm alone with my thoughts, I take a seat behind my new desk. This place is better than working on my own.

I've always felt connected to my family, but I've been disconnected from my purpose for a long time now, and Kate has done an amazing job making me feel like I belong here.

My old cardboard box sits in the corner of the room, holding the life I stepped away from, and it's going to stay there for a while longer.

When I open the desk drawers, sticky notes, pens, and half a stationary store fill each one. On top of everything is the piece of paper the guy from IT wrote my passwords on, and I click the mouse, powering my computer on. Then I follow the instructions in an email marked "urgent" and change my passwords to something permanent.

As I'm finishing up, Kate breezes into the room carrying two mugs of coffee. She sets one down for me as she informs me Jax is in if I need him, and she's gone with the other, which is probably for him.

I know Kate is excited to have me back, and I chuckle into my cup as I take a sip.

I give it a week before she's telling me to get my own damn coffee.

To pass the time before Kill arrives, I open my internet browser and do a regular search, starting with Gregory Pasternak. Social media profiles display at the top of my results, and I click on a few before reaching into my desk drawer and pulling out a notepad.

I have no idea which Greg I'm searching for, so I expand my terms to "Gregory Pasternak" and "convicted." This brings up a few news articles, but I need to click on two of them before I get a picture. As reported, he was charged with one count of human trafficking that crossed state lines and was sentenced to two years.

The charge doesn't sit right with me. I'm no lawyer, but I've been around the criminal system long enough that I know a charge like this should carry a minimum of ten to fifteen years.

The first photo of him is his mug shot. The guy looks rough, but he probably cleaned up pretty good before he got caught. I do a reverse image lookup and find links to more photos, which confirm my assumption.

It turns out Greg worked as an armored truck guard. He's in his mid-thirties and single, and this is where the information starts to repeat itself through various news sites. However, I don't find any personal profiles on any social networks. The guy prefers his privacy.

I open a new browser and go to work on Remy Larsen.

His picture comes up immediately.

The guy loves the spotlight, and the first five links I find are all his own social network accounts. Picture after picture of him with celebrities and sports stars litter his social feeds. The guy just can't take a bad selfie—or, if he does, he doesn't post it for the public to look at.

Remy has managed to stay on the right side of the law. No convictions to speak of.

These two couldn't be further apart from each other, which makes it both easier and more difficult to create a profile and determine if Elle is in any danger.

If they were similar, I could ask Jax to help me work on one profile, then start omitting one or both of them from the finer details. Since they're so different, I have to start on two profiles.

I consider creating a profile for Elle, but that makes me uncomfortable. I may need to ask for Jax's help on that, since he is not personally invested in her like I am.

"Hey." Kate pokes her head through my open door. "Kill is here. We're going to meet in Jax's office."

I check the time. My search ate up forty-five minutes. "Sure." I hold up my coffee cup. "I'm going to top off. I'll be right there."

The doughnuts are almost gone by the time I join everyone in Jax's office.

His desk is empty, and my siblings all sit on or around the couch in his office, drinking coffee and chatting like we're a normal family.

It's all a bit surreal.

Judging by the awe on Kate's face as she looks at each of us, she's thinking the same thing I am.

"Hey, man. It's good to see you here." I approach Kill, and he stands to give me a hug.

"I'm not gonna lie, it feels pretty good to be here."

Jax grabs a doughnut before pointing at an empty seat. "We were waiting for you to get started." Once I'm seated, he looks at Kill. "So, spill. What's going on, Kill?"

He takes a sip of his coffee then sets it on the table. "It's pretty much like I told you on Saturday. One of my jobs fell apart. Like, it was bad. I lost some people I was really close to, and I was found out. I made it out, but as far as everyone else knows, I was in the wreckage after the blast went off. My alias is dead. Ten fucking years undercover just to start over. Because of the scope of my connections, I am limited to two choices: take a remote job somewhere where those guys don't exist, or go off-grid and retire." He pauses for a long time. Then he shows where his heart is when he says, "I can't be even farther away from my family than I've been. At the same time, we all know I can't retire. I'm not built like that."

Signs of life have drained from Kate's face. Before Kill had to go into seclusion, they were really close. They shared the same type of dark humor, and he was the only one she could convince to watch her favorite soap opera so she had someone to talk to about it.

Jax breaks the silence. "What do you need from us?"

The way he says it makes it sound more like, *We will give you anything you need*, and Kate and I nod in agreement.

"A job? Something that puts me so far in the background that no one ever sees my face?"

The four of us went into Wolfe Security with equal shares,

so he has as much right to walk in here and ask for an office as I do.

"It's yours. Kate will set you up with a space here, and we'll get you anything you need for working remotely. We could use your skills."

Kate shifts in her seat, obviously excited. Not only does she have her last brother with her, but she has another office to order stuff for.

My phone vibrates in my pocket, and I pull it out, glancing at the lock screen to see a message from Elle.

ELLE

Why do I have a text message from Kate asking if I'm free on Thursday?

I look over at my sister, who quickly looks away.

Kill speaks up, stopping me from confronting Kate.

"Thanks, Jax. I'm looking forward to it. I have some final exit and debriefing interviews this week, then I should be out."

"Great. Give Kate the week to put an office together, and let's meet back here at the same time next Monday. Marcus is back as well, and we can catch up more then."

"Actually," Kate interjects, "I was talking to Mom and Dad, and they were hoping to have a family dinner on Thursday night. Kill can make it." They exchange a glance. "And maybe, if there is anyone we want to bring...like to meet the family..."

Now the text to Elle makes sense.

I shake my head.

She's planning on inviting you over to my parents' for dinner.

Let me be clear: I just found out. So I'm officially inviting you. If you feel comfortable, I would love to introduce you to everyone.

ELLE

I'm free. I would love to.

"I'll be there, and Elle will be joining me." I level Kate with a glare that she breaks away from.

She knows what she did.

"Great. I'll let Mom and Dad know."

If Kate hadn't texted, I probably wouldn't have invited Elle so soon, but it doesn't mean that I don't want her there. I just wasn't sure if it was too fast for her, especially after the whole flower incident.

"That's all for now, Kate." Jax excuses her.

I wait until she's at the door before asking my brothers to stay. "We have a couple of things to discuss." I look at Kill. "Were you able to find anything out about Gregory Pasternak? The human trafficking case?"

"Yes and no. It's a little more complex, so I need more time." He must notice my frustration, because he elaborates. "The case isn't as simple as you made it out to be."

I agree with him. "I looked it up just before you got here. The guy's sentence doesn't match the crime. Elle is under the impression he was convicted of human trafficking, but his sentence is well below the minimum, and I saw the news reports. He crossed state lines, and all he got was a couple of years?"

"Yeah. I need you to leave it with me for a bit longer. I have a call into the DA's office. I'm hoping to get answers before my clearance expires. I'll let you know as soon as I hear anything."

"One last thing: No mention of this on Thursday night around Elle, okay? If we find anything out, I want to bring her into the office for it. I don't want her associating our family get-together with her case if it comes to that."

My brothers answer in unison. "Understood."

According to dating etiquette everywhere, I'm pretty sure I answered Marcus's text inviting me to meet his family too fast, but I don't care.

I've already met all of his siblings, unless he has a few others he hasn't told me about yet.

Judging by comments Marcus has made, it's rare that his family is all in the same room together, and I don't want to pass up the chance to be there for it. Also, just the fact that he wanted me to be a part of it is a big deal.

So when Daniel knocks on my door asking if we're still on for Thursday night, his question catches me off guard.

"What's on Thursday?" I wave him in, and he takes a seat at my desk.

"It's the yearly audit."

Dammit. I forgot.

"Can we reschedule it?"

"Do you have a meeting? It's after hours," he reminds me.

"No, I know. It's just that I made plans—for dinner—with

Marcus's family." I pinch my eyebrows, wincing and hoping he'll be up for another night.

"I see." He glances out of my office window. "It's getting close to the deadline. We kind of pushed it way back this year."

"How about I make up for it by coming in on Saturday and Sunday, on my own, and collecting the files we need then?" I offer, hoping it's a fair compromise, but making it clear that I won't be missing the chance to meet Marcus's family.

"No. I'll come in on Thursday and gather the files for you. Then we can start reviewing them when you're back in the office next week."

"Are you sure? I don't mind."

"I'm sure. Go and enjoy your time. I'm here for you."

"Okay, but I'll have my phone on me if you need anything. Thank you, Daniel."

That's one thing off my plate of things to worry about.

When Marcus, Jax, and Kill are in the same room together, it is easy to see the similarities. They all have kindred personalities, yet they don't dominate or conflict with each other. Maybe it's because they grew into the people they are together.

Kate hasn't stopped smiling, and neither has their mother.

We arrived a few minutes late because Marcus walked into my room to grab his jacket off my bed when I was getting into the shower. Forgetting the door separating us was glass, he watched me until his self-control snapped. Then he joined me, pushing everything back by half an hour, so I had to rush getting ready.

Kate accused Marcus of being late on purpose so he didn't have to help set the table, and they bickered until I volunteered myself and Marcus for cleanup duty.

Cillian pulled Marcus aside to speak in private. When they returned, Marcus looked a little tense, but he brushed it off when I asked if everything was okay, saying it was an issue for another day.

I have no idea how those brothers finished eating before me, because they talked all through dinner. It was mostly reminiscing about growing up. Everyone particularly enjoyed sharing stories of when Marcus was a kid—everyone except for Marcus, who often just rolled his eyes at me.

"I think that's the last of the dessert plates. Are you sure I can't wash the dishes for you? I feel kind of responsible since I'm the one who volunteered us for this."

"Oh, don't you worry. You'll pay for that, but in other ways." Marcus winks at me, then juts his chin at a dish towel on the counter. "You can help clear some of these by drying them though."

"None of that, you two. Here." Mrs. Wolfe opens the fridge and removes a bottle of white wine, then hands it to Marcus as he finishes drying his hands. "Those dishes can wait. Family time can't. Help me with these?" She opens a cupboard and pulls out some small wineglasses. "The wine is sweet. Perfect for after dessert. Follow me."

Marcus and I do as we're told, and I'm not surprised to see two empty seats beside each other once we reach the living room.

Marcus pours the wine, and his mother hands the filled glasses around the room. Jaxon and Cillian pass since they still have their drinks from dinner with them. Their father takes a glass but sets it aside, and Marcus pours his last. It's nothing more than a sip. So that leaves Kate, their mother, and me.

"So, Elle, Marcus tells me you own your own company? You throw parties?"

"Ma, that's not what I said." Marcus angles his body toward

mine, draping one arm along the seat behind me to explain. "I told her you own an event-planning company."

"And it's the best one in the city." Kate backs him up. "We were at one of their events last weekend, and it was amazing."

The brothers look at her in warning, and they all shift uncomfortably, as though they know what's coming next.

"Oh? And what was it for?" Mrs. Wolfe asks.

Kate's eyes bug out. It's clear she wasn't thinking ahead.

"Oh, um. I don't remember. I think it was a new club or something."

The version of Kate she shows her parents is the polar opposite of the woman who was going on about sex toys and circle jerks on Saturday night, and I giggle so hard into my wine that I blow bubbles.

When her mom looks away, Kate snickers with me.

She is the classic baby of the family (and only girl) who gets away with everything her brothers didn't.

Mr. Wolfe spent most of the dinner silent. He enjoyed the conversation, laughed along with everyone else, and answered questions that were asked to him, but other than that, he is a man of few words.

He reminds me most of Jax. They both seem to prefer observation to communication, so when he speaks up, everyone pays attention.

"Kate tells me you boys are all at the office now."

Jax looks at Cillian for confirmation before he speaks, and Cillian answers the question. "I start next week."

Their father nods. "Your mother and I are happy you're home, son."

It's a tender moment between father and son, and it sheds more light on the loving family Marcus is a part of.

As if sensing my thoughts, Marcus moves his arm from the couch to my arm and hugs me to him. Kate watches us out of the corner of her eye with a sneaky grin, and his mom smiles before standing up and gathering some of the wineglasses.

"Coffee's goin' on," she announces as she walks toward the kitchen. "Anyone up for cards?"

"I call Kate." Cillian speaks up, pointing at his sister as though his answer makes sense.

At least it does to Kate, who shifts far enough out of her seat to hold up her hand for a high five when she says, "Heck yeah!"

Marcus lowers his voice. "Have you played canasta before?"

I shake my head. "Is it easy to learn?"

"It'll take some time. Why don't you sit with me, and I'll teach you while we play?"

Their father is already heading over to the table and moving things around. It looks like this is a family tradition, and I'm excited to be a part of it. "Sounds great."

Marcus takes my hand as we circle the table, with everyone claiming the same seats as they did to eat. Marcus sets a chair beside his for me.

"There's no talking during the game." He raises his voice so everyone can hear. "However, Kate always forgets that rule."

"I do not." She looks at me and clarifies, "There's no talking *to your partner.*"

Jax points at his sister. "Also, she is an aggressive card player."

Kill laughs at that. "Why do you think I always want her on my team? Better my partner than my rival."

The boys help their father remove the center leaf from the table, making it smaller, and they take their seats. Each person sits across from their partner, and I sit off to the side and slightly behind Marcus as the cards are dealt.

Their mother calls into the dining room from the kitchen,

telling everyone that coffee is ready, and they set their dealt cards facedown and head in. Marcus squeezes my leg, telling me to stay put and he'll get us a cup to share. He returns with the largest mug, handing it to me, and I take a sip before setting it down for him.

The deck of cards looks a little different than a regular deck, and there are more cards in play. As they take turns around the table, Marcus leans over, whispering what each move means.

I'm learning quickly that it is a game of strategy. Sometimes cards are held back until the perfect time to play them; other times they go all in right out of the gate.

Jax and Marcus are pretty laid back when it comes to playing. They shoot each other questioning glances now and then when they don't agree with a choice the other made, but overall, they just play. Their parents are seasoned pros and are focused on playing their best hand. No, the only pair out for absolute domination is Kate and Cillian—but mostly Kate. She sizes everyone up, and her smack talk is on point. She can rile her brothers up like no one else can, and I get so swept up listening to her egg them on that I forget to pay attention to what's happening when Kate looks across to Cillian and asks, "Can I go out?"

Cillian nods, and everyone groans when she lays down the rest of her cards.

I tug Marcus's sleeve then lean in. "I thought you can't talk to your partner."

"That's the only time you can."

Everyone except Kate starts counting the cards in their hands and shouting numbers to Mrs. Wolfe, who is keeping score.

Marcus tells me that the cards they're all still holding count against them, while the cards Kate and Cillian laid down go toward their score. He reaches for his coffee, then hands it to me, and I take another sip.

"So they win?"

"They won this round, but it's the first team to hit five thousand points who wins the game. Sometimes we go to ten thousand."

All of the cards are compiled and passed to Jax to shuffle. As he deals, my phone vibrates in my pocket. I really don't want to answer it. I wouldn't even have it turned on if I didn't promise Daniel I'd be available for any questions while he was doing audits tonight.

When it vibrates again, I whisper in Marcus's ear, "I need to answer my phone. I'll be right back."

I excuse myself from the table and step away from the conversation. I don't recognize the number on my display.

"Hello?"

"Hi. May I speak with Elle Sinclair?"

"I'm Elle Sinclair."

"This is University Hospital. We have a patient here who has listed you as their emergency contact—"

I sway and recover quickly as the woman explains as much as she knows about the situation. By the time I hang up, Marcus has already stood and crossed the room to me.

"Elle, what's wrong?"

I meet his eyes, then glance over his shoulder as his two brothers watch from their seats. Everyone else seems oblivious to my inward spiral.

My mind goes into overdrive running through bits and pieces of my day.

"That was the hospital. I need to go. Daniel was attacked tonight—at the office. Marcus, I was supposed to be there with him."

Elle hasn't said a word since I threw my car into reverse at the house. She's slouched into the passenger seat with one arm wrapped around her midsection. The other is braced against her arm, and her fist is propped against her lips as I drive toward the hospital.

We're both deep in thought, but probably for different reasons.

She's worried about her friend and coworker.

I'm worried about what all of this means for her.

When we first arrived at the house, Kill pulled me aside to update me. It turns out that shortly after Gregory Pasternak's conviction, he was quietly moved out of state to serve his time in a facility in Wisconsin, a couple of hours away. His lawyer cited an ailing mother who wanted to be closer to him for visitation.

The case was originally brought forward as a Class A felony for first-degree kidnapping, which carried the possibility of life in prison. That charge was dropped down to a Class B felony and was further lowered to aiding and abetting only, which carries a minimum sentence of only two years in prison.

That isn't the worst of it. As of a month ago, Gregory Pasternak is a free man, released on early parole for time served, or something like that.

So now both Elle and I are sitting quietly in the car, simmering in our guilt. Her for leaving her coworker and friend alone, and me for not telling her this information as soon as I got it.

I just finished explaining to her how important open communication was, and I decided to hold this back from her so she could have a carefree time at my parents' place. I figured she was with me, so she was safe.

The lot beside the ER has emptied out since most are not permitted after visiting hours. But Kill called in a favor, and we should be let in.

The nurse who looks up from behind her computer screen already has a look that tells me she's prepared to give us the same spiel she tells countless others. "Visiting times are over."

I gently move Elle to the side so she doesn't have to deal with this right now. "A patient was admitted earlier." She rolls her eyes, unimpressed that I don't know how to follow simple rules. "There are police with him, and I've been called in. They're expecting Marcus Wolfe and Elle Sinclair."

Her demeanor changes. "Hold on."

She walks to the hall, waves, and then returns.

As soon as the uniformed officer joins us, I take the lead. "I'm Marcus Wolfe."

The guy looks past me to a visibly shaken Elle. Then he starts walking down the hall, and I fall into step as she trails behind.

"Right. We're just wrapping up here. Mr. Hawkins doesn't

want to press charges, so there isn't any reason for us to hang around."

"Can you give us five minutes with him before you go?"

"Sure. I'll grab a coffee and circle back for my partner."

The officer opens the door and tells his partner to hang tight for five before he leaves. I hold the door open for Elle to go first.

The gasp she makes as she clears the curtain hits me in the heart, and I understand when I get my first look at Daniel.

Judging by the cuts and the amount of swelling, his nose is going to take some time to heal, and he's sporting a black eye. There's a laceration along his forehead.

I listen as Elle rounds the bed, taking a seat by Daniel's side as I step over to his clothes, which are folded neatly beside him in a large plastic bag. His shirt is soaked in blood, but I won't pick it up. The officers have bagged it, but he probably hasn't given them permission to take it. So they are leaving it for now.

"What happened, Daniel?" Elle reaches out to take his hand, and he holds on to her.

"I don't really know. I was in the office, working on the files we needed, and I went to the file room to gather more folders. The room was dark, and I didn't think I turned off the light because we always keep it on. I went to turn it back on, and someone pushed me inside. I didn't get a look at them. They grabbed me and pushed my face into the shelf. I couldn't see right, and everything started going dark. They hit me a few more times." He attempts to lower his voice for privacy, but he chokes once he says the words, and everyone hears him. "I thought I was going to die, Elle." He clears his throat; his exhale is shaky. "When I came to, I was on the floor and alone. I called 911. That's all I know. That's what I told them."

"Daniel, I don't know what to say. I am so sorry." When

defeat enters Elle's tone, I place a hand on her shoulder for support, and Daniel watches me in silence.

"Are you sure you don't want to press charges—or at the very least have these officers open a file?" I ask.

His eyes flit from me to the officer who is still in the room and listening to everything. "Do you think we can speak alone?"

I glance over my shoulder at the officer. "Can we get a minute with him?"

His answer is already written on his face. "I can't. Not until a decision on the charges has been made."

I look at Daniel and Elle before turning back to the guy. "Is it the bag?" I tilt my head in the direction of Daniel's clothing, indicating chain of custody.

"It is."

I explain it to Daniel. "He can't leave until charges have been decided and you sign off either way. Your clothing is evidence, and he needs to have eyes on it at all times for it to remain admissible in court. Can you give him permission to take it with him out of the room? Then he'll go. He'll bring it right back if you still don't want to proceed."

Daniel glances at Elle, who nods her head.

"Sure. That's fine."

The guy groans as he stands, and he nods his thanks to me before taking the plastic bag out with him.

When the door shuts, Elle asks Daniel why he won't open a file.

He looks up at me instead of answering. I think he's about to ask me to leave as well before Elle assures him that I'm here to help and I'm staying.

"I just...remember everything you went through—last time. Elle, if I open a file, I'll need to tell them about you being stalked. Then they'll ask you about your ex, and you'll have to tell them about the club, and I kind of thought you wanted to put that behind you and move on."

I stand helpless beside Elle, watching in real time as she slips into the past she was trying to forget.

What Daniel says is true.

Those cops will ask questions, and Daniel's answers will lead them to Elle. She'll have to tell them, in detail, what her involvement at the club entailed and about her relationship with Greg. They'll paint an inaccurate picture of her life, and it will bias the whole investigation. Neither of them even realize that the police may have to ask questions around the office, which, if done incorrectly, could put Elle's past front and center.

"I don't care about that, Daniel. You were attacked. I should have been there." There's a tremble in her voice.

He releases his hand from hers and sets it on top of her closed palms, comforting her. "I didn't see a thing. Opening a file will only hurt you, and I won't do that to you."

I scan Daniel's cuts as I list our options in my head.

"I don't think he should open a file." I surprise Elle, then look at Daniel. "Will you turn your clothes over to me?"

Elle sits up straight, shifting her attention square on me. "What are you going to do?"

"I'll take care of it."

I leave it at that, and Elle accepts my answer, turning back to Daniel with a hopeful look.

He levels his eyes on me as he weighs his options in his head before reluctantly agreeing.

We're interrupted by the night nurse when she tells us we can stay, but Daniel needs to rest. She steps to his side, hands him some pills, and holds a straw in a cup of water up to his mouth for him to drink.

As soon as the police inform the hospital staff any evidence they collected isn't needed, they'll wrap it up and file it away.

I tell Daniel to take it easy and leave Elle with him to say goodbye. As I step out of the room, I pull my phone from my pocket.

Before we left my parents' to come here, I texted Swank's address to Kill. He knows enough people in the right places, and he can get around a lot of things. He and Jax left shortly after we did and went to Elle's office to look around on their own.

When I open my messages, there are a couple of photographs from Kill, followed by a text telling me the cops cleared out of there about fifteen minutes ago. Apparently, they've already been informed it is no longer considered a crime scene.

In one of the photos, there's blood all over the edge of a shelf, and I'd say it's consistent with the damage on Daniel's face, but that's not what makes my blood run cold.

The next image shows flowers tossed all over the floor, as though they were torn apart in the scuffle.

> Was there a card with the flowers?

KILL

> Jax found something sticking out from under the shelf, and it's the kind of card that usually comes with flowers so...

> What's on it.

I'm already sure I know what's written on it, so when Kill sends me the picture, it takes me a moment to realize we have a new message:

Imprison me in your waning light

The cop I sent out of the room approaches me. I tell him that they won't be opening a file and he'll need to move fast if he wants Daniel's signature on the release form before he falls asleep. I offer to take the bag of clothes from him, and he hands them over.

The officer enters the room as a distraught and sniffling Elle exits, joining me in the hall.

"I don't know what to do. If you weren't here, I—don't know."

"I want you to stay at my place tonight, but I also want to go by your office and check it out."

"I want to come with you." She looks at me with hopeful eyes.

"That's not a good idea. Cops don't clean up. Jax and Kill are there now, and there is still blood everywhere."

"Oh, God." She pales, and I wrap my arm around her to lead her out of the hospital before she faints. "Why are your brothers there?"

"I asked them to go by. If anyone is going to find anything, it will be them. I'm taking you back to my place, but first I'm texting Noah and Hazel to see if they're home."

"It's late. I don't want to be a bother."

"You're never a bother, Elle. Let us help you. Noah and Hazel went through something similar about a year ago. They may be great people to talk to. At the very least, they'll stay with you while I take a look around your office and clean it up, so your employees don't show up to a crime scene in the morning."

She slumps into the car at that thought.

It's on the tip of my tongue to tell her what I know. I stop at a red light and glance at her out of the corner of my eye.

I would be going against everything I asked of her if I don't tell her what Kill found out.

"The light's gr—"

Elle is cut off by the driver behind us when they lay on their horn, drawing my attention to the green light.

I step on the gas and pull over to the side of the road.

"Why are you stopping?" Elle glances up and down the street, as if looking for trouble.

"There are some things you need to know."

My arms hang heavy at my sides. When Marcus opens the door to Swank's offices, I wrap them around myself in a hug, as though my limbs will fall off if I don't.

Everything is quiet here after hours. It's so quiet, I swear I hear the sounds of Daniel's attack as we approach the file room at the end of the hall, but it's not him, because he's currently recovering in a hospital bed.

It must be Jax and Cillian.

"We should go to your office. Let me take a look in there first."

The world dropped out from under me when Marcus told me that Greg had been released. All of this time, I assumed he would serve his sentence. I wasn't listed as a victim, so no one had any obligation to inform me that he wasn't locked up anymore.

I wanted to live in ignorance. I went out of my way to keep myself sheltered, and Daniel has a fractured nose because of me.

I know Marcus wants to protect me, just like I've been trying to protect myself, but I can't look away from what is obviously happening.

I don't stop walking toward the file room. "No. I want to see it."

Marcus makes one last-ditch effort to turn me away at the door, and my throat tightens at the mental image of what the room must look like. Now I need to see it to replace what my brain is conjuring.

He makes sure he's standing as close to me as possible when he pushes the door open. Jax and Cillian turn from their place in the corner of the room, and I fail to hide the choked gasp I make when I see the blood, most of it now dry, on the floor.

Their expressions are reserved. Gone are the smiles from only hours ago while they played cards and laughed around the table at their parents' house.

"Hey, Elle. Maybe we should talk—in your office." Jax gestures to the hall behind me, but I'm not ready just yet.

I close the distance to one of our shelves, careful to step around the splotches of blood. A few papers and folders are out of place, and more blood covers the edges of the shelf at eye level. This must be where Daniel's nose was bloodied.

When I look down to the floor to see where he would have fallen, something catches my eye. It's a dark red rose petal, and it is soft between my fingers. I hold it up and look at the brothers.

Jax is the one who answers me. "We found about a dozen roses all over the floor. Marcus told us about the odd delivery you had, and we wanted to get them out of here before—"

Before I got here.

I nod, holding up my hand and telling him I get it. "Did you find anything?"

They look at Marcus instead of answering me, and it's the first time since I arrived that I feel like I'm being kept out of things.

"I told Elle everything. I think she has a better chance at staying safe if she knows what we know." Marcus looks at me.

Cillian agrees with him. "I think you're right."

Jax walks toward us. "I'm not suggesting. Let's go to your office and sit down. We'll talk there."

The elevator dings down the hall, and I look at Marcus, bracing myself.

What if whoever did this came back?

Jax quickly settles my nerves. "We have a team coming to clean this up. It'll be cleared by morning."

"Oh. Thank you." I glance down at my watch. I didn't even think about what happens when the employees show up for work—in six hours.

A man and woman dressed in white hazmat suits pass us in the hall, nodding at the brothers, and Marcus walks beside me as we lead Jax and Cillian to my office.

I break away and walk to the couch at the back of the room. I sink into it, and it wraps around me. The cocooning sensation is comforting.

Marcus joins me on the couch, and his brothers pull up chairs from my table and join us.

Jax reaches into his pocket, pulling out a small plastic bag with a piece of paper in it. "We found this in the file room."

Imprison me in your waning light

It's a little more poetic than the last message. "What does it mean?"

"We're not sure yet. Nothing came up in a quick search

online, but we'll keep looking." Jax holds his hand out for the bag.

Cillian leans forward, bracing his elbows on his knees. "We're following up on Gregory Pasternak, but it's been slow getting information since he was transferred out of state before he was released. Is there anything else you can share that might help us?"

I draw my lips wide in a grimace.

This is exactly like when I tried to go to the police when I first felt like something was wrong. As soon as they found this stuff out about me, I was on my own.

Now it will be worse, because this time I'm airing my dirty little secrets to Marcus's family, and I want them to like me.

Marcus covers my hand with his, squeezing until I look him in the eyes. "They'll tell you everything they find out, but you need to tell them everything too. There's nothing you can say that will damage this." He points between us with his free hand. "Trust me, my demons are darker than yours."

Jax clears his throat. "Keeping secrets won't keep you safe."

They all sit in silence, waiting for my answer, and I nod in understanding before taking a deep breath.

"Greg was a dominant I met at a club—a sex club. We weren't serious—um, like in a committed relationship. Actually, I remember being shocked when I found out he was arrested. Even though there were weird things happening to me around the same time, it never occurred to me that they had anything to do with him. He just didn't seem like he wanted to pursue anything beyond what we had going on at the club. That's the only place we saw each other."

"What did your relationship with Greg entail?" So far, Jax is asking the same questions the cop asked me a year ago, but I don't feel the same level of scrutiny that I did then.

"Well, he was—uh, dominant, so that means I was—"

"Submissive," Cillian offers, probably to get the conversation moving along.

"Kind of, but I wasn't really submissive to him. We weren't exactly a m-match, but we found some common ground that worked for both of us."

"What was the common ground?" I don't know why, but I'm thankful it is only Jax asking the questions right now. I'd feel under fire if they all jumped in.

I wonder if this is a tactic when trying to get people to open up.

"You're doing great." I inhale deeply at Marcus's encouraging words.

Anxiety is making it difficult for me to swallow, so I clear my throat.

"We set up scenes where he could impose control over me. We agreed to everything before: what he would say, how I would challenge him, what we would and wouldn't do, and he never strayed, not once. We always talked about it afterward: what worked for both of us, what didn't, and then we'd adjust things for the next time."

Jax's eyes lower to my hand that Marcus isn't holding, making me aware that I'm fidgeting, and I stop.

"Let's switch over to Remy Larsen for a minute. He's the other man who was bidding on you at the charity event we attended. Is there anything out of the ordinary about him?" Jax and Marcus exchange a quick glance while I think about his question.

"Remy? I guess he's always been a bit pushy. Now that I think about it, I've become used to his advances, maybe conditioned to expect them as part of our regular interactions, so I've started playing it down as normal."

"How long have you known him for?"

"It's been years. He was starting out as an agent when I

started Swank. It was around the time Daniel and Julie started with me. I think he went to the same school as Daniel; that's how he started coming to our events."

Marcus squeezes my hand, sliding forward in his seat to get my attention. "Daniel mentioned Remy dropped by your office a while ago, asking you out for a drink."

I'm not sure when they spoke about me, but I appreciate the concern.

"He did. Um, I wasn't expecting him. He stopped in and kind of hinted that, since he went out of his way, I owed it to him. But that's just Remy. He's the kind of guy who talks a bigger game than he has and hopes that someone buys what he's peddling. He's attractive, he knows the city's best athletes, and he can open doors. That works for a lot of people. It's just not what I was ever interested in."

A yawn slips in, and Jax must take it as a cue to give me a break. "I think that's enough to start with. Thank you for being open with us. Nothing leaves this room, and it doesn't change anything. We're happy you're an honorary member of the family. At least until this one"—he gestures to Marcus—"makes it permanent."

The mood relaxes. This wasn't as bad as the last time I was questioned, and that gives me courage.

"Maybe I *should* ask the police to open a case."

Marcus's hand over mine tightens, and Jax examines me with an unreadable expression on his face.

Cillian tilts his head to the side. "Leave it with us."

His tone is halfway between a command and a question, and I harden my gaze, trying to figure out which it is.

Marcus doesn't leave me hanging. "Daniel signed off on not proceeding. His clothes are in my possession now, making them inadmissible in court, and the file room is being cleaned up. They most likely won't proceed, but they will take his clothes back as evidence, which means we won't be able to do our own due diligence in testing them."

Cillian picks up when Marcus takes a break. "What you've shared with us—about your history—stays here, and none of us will hold it against you. We'll do our job. I trust the department, and all of the fine people who serve, but they don't know you, and everyone makes mistakes. If you open a file now, after agreeing not to...well, it doesn't look good. I acknowledge that assumptions can be made based on victim information that comes to light. I don't agree with it, but it happens."

"So what do I do?"

I don't like this feeling. It's clear that there is a threat, and the three men sitting in front of me, all with law enforcement backgrounds, have all but come out and said that the police are not in a position to help.

Jax stands, and I strain to look up at him. "Now you leave it with us. Marcus is going to take you somewhere safe—your home or his, and he's staying the night. We'll work out a longer arrangement if necessary. You're okay at work provided you're here only within office hours and you contact us if you're leaving the building. Can you send Kate a copy of your business calendar?" I nod. "Good. We're going to test Daniel's clothes, and we have samples from the file room. Kill has a call in; any evidence the hospital gathered will be sent over to us. But for now—and I can't stress this enough—get some rest. We're here for you."

When we leave my office and walk toward the elevator, it's clear that his brothers aren't coming with us. They walk down the hall, returning to the file room.

The doors slide open, and Marcus ushers me in, pressing the ground floor button. "I'll leave the decision to you. Do you want to stay at my place or yours?"

"Can you stay at my place? I haven't been home for a while,

and I want to make sure the cat is okay." I glance at him, embarrassed. "It's kind of a small thing to worry about, but—"

The rest of my sentence is muffled by Marcus's chest as he pulls me into a hug. "But it's who you are, Elle, and it's why I won't stop until I find who is doing this to you." He kisses the top of my head.

Knowing, just knowing that he is in my corner, that he believes me and is here to support me, is what wrecks me. I push my hands into his jacket, wrapping them around his waist as I finally let myself break down and sob against his chest.

He lets me, and that makes all the difference.

He folds his arms around me and lets me hide myself away from the world for just a little while, and I take it. I take this comfort even though I have a feeling it's going to get worse before it gets better.

CHAPTER 27
MARCUS

I'm working on a few hours of sleep, which is a couple less than Elle is. After our late-night visit to her office, I drove her to her place so she could check on her tenant's cat, and we climbed into bed. She couldn't settle for the longest time. Finally, I played with her hair and told her about everything we would start doing to help her find who did this to Daniel.

Elle is a focused woman. She is powerful at work, and she does well when she feels like she is in control. The more I told her, the more her body relaxed, until she fell asleep with little snores against my chest.

She set her alarm early this morning so she could beat everyone into work, and when we arrived on her floor, she went straight to the file room.

It was like the attack never happened. Although, judging by her pale complexion, she vividly remembers what was in there only hours ago.

I stuck to her like a shadow, moving from office to office. Then I sat in a chair off to the side of her desk as Elle read her email and ever so slowly slipped into the composed businesswoman she portrays. By the time her employees filed in, she was ready to get back to work.

"Should I call a meeting? Tell everyone what happened?" she had asked. I advised her to wait and said I would help her work on an announcement for later in the day. While we don't want to create an atmosphere of panic, we should inform her staff.

She agreed to wait until I returned to her in the afternoon.

The mood at the Wolfe Security office is different than earlier this week.

Kill ended up moving into a temporary office this morning. Kate rescheduled as many meetings as she could, and Jax is now returning from the only meeting he had to have today. And he's bringing lunch, which is good, because I'm not sure I would stop to eat otherwise.

I've been jumping around in my focus all morning. I start looking into something on Gregory, then switch to Remy, hoping that one of them will finally rise to the surface and I can narrow my focus.

The longer they both stay on my list of suspects, the more frustration gnaws at me.

This isn't a simple attack on Elle and Daniel; it is designed to create space between Elle and possibly me.

When we left her office last night, she gave in and cried in my arms. She searched and asked for comfort. As soon as the doors to the elevator opened on the main floor, she froze up and made sure there was space between us as we walked to the car.

Unchecked, this distance between us will likely grow, and I'm angry that whoever this is is trying to take her from me.

Even if they do nothing else, Elle is scared enough that she's already pushing her needs down. They hit her hard where she is most vulnerable—her heart—and now all they have to do is sit back and watch as she retreats from her desires.

"Hey." Kate is already two steps into my office by the time I look up. "Didn't you hear me knocking?"

"No. Sorry. Just thinking."

She drops her shoulders, cutting me some slack. "Yeah. We've set up lunch in the conference room. The guys want to talk."

Deli sandwiches are piled on a platter in the middle of the table, and a carafe of coffee has been placed conveniently next to the empty chair I assume is for me. As I circle the table to grab a sandwich and sit down, Jax stands and turns to the table behind him, grabbing a bottle of water and reaching across the table to hand it to me.

Kill tells me to eat while they update me, and Kate pulls a seat up to the table across from me.

Kill shuffles some papers until he finds the one he's looking for. "I've had some back-and-forth with Gregory Pasternak's lawyer. He's adamant that the charges laid a year ago were too serious for the intent of the crime. It turns out it was a domestic dispute between Mr. Pasternak's younger sister and her then husband. His sister was trying to flee an abusive marriage, and Mr. Pasternak had offered to drive her back to their family across state lines to help her out. He had taken some pictures of the beatings—bruises and whatnot, so she would have documentation— and had them on his phone. Well, the abusive husband just so happened to be some hotshot businessman. He called the police and had them picked up, and Gregory was arrested. His sister was returned to her husband, who threatened her, and she changed her story out of fear of retaliation against her family.

"So here is where the courts got a little nervous. Because she was eighteen, she was considered an adult. However, it was still really close to the child pornography age, and the images found on his phone were held against him. Courts don't like that. The husband was out for blood and really pushed this girl. The lawyer told me, in the end, Mr. Pasternak just wanted to get his sister away from her abuser with as little damage to her or their family as possible, so he agreed to plead to the lesser charge in exchange for him signing the divorce papers and allowing her to return home to her family."

Jax groans beside me, and I already know what it means. While it doesn't clear Gregory, it does shine more light on the profile I'm assuming Jax has been working on, and it is probably in Gregory's favor.

"Can anyone vouch for Gregory's location at the time Daniel was attacked?" I ask between mouthfuls.

"Well, that's a little trickier. I sent that question back to his lawyer, but I haven't heard anything yet. See, it's his job to keep his client out of jail, and I'm snooping around about a current crime. If I don't hear back by next week, I'll follow up."

For a long time, I stare at the lines on the notepad I brought in with me, contemplating the question I want to ask. But it comes back to what Jax told Elle last night: keeping secrets won't keep her safe.

"Can you profile Elle?" I don't look at my oldest brother directly, but everyone around the table knows who I'm asking. I feel like I need justification, so I keep talking. "I mean, not her directly, but can you create a profile that might tell us who would target her or why? But keep it between us." I look around the room. "I mean—shit, we shouldn't know this much about her, but I don't want to be in the dark here. I can't—"

Lose her.

When I do look around the table, my siblings all stare back at me with sober understanding.

Jax breaks the silence.

"I can do that—for now. But only because Elle is dealing with a lot at once. You will have to let her know eventually."

When I only nod in understanding, it isn't enough for Jax. "Hey. We'll figure this out."

Kate clears her throat, asking for her turn, and we all look over at her.

"So, Jax asked me to look into the messages on the cards that came with the flowers. The first one"—she picks up a plastic bag with the card in it—"was really generic. *The time has come.* It could be any number of things: song lyrics, a quote from a book, a movie line, or even just an announcement. Like the time has come to send those flowers." She exchanges the first bag for the second. "The last message, *Imprison me in your waning light,* is a little more poetic. Still, nothing comes up online. However, this only means it isn't song lyrics, or a short poem. I have a friend who has her master's in English lit, and I sent the quotes off to her, asking if she can help me out. She's going to look into it. If either message is part of something published, she'll find it."

Jax stands from his seat, stretching out his back. "We all have our tasks. I'll try to find out where Remy Larsen was last night when Daniel was attacked, and I'll get started on Elle's victim profile." I wince at the term. Elle is not a victim. Jax must notice my distaste, because he leans over as he gathers his papers, saying, "You know what I mean."

"Yeah, man. I know. I'm going to head back to Elle's office to help her work on what to say to her staff."

Kill and Jax both leave with extra sandwiches, and Kate carries the tray to the front of the office for the rest of the team.

By the time I arrive at Swank, everything has gone to shit.

"What do you mean the whole office knows? I thought we agreed to work on an announcement together." I settle into the chair in front of Elle's desk.

"We did, but Daniel was released this morning, and he stopped in today to see if he could grab some work to do at home while he recovers since he doesn't have an event this weekend. It's mostly phone calls and emails. Julie saw him before he got to my office, and that was it."

"Where is Daniel now?"

"I had him in here with me for a while, then I asked Nat to grab the files he needs. He can access company email from anywhere, so he has most of his stuff online. He's at home now. He says it doesn't hurt as much, but he looks way worse than he did in the hospital."

I only nod. Usually when you see someone in the hospital, you expect it to be bad, so it doesn't look as bad as you think. Elle wasn't expecting to see Daniel here, in the light of day, so he's going to look worse. The swelling and bruising have also probably started to set in.

"So what did you say happened?"

"I didn't say much. Daniel told them he was attacked but didn't want to talk about it. He said it was late at night, and he didn't tell them it happened in the office. I think he was trying to be vague to protect my privacy."

I glance at my hands, almost forgetting I brought Elle one of the sandwiches from our office. "How are you doing?" I reach across the desk and hand her the food. She takes it with a smile.

"I feel awful. This is all my fault. Daniel had to lie to everyone here because he felt he needed to keep my secret. The worst thing is, I let him. I was so afraid that my staff would find out about who I am that I let a man who was attacked lie for me. I owe Daniel more than that."

"You can't do this to yourself, Elle. Someone out there is determined to make you think this way. We are going to find out who it is. Eat something." I nod at the sandwich I brought her.

"What? Oh, I'm not hungry."

"It's not a suggestion. And before you brush it off, I asked Nat before I came in here, and I know you did not eat lunch. Take a bite, or we're going to have a problem."

Elle's eyes flash to her closed office door before she swallows hard and looks back at me.

I'm asserting dominance over her at her place of work because she's not taking care of herself. I know how badly she wanted to relinquish herself to me last night and how she separates herself from her needs when she's in the office.

I'll back off if she steps up, and I wait, tapping my forefinger against the arm of the chair I'm sitting in.

She reaches over and picks along the cellophane that holds the sandwich together until she finds an end and unwraps it. Then she takes a bite and groans, telling me it tastes good.

Satisfied with her choice, I lean back in my chair. "What are your plans for the weekend?"

"We have events on Friday and Saturday. I can skip tonight, but I should be there tomorrow. It's an awards dinner, and I'm a little more hands-on for this one because I've been training Julie for a more senior role. I'm thinking about expanding an office into another city."

"I thought Daniel was your second-in-command. Hasn't he been with you since the start?"

"Pretty close to it. I met him almost seven years ago. Just after his divorce. He would be my first choice, but he says he's happy in Chicago so I've been training him to take on a senior role here."

"Are you able to secure a couple of extra tickets? I'll bring Jax or Cillian along—you won't notice we're there."

Elle reaches into her desk and pulls out an envelope. "I had a feeling you'd ask. I put four tickets in there. Take what you need."

CHAPTER 28
ELLE

I probably didn't need to be here tonight after all.

Julie has been doing an amazing job as lead on this event, and I haven't had to get up once.

True to Marcus's word, I haven't spoken to either him or Jaxon yet this evening, but I know both of them are here. A couple of times, I found myself trying really hard to find them in the room.

Beside me, Nat takes a sip of her wine.

"Oh. Found him again." I think she's turned locating the Wolfe brothers in a crowded room into a drinking game.

One of the women seated at our table won an award earlier, so people have been dropping by all intermission to congratulate her. It's given Nat and me a chance to talk amongst ourselves.

Marcus swings by the table, getting closer to me than he has all evening. When he passes the back of my chair, he sets his hand on my bare shoulder, sending chills across my skin. Leaning down, he lowers his voice. His breath is hot against the shell of my ear, and I shiver as he speaks.

"Ms. Sinclair, I am looking forward to getting you alone later." Then he stands, smiles at Nat, and walks away.

"That man is *hot.*" She breathes the last word. "Found him again." She takes another sip. "Seriously, Elle, I don't know what it is about those two brothers, but every time they talk, I need to make an effort to listen because all I hear is *bow chicka wow wow* in my head, and I can't stop picturing them naked and strutting around holding their belts. I mean, I'm a married woman, and every time he looks at you like that, I want to spank myself."

I burst out laughing, startling the people across the table. Mouthing an apology, I grab my glass of wine.

Now that, I will drink to.

"You should see their other brother."

Nat's eyes bug out. "Seriously? Don't. That's not even funny. There's another one?"

"There is—and he's the mysterious one." I chuckle.

Nat's eyes go up to the ceiling, and I imagine she's trying to picture Cillian in her head. After a few seconds, she gives up and returns to our conversation.

"Hey, how's Daniel doing? A few of us around the office want to get him something."

"I spoke to him today. He said he was trying to get out and run some errands, but mostly he's resting. I think he'd love to know you're all thinking about him. Let me know what you come up with. I'd like to contribute."

The lights dim again, and as dinner arrives, we fall back into work mode. We are trying out a couple of new vendors we haven't worked with before, so while Julie is running around and coordinating the hired staff, it is our job to assess everything from an attendee's point of view.

We are the "special requests" and the eyes of the evening. I have a special food request for a vegan meal, and Nat has advised our server of a lactose intolerance, which she does have.

I forgot to follow Marcus and Jaxon to see where they're sitting, but I sense them nearby.

The din in the room slowly rises into a white noise of chatter and utensils clinking against porcelain as I take my first bite of my portobello mushroom steak, which tastes better than many actual steaks I've had in my lifetime.

"How are the lactose-free whipped garlic potatoes?"

"Well, I'm not farting." She takes a sip of her wine. "Hey, remember that time the caterer convinced me that their dessert was lactose-free, and it was so good I ate two of them, then I couldn't leave the bathroom for like an hour?" When I laugh, she shakes her head at me. "God, that was so bad."

I lift my glass to her. "You took one for the team. I salute you."

"Yeah, right. None of you wanted to drive me home that night."

"Hey, I stepped up!"

"After they all left me! Ugh, and the car smelled like a frat house the day after they served chili cheese dogs at an all-night kegger. I was so embarrassed."

When we get to the last few bites on our plates, the lights come back on, and speeches start up again.

"Luckily, my stomach is happy. I can confirm my main course had no lactose in it."

"Yeah, this mushroom steak is amazing. Want to try a bite?"

Nat forks one of my last pieces off my plate and groans as soon as it hits her tongue. "That tastes better than my steak did. Next time, I get to be vegan." Then she looks over my shoulder as she reaches for her wine. "Found him again."

"I don't think they're trying to hide from you." I glance over to see Jaxon walking out of the room toward the main hall.

She shrugs. "It passes the time. So tell me more about—" Her eyes leave mine and round, but she holds her smile on her face. "Keep looking at me; Mr. Larsen is coming this way. I don't know if he sees—ugh, yup, okay, he sees you."

"Elle, I thought that was you." He steps between our chairs with his back to Nat.

"Oh, hello, Mr. Larsen. You remember my assistant, Nat." I extend my hand toward her.

"Yes, hello." He quickly returns his attention to me. "How are you doing? I ran into Daniel, and he told me all about that unfortunate business at your office."

Even Nat doesn't know the full truth as to where the attack occurred.

"Excuse us for a minute, Nat. Can I get you anything from the bar?" I speak as I stand and gesture for Remy to join me.

"I'll try that signature cocktail they were pushing before." Nat shoots me a concerned look that I shut down.

Jaxon and Marcus are around, and I know I'm safe.

Remy walks behind me while we navigate through the tables, then he steps to my side as we cross the floor.

Before we approach the bar, I turn with a smile. "Where did you see Daniel?"

"He was at the club yesterday. I was there for my weekly lunch meeting. He said he was dropping off a final invoice for your client. What happened?"

I know Remy is a possible suspect. I'm probably looking at him more than I ever have, and I hope I'm not sending the wrong message, but I just don't see it, except—

"Why are you here tonight? This isn't a sports event."

He looks around the room before throwing his hands into the air as though he's playing around. "You got me. When Daniel told me what happened, I thought I'd check on you. I wanted to make sure you were okay."

"I'm fine, Mr. Larsen, but you could have called the office."

A bartender opens up. I order two of the strawberry champagnes, and Remy orders a Jack and Coke.

"I was hoping this would be enough of a grand gesture to show you that I was worried about you."

His admission makes my skin crawl. He isn't as concerned about my welfare as he is about getting some. Using this traumatic event to weasel his way close to me is low-level.

"While I thank you for your concern, I have many people around me, and I am fine. I'm more worried about Daniel, who actually was attacked."

"Oh, yes, yes, of course. I'm just saying that I could take care of you."

Now I want to play the game Nat was playing earlier. I scan the room, looking for a Wolfe.

"Mr. Larsen—"

He takes a step closer. "It's Remy."

I put my hand up. "No. It's Mr. Larsen. I am involved with someone else, and I have many people I am close to who take good care of me."

"Are you sure about that?"

"Pardon me?"

"I'm just saying: Daniel was attacked, and it happened in your office." The bartender sets our drinks on the bar, and Remy reaches over.

For a moment, I think he's going for our drinks. Then he settles his hands on my bare shoulders, squeezing my skin, and I stare dumbfounded at his hold on me. The whole situation catches me off guard, and I freeze as his grin slithers across his face.

"Get your hands off her." The voice from behind me is low, demanding, and barely contained.

Remy tries to reason with Marcus. "We're just having a friendly conversation."

When he smiles down at me with his lecherous grin, I slowly shake my head and take a step back. He has no choice but to let go or take a step with me, which we all know would be an obvious sign of aggression.

Reluctantly, he pulls his hands back, but I think it might be too late when Marcus clenches his hands into fists beside me.

Being the eternal prey that I am, I sense he's about to lunge, and I panic, stepping between the two men.

"As I said earlier, I am well-protected, and I am fine, Mr. Larsen. I believe you remember Marcus Wolfe—my date." I add the end just so there's no confusion.

Neither man makes an attempt to shake hands when Jaxon joins us.

"I was just looking for you," he says to Marcus with a carefree smile. Then glances at Remy, takes a step back, and points. "Hey, didn't we meet at that charity auction? Remy Larsen, right?" Jaxon reintroduces himself and tells him he is a huge fan of the quarterback Remy represents. Then he starts asking him something obscure about sports and money—two of Remy's favorite things.

Once Remy relaxes, Jaxon asks if he can buy him a drink, and he leads him away from us, diffusing the whole situation like the professional he is.

Marcus reaches behind me, taking the two glasses of champagne and leaving the third drink behind.

I thank him when he hands me one, but he doesn't answer. His eyes track Jaxon and Remy as they stroll to the bar farthest away from us.

"What are you thinking, talking to him like this?"

"What? He started talking about Daniel at the table, and I

didn't want to worry Nat. I knew I was safe because you were here."

"But I wasn't. Not for a moment. I had to step out to use the bathroom. It only takes one mistake." When I examine his face, I find chaos in his eyes.

It's the exact opposite of the control I know he centers himself in. For him, losing me is the same as losing control.

"I—we were in public."

"I saw you freeze, Elle."

"What?"

"When he put his hands on you, I watched you freeze, and it broke me. People think there are only two modes when you face a threat"—he holds up two fingers, counting them—"fight or flight. But there's a third: fright. There is going into shock and doing nothing, and that is the deadliest one of all. If Jax didn't show up, I don't know what I would have done." He looks almost scared of himself.

He's right.

I froze.

If we weren't in public and Remy is my stalker, I would have slipped right into fright mode, and I don't want to think about what would have happened to me.

"You placed your business reputation above your personal safety, and I won't allow this to go unaddressed."

"What does that mean?"

"It means it's time you learn that it isn't only actions that have consequences. Inaction has its own repercussions as well. How much longer are you needed here?"

"I'm not. Needed, I mean. Just let me tell Nat so she can go hang out with Julie. Are you taking me home?"

"No. You and I have some things to sort out. Say your good nights, and meet me at the front in five minutes."

Elle is quiet in the seat beside me as I drive toward downtown. She hasn't asked again where we are going, and I haven't offered.

Remy Larsen putting his hands on Elle didn't bother me. Well, it did, but it was her reaction that set me off.

I'm not the least bit concerned that Elle doesn't know who she belongs to—she knows she's mine, but I am livid that her instinct was to freeze.

The expression on her face drained the life out of me. For a flash in time, she was terrified, but her fear paralyzed her. She was in a roomful of her peers, her employees, and her clients, and she cared more about keeping up appearances than she did about protecting what I treasure.

In that briefest of moments, I was angry—at her.

I slow to a stop at a red light and keep my eyes on the road ahead. "What were you thinking?" I ask the question again.

She waits until the light turns green before she speaks softly while she stares at her hands, which are clasped in her lap. "I wasn't."

I drive in silence the rest of the way and let her answer sink in for the both of us.

She knows where we are when I stop. I step out of the car, then circle around to her side, opening the door and offering my hand to help her out.

I stare at the words above the door, reminding myself of why they are there and how I vowed not to fail again. WOLFE SELF-DEFENSE: ADELAINE CENTER.

It's the only sign Adelaine can still give me, because she's dead and gone.

I unlock the door and hold it open. Elle lowers her head as she enters, and I lock the door behind us, then enter the code for the alarm.

I break the silence, and she startles.

"I don't care where you are. If you feel threatened, you react. Do you understand me?"

She rounds on me. "It's not as simple as that."

I am not in the mood.

"It's exactly as simple as that. Predators rely on their prey wanting to keep the peace." I raise my voice. "Women are the perfect targets because"—I point right at her—"all of your life you've been raised not to be aggressive. In a society where docile women are considered ladylike and those who speak up are scorned, the world around you has taught you that in order to be liked, you need to shut the fuck up and take it." Elle pales the more I talk. I know I'm right, and I challenge her. "Go ahead—tell me I'm wrong. Tell me you've never been called a bitch when you've turned a guy down, or sensitive when you speak your mind." I step closer to her. "Tell me that you don't love hearing me tell you what a good girl you are, and now think about the things you'd be willing to do for me just to hear me say it."

It's a low blow, but I'm making a point.

"That's not fair." She blinks rapidly.

"It's never fair when you are the one who is being hunted."

She tears up.

I ease off.

"I want the spitfire who told me to call her Ms. Sinclair in front of a roomful of people. The person you were before you backed down because you didn't want to rock the boat. Rock the fucking boat, Elle. I'm giving you permission if you feel you need it. I'm in your corner. I've got my life jacket on, and I don't give a shit if the ship breaks apart as long as you're safe. When you feel threatened, I want you to act accordingly. Do you understand me?"

"I understand." She matches my raised voice, showing me a little bit of the fire I've been missing from her eyes since Daniel was attacked.

"Good. Now, the women's room is at the back, down the hall. It's marked. Kate has some workout gear in there, in a bag in locker thirty-six. Get changed; we're training." I turn my back on her, slide the keys to the door in my jacket pocket, and toss my coat behind the counter while she watches me.

"Right now?"

"Yes. Now. And we aren't leaving until I know you won't hesitate next time. Now go!"

When she's halfway across the room, I move quickly to the bag I always store at the counter. My pants and shoes are off, switched with a comfortable pair of sweats, before I hear the creak of the door to the bathroom. I tear off my dress shirt and replace it with my workout shirt, then carry my belt as I cross the room, taking the same steps she did.

I wait outside of the door, counting out another minute before I open it and step into the women's locker room.

As I expected, Elle spins around, caught in her bra and

panties, and she points at the open locker. "There's no clothes in here."

A wicked grin crosses my lips.

This is going to be fun.

"Lesson number one: your predator will always wait until they have an advantage."

"Oh—kay. But I thought we were training."

"You don't understand. We are training. Your goal is to get my keys and open the front door. Then this stops."

"This?"

Elle startles at the snap of leather against flesh as I test my belt against my hand a little too eagerly, and it stings. It makes my point, but I spell it out anyway. "If I catch you, I will punish you. First with my hand, then it will increase each time, until I move over to my belt. Get away from me and stay away and you're safe; get the keys and open the door and we're done. You saw where I put them?"

She looks like she's searching her memory before she nods.

"Good. Say your safe word. We're using it here too, if you need it, but I really suggest you push yourself to learn this lesson."

She grits her teeth, preparing for a fight. "Bowling."

I allow the tension to drift between us before giving her my final warning.

"I mean it. I won't lose you because you freeze up. Stay away from me and open the door. And, Elle—rock the fucking boat."

She exhales a steady breath as she adjusts the positioning of her feet, spreading them a little farther apart to steady herself.

I'm not playing around.

She asked me once if I could train her, and I intend to teach her a lesson she'll never forget.

Her eyes flit around the room.

I turn my attention away from her, and I'm about to tell her I'll give her to the count of twenty to find a place to hide when one of her heels goes flying past my eye. I turn to watch it connect with the wall behind me, and her second heel hits me in the back of my head. I look up as she clears the corner of the locker room and heads toward the showers.

Anger and desire battle for supremacy as I crack my neck and rub the spot where she got me.

I really love it when she runs from me, and this is one hunt I'm going to thoroughly enjoy.

I raise my voice.

"An apex predator learns from their mistakes. They grow. They evolve. They use their setbacks to become stronger and faster. Whoever is hunting you will make sure they've cornered you before they make themselves known. They will have the advantage, just like I do." I stay where I am, speaking in the direction where Elle ran to give her a false sense of hope before I start tearing away at it. I take slow steps toward the back in my bare feet. "Take me, for example." In the distance, Elle turns a shower on, then a second and a third. "You don't think I'd let you get a head start if I didn't know that the only exit is the one I came in through, so you have to go through me to get out."

Adrenaline sparks to life in my veins. Since I'm starting with my hands, I drop my belt on a bench and turn the corner, following the wafts of steam into the women's shower area.

The place is fairly clean, except for a large hamper of used towels. I stand at the edge of the showers for half a minute in silence, but I'm unable to hear anything over the running water.

"Such a smart little mouse my girl is." A wicked grin creeps across my face, and I bare my teeth, licking my tongue over my lower lip.

Grabbing a folded towel from a shelf, I walk through the water.

I turn off the first shower, then the second and the third.

The water warms my feet.

I stay still and quiet, listening to the water drain out around me.

There's a sauna and a storage room beyond the shower area, and I've got her.

I turn, walking the rest of the way through the showers before drying my feet on the other side.

I have one hand on the door to the sauna when I say, "I'm going to be extremely disappointed if I find you in here."

I have the door halfway open when a commotion across the room catches my attention. The hamper I just stood beside tips over, and Elle dives out of it, running toward the exit I opened up for her.

"Shit."

Forgetting my surroundings, I run through the showers, slipping on the wet floor and going down hard. I hit the tiles and slide into the wall, soaking my clothes.

A string of profanities follows as I haul my ass off the floor and run toward the locker area, reaching for my belt as I go.

But it's not where I left it.

Pride explodes along my nerve endings. I finally have someone worth chasing, and she just might get away from me— and she's got my belt.

I hit the corner at a faster pace than I'd like, slamming into a row of lockers, but I already told her not to hold back, and I won't either.

When I reach the main room, everything is quiet. The door is still locked, but my jacket has been moved from the spot where I left it.

She didn't have enough time to get my keys and get out, so she's hiding somewhere.

I'd be lying if I said I wasn't entirely turned on by this.

I look around the large area, waiting for even the slightest movement to catch my eye.

I speak into the room. "Since you did such a good job of making it out of the locker room, I'll tell you a secret: the key to the front door is on its own key ring."

I listen carefully.

For a moment, the sound of the ventilation is the only thing I hear, until the small tinkle of a key ring coming from the back training rooms makes my heart beat into my rib cage.

Gotcha.

It's a good bet that Elle is a creature of comfort. If she was running from me and had to make a quick decision, she would go to the room she knows, the one I met her here in.

I close the distance with each step. My mind swirls knowing I have her one way or another, because I'm the big bad wolf, and her demise is just a matter of time now.

I open the door, step into the room, and reach to the side to turn on the light.

"Ready or not, here I co—"

The door to the room beside me bursts open, and Elle runs at her top speed. One hand is gripped tight around the one key on its own ring; the other hand is holding my belt. I spin on my heels and run after her, closing the distance between us as she hits the front door, jabs the key at the lock, and screams when I grab her.

By the time I reach her, my cock is rock hard. I'm not sure I'm going to be able to keep playing this cat and mouse game any longer.

I haul her off the door and push her into the room, and she goes down on a mat. I stalk toward her as she rolls onto her back and attempts to crawl away from me on her hands and feet.

"The key. It—" She holds up my belt to block me, and I tear it out of her hand.

"Didn't work. There's your next lesson. Never trust anything a predator tells you. You are prey. You are meant to be trapped, and I will do and say ANYTHING to make sure I have you."

When I reach her, I kick her feet out, and she falls on her ass, legs sprawled, sealing her fate.

"It's time to accept your defeat."

I sit on the floor beside her and drag her across one of my thighs, trapping her legs under the other one. I fold my belt over itself and settle my free hand on her back, pushing her down before I bring the belt down across her ass.

Her first cry is the sweetest thing I've ever heard.

She kicks her feet and struggles in my hold. "You said you would start with your hand."

"Lesson three. There are no rules. A predator can and will change the way they play the game to suit their needs every damn time."

I spank her again, then again, and her ass reddens around her panties for me. My first strikes are the worst. I did lie. There's no way Elle can get out of this hold, and we would be here all night until she screamed her safe word, so I'm starting off rough.

She shudders as her fight leaves her, but it isn't fear. I'm not sure if Elle understands, but she's just crossed a line and surrendered herself to me.

I drop my belt beside her and caress her hot flesh with my hand as she stills underneath me. As I appreciate her submission, I murmur, "Training is done for tonight."

When I roll her over, meeting her eyes, she bites her lip, breathing heavily before she lunges for me. She wraps her arms around me and buries her face in me like she needs this to survive.

Maybe we both do.

I roll us until I'm on top of her, pinning her arms to the mat above her head with one hand. I explore her body with the other as she squirms. When I slip my fingers into the seam of her panties, her pussy is warm, inviting, and wet.

"Please, Marcus. I need you."

I pin her to the ground with the weight of my body as I reach for my belt. Looping it on itself, I run the end through the buckle before slipping it over her head and securing it like a gag between her open lips.

My pants are only halfway down my thighs when I push her legs open and up against her chest. Pulling her panties to the side, I slam into her in one unforgiving push.

Elle's back arches off the mat as she cries out against the gag.

I grip her wrists in one hand, facing her palms together.

"Clap your hands together or snap your fingers instead of your safe word if you need it." I pull back to my tip and slide myself all of the way back in. I let go of the belt now, muting her voice, and she bites down on the leather as I wrap my fingers around her throat.

"That's it, Elora." I use the name that makes her mine. "You fucking bite down hard and take it. I want to remember how fucking good my girl is every time I see your teeth marks on my belt."

She whimpers under me, spit dribbling out of her mouth around the leather, and I fuck into her like the apex predator I am, claiming my victory.

Our chase heightened everything, and it isn't long before Elle's thighs are clamped tight around my waist as I rut into her over and over again.

Her bite marks are clearly visible all over my belt, and my balls draw up tight at the sight of them as she spasms under me, drifting away on her orgasm.

When her pussy grips my cock one last time, I follow her over the edge, releasing all of my tension into her. Then I roll us both onto my back, so I don't crush her with my sated weight.

I loosen the belt and remove it from her mouth, tossing it aside and brushing her sweaty hair away from her face with my fingers.

"It's a good thing there are showers here." I kiss the top of her head.

Her body vibrates against mine as she laughs, then props her arm on my chest, lifting herself enough to look at me.

"Can I start taking classes with you—to train for real?"

Relief that she's taking this seriously floods through me. "Sure, but if anything happens before then, that move you tried on me the first time we were here—the one to the nose—that will definitely work. We'll set up a schedule on Monday. Right now, though, I really want to do some kinky shit with you in the showers."

She laughs again, but this time I'm not joking.

"Are you sure you're okay coming back to work?" I've asked the question so many times this morning that I sound like a broken record.

It's only been a week since Daniel was attacked, and I'm not sure I agree with his doctor's assessment that work is the best place for him to be right now.

"So far, I've been okay. I can't sit at home, Elle. You know I like to keep busy."

"I know. But seriously, feel free to just hang out around the office this week. I'll clear your schedule. Julie has our intern working with your clients, and she's doing all of the face-to-face meetings." I wince as I say the words. The bruising around his eyes has started to yellow around the edges.

As if hearing my thoughts, Daniel reaches up to his nose. "It looks worse than it feels. Really. How are you doing?"

"I've been better, but it's been quiet around here—since that night. I mean, work is busy, but nothing else has been off."

"Maybe it was just a random attack." He looks hopeful as he offers his thoughts, but I know it wasn't random. I haven't told him yet that more flowers and a card were found in the file room.

"Maybe. I wonder now if we should have opened a case. I know you did that for me, but still. Someone is out there, and they're getting away with doing this to you. It isn't right."

Daniel reaches across the table, covering my hands with one of his. "Hey. I'm okay, and we're not going to let this happen again, right? I'm here for you too. We'll get through this."

I pull out one of my hands and cover it over his. "Thank you, Daniel."

Nat calls through to tell me that my lunch meeting is here, and I tell her to let them in.

I circle the desk to help Daniel stand, and he waves me off, telling me he needs to do these things on his own—doctor's orders.

Marcus and Jaxon enter with Nat trailing behind them, carrying a carafe of coffee. "I'll be right back with the tray."

"Daniel, it's nice to see you up." Jaxon extends his hand to shake Daniel's, then points toward the desk. "Would you like to join us?"

"A few of our coworkers are taking me out for lunch. I was hoping Elle could join us."

"I'm sorry, Daniel. I'll make it up to you by taking you out next week."

"It's a deal," he says as he steps away from the chairs and moves toward the door. "Have you found anything out yet?"

"We're still looking into a few things. I'm confident something will come to light soon. It's always a matter of time with these things." Jaxon offers a sliver of hope without saying anything definitive.

Marcus joins the conversation. "How are you doing?"

Daniel shrugs it off. He's been asked that a lot this morning.

"It doesn't hurt so much. I'm just happy Elle wasn't there with me. Who knows what might have happened." He looks back at me, and my heart feels heavy that I left him here alone that night.

"You're a good friend to her."

Daniel looks between us. "Yeah, well. She helped me through a difficult time." He points at the door. "I should get going."

Nat returns and sets the platter of deli wraps on my table. They thank her and wait in silence as she leaves us, closing the door behind her.

"A difficult time?" Jaxon asks as he pulls out a chair.

I turn to my desk, grab my mug of cold coffee, and join them at the table. Marcus beats me to my chair and pulls it out for me.

"He was going through a divorce when he first started working at Swank. He likes to keep busy, and he threw himself into his work. Kind of like he's doing now." I grab a wrap off the platter. "So, Kate said you have some questions for me?"

Jaxon stares down Marcus for a moment, waiting for him to do the talking.

"Before we talk about anything, I need to tell you that I asked Jax to include a profile on you, to determine what it is about you that someone might obsess over. I didn't tell you last week because you were already dealing with the attack."

"Okay. What did you find out?"

Jax sets a notebook on the table. "Well, I'm running what I know about you against both Remy Larsen and Gregory Pasternak. Greg's lawyer is cooperating, but it's limited because he's worried that he'll implicate his client. I had a chance to spend some time with Remy last weekend at the awards dinner. I have some questions for you that should help narrow things down."

I had a suspicion that Jaxon was talking to Remy to gather information.

"Sure. Ask away."

"You're positive you'd never met Gregory Pasternak before he approached you at the club? And you don't have any friends in common?"

"Yeah. We didn't know each other, and we never spoke of any mutual friends."

"And you mentioned that Remy went to school with Daniel, and that's how you met him?"

"Yes. Although I'm not sure. You'll have to check that with him."

Jaxon nods and jots down a note. "Go back as far as you can in your mind and tell me about the first time you can remember feeling like you were being watched."

I puff my cheeks out on a long exhale as I travel back through my memories. "I'm pretty sure it was a little while after I met Greg."

Jaxon and Marcus both nod as I talk, and I wonder what is going through their minds.

"Tell me about who you dated before Mr. Pasternak."

"I dated a couple of men here and there when I first moved to Chicago, but there wasn't anyone I fit with. I'd have to say before Greg would probably be Ben, my boyfriend from high school back home. I was kind of hardcore with my studies in college. Then I moved out here and started Swank. I guess I didn't have time to date."

That part is a lie, but I'm not going to elaborate here. I had time. We make time if something is important. I just didn't meet anyone who filled my needs until Greg came into the picture, so I didn't make time.

I wonder who my answers are leading Jaxon to since he switches between asking about both Remy and Greg.

"After you started seeing Greg, did he ever show up unannounced or try to insert himself in other parts of your life? Did he instigate taking your relationship to another level?"

"No. We had an arrangement, and we stuck to it." I glance at Marcus, feeling weird about discussing a past lover, but his soft expression tells me this information is more important than his pride. "He never pushed for more time, and he was fine when I said I wasn't interested in pursuing an emotional connection. At least, that's the impression I got."

"Does Remy insert himself into your life in a way that you feel oversteps the boundaries of your relationship?"

"Well, we only have a business relationship, but he has. He told me he showed up at the event last Saturday to make sure I was okay."

"What made him think you weren't okay?"

"He said he ran into Daniel, who told him about the attack. It felt self-serving. Like, he told me that he came to check up on me, but I felt like he thought that meant I owed him something in return. The whole thing felt weird."

"Does he do this often?"

"He came by my office the other week, wanting to go out for a drink. But other than that, no. He approaches me at events, but after I turn him down, I often see him at the end of the night leaving with other women."

"These women, is it clear he has a certain type? Same hair color, body shape, age range?"

I run the women through my head as I swivel it from side to side. "I'd say the only thing they have in common is they buy what he's selling."

"Okay. That's probably enough to start with for now. We have a meeting this afternoon. I'll let you know if we learn anything new."

I finish chewing my mouthful before reaching for my coffee

and swallowing it down. If I don't ask the question I want to ask, I won't stop thinking about it all day.

"So—um—what did you learn about me? My profile? What does it say about me?"

The brothers look at each other again before answering. Jaxon's expression seems to say *I told you this would happen.*

"Well, until I can fit the pieces together, it doesn't tell me much. Remember, I'm profiling the obsession, not your character."

"Still, my character factors into it. Tell me what you know. I can correct anything you might be wrong about."

"Oh, I'm not wrong. I just don't know where it fits yet."

I level my gaze on Marcus but speak to Jaxon. "I want to know."

Marcus stares at me in silence before breaking away and nodding to his brother.

"Okay. I just want to remind you that these profiles strip everything away. They remove how we feel about you as a person and focus on your core makeup, so they are a lot colder than a personal opinion would be."

"I get it. And?"

"You are highly respected and loved by those closest to you. Equally, you love those around you, often putting others first and never for your own gain, so you lean more toward selfless than self-serving. So it isn't likely you are being targeted because you are hated. You are driven and successful, so it could be jealousy. However, the flowers and the cards suggest it's more likely either an admirer or a scorned lover." Jax glances between Marcus and me for a few seconds as he considers his next words. Then he points at his brother. "Marcus is a dominant personality, and based on what you've shared about your time with Greg, you are submissive, so we're looking for someone who is in control and dominant in nature.

As for the rest, I need to eliminate Remy or Greg to complete the profile, and I promise you, we are doing all that we can."

It isn't lost on me that Jaxon is saying the bare minimum without committing to anything. It's the same way he answered Daniel's question earlier.

When I look over at him, he leans forward. "Listen, *those parts* of your profile are none of my business unless they need to be, so I haven't looked at them. You are among friends and family here. We are rallying around you, and we won't stop until we solve this. Don't invest your time in worrying about what we know or might find out about you. I guarantee it won't change how much we all like you. You will only alienate yourself from your pack, and that is what this person is waiting for."

When he says it this way, it makes sense.

When lunch comes to an end, Jaxon asks if he can drop in to verify a few things with Daniel, and Marcus hangs behind.

He locks the door after Jaxon leaves, then closes the distance and reaches out for my hand, pulling me with him to the couch and settling me on his lap.

He doesn't cuddle me into him, but he does shift his body so he's open if I wish to do it myself.

"How are you? Really?"

I circle my arm around his neck and lean against his chest. "I don't know." Marcus makes a face at my answer. "Really. I'm just trying to move along. It's hard to explain. I know there is a threat, but I don't know what it is, so I'm locked in this strange loop where I just go through the motions of my daily life. Every time I look at Daniel's bruises, I feel responsible."

He hugs me a little closer. "Those are all valid feelings, Elle. At the same time, though, do you understand that you are not responsible? There's a difference between feeling it and knowing it."

"Yes. I understand I am not responsible."

"Good. I'm going to go find Jaxon and get back to the office. We have a couple of people dropping by later to shed some more light on things, and I'll contact you if we learn anything. I'll pick you up after work?"

I nod in agreement, and I walk him out to find Jax talking to Daniel near the elevators.

Marcus must sense my unease, because he turns to me and assures me that he's not going to stop until I'm safe. He says it's just a matter of time before something falls into place.

He kisses my head as the elevator dings, and I don't object.

I'm at work, but I don't care anymore, because I need this connection. I need to know they are here for me and I'm not alone.

CHAPTER 31
MARCUS

Jax is quiet for most of the drive back to our office until he mutters, "I'm missing something."

"How so?"

His forehead creases as he grips the wheel. "I don't know. Something isn't right about this."

He goes back to his thoughts for the remainder of the drive, and I leave him be. If it means he'll figure out who is doing this to Elle, I will shut up around him for as long as I have to.

Kate greets us as we pass her desk, handing Jax a small stack of paper. He flips through his messages as we trail behind him down the hall to his office.

"My friend Helen—the one in English lit—is on her way over to talk about those quotes I sent her. Are you free to talk to her?"

"We are. Let us know when she gets here. Is Kill in?"

"Yeah. He's in his office, following up on some things." The front door chimes, and Kate turns and leaves us.

Jax pauses outside of his office, stopping me from entering

along with him. "I need some time to figure this out. Can you give me a bit until Helen gets here?"

"Yeah, sure. I'll be in my office if you need me."

He steps in and closes the door. I don't take it personally. Jax's manners have always taken a back seat when he's deep in thought.

I turn my attention to looking at everything we've gathered from other angles. First, I contact the building where Swank is located to ask their security department for any footage they have for the night of the attack. Then, I go back over every piece of information I gathered on Remy and Gregory and reread it until my eyes go blurry.

I think about calling Elle a couple of times, but I don't want to get her hopes up since we are no closer than we were before. She's also busy wrapping up her work, and I'll have her to myself in a couple of hours anyway.

Kate pokes her head into my office. "Helen is waiting in the conference room. The guys are going in now."

I waste no time sauntering over, and Kate has to jog to catch up to me.

"Hi, Helen. These are my brothers." She points around the table at each of us. "Jaxon, Cillian, and Marcus. This is my friend Helen."

We all exchange a greeting before she sets her bag on the table and opens it, pulling out a binder with sticky notes poking out of the pages.

Jax ushers her along. "Kate tells us you have some information on the phrases?"

She sits down, sliding her chair to the table. "I do. Okay. So, the first phrase on its own could mean anything." She splays her fingers over her closed book. "But the second phrase was really helpful because both of those lines do appear in some works by a Roman poet, Costa, who lived a long time ago—like we're talking around the birth of Christ here. Anyway, his works have since been translated into English a few different times, and these two phrases appear in one of the more popular translations. The piece is titled 'Per Sempre,' which very literally translates to 'always, forever, or everlasting,' and it was about a woman named Calypsus."

"So it's a love poem?" Kill asks as Jax jots down notes.

Helen's face pinches at the question. "Yes and no. It's an elegy."

"What's an elegy?" I can't be the only one who has this question.

"In a nutshell, it's a poem for the dead. Like a eulogy, but it's more reflective."

"So Costa wrote this because he lost Calypsus?" Jax asks.

"Well, actually, according to history, Costa killed Calypsus."

That gets everyone's attention. When we all sit in silence, Helen takes it as her cue to explain.

"It's written that Costa loved Calypsus, but she had eyes for someone else. As the elegy continues, Costa decides that he thinks maybe Calypsus didn't notice him because he was always too afraid to make his intentions known. The part in the first message, *The time has come*, is when he decides to make some type of grand gesture, hoping to show her how they could be together, but it turns out what he was offering was not what she wanted, and she chooses another. He takes this to heart because he had never dared to be vulnerable with anyone but her, and her rejection cut away at the very fabric of his soul. The elegy devolves from there. He writes about watching her with other men and still believing she was meant for him, until near the end of the story."

Worry covers Kate's face. "How does it end?"

Helen taps the piece of paper. "*Imprison me in your*

waning light. This ends the part where he talks about luring her away to try to reason with her one last time. It's believed that the *waning light* is her dying breath, because it's written as *your* waning light instead of *the* waning light. She rebuked him one last time, and he wanted to live in her forever. The story goes that he strangled her, and the last thing she saw was him. He hoped it meant she would carry him with her always, as his heart had forced him to carry her."

No one moves a muscle when Helen stops talking. The level of this obsession is higher than I expected.

Jax stands. "Helen, thank you for coming in." When he meets my eyes, he looks more lost than before. "I have another meeting arriving shortly."

"I need to make some calls." Kill stands and leaves Kate and me with Helen.

"Um, I'm leaving in fifteen minutes. We're going to grab dinner." Kate doesn't sound like she wants to go now. "Unless you need me to help out with anything?"

"I think we've got it. I'll call if there's a problem."

I walk the women to Kate's desk and head to my office, where I find an email from Elle waiting for me. It turns out Alexandra stopped by to check on her, and they are going for dinner. This will give me a couple of hours to look into this new information, but I don't know where to start, so I make my way back to ask Jax if I can shadow him for a while.

"Sure. Grab a seat. Listen, I don't know how to tell you this, so I'm going to come out and say it: I don't think it's Remy Larsen."

"How can you be so sure?"

"I spent time with him on Saturday night. The guy is shallow." He holds up three fingers. "He loves three things: money, pussy, and himself." He puts a finger down for each item he lists.

Kate buzzes through and announces that Mr. Larsen is here for Jax, and I glare at him accusingly. He tells her to put him in a conference room and looks at me. "I still have some questions for him, to make sure. Now, you are welcome to join me, but you sit quietly in the corner. Am I making myself clear?"

I don't like this one bit, but I remind myself that Elle is safe at work. So I agree, and I follow Jax into the conference room.

He stops outside the door. "I mean it, Marcus. This is Elle's life on the line, and you fucking do this for her. You push down this pissing match between you and Remy, and you sit there with your mouth shut. You got me?"

He's right. If I push Remy, he could shut up, and we won't get what we need out of him.

"I got you."

Remy's smile for Jax falls from his face when he sees me enter the room behind him. I walk to the far side of the room and slide my chair back, almost into the corner and out of my brother's way.

Jax drops his aggressive tone to a more accommodating one. "Remy, thank you so much for offering to help us out."

"Sure thing."

"So, as I told you on the phone, we could use your help in clarifying a few things."

As they break the ice, I glance at my watch. Business hours are almost over. Elle must be getting ready to head out with Lexa by now. I make a mental note to call her as soon as we are done here.

My thoughts of her take me away from the conversation for a moment.

"—and this means we need to look into everyone who is close to Elle, not as suspects, but as people who can offer us better insight."

I roll my eyes, thankful that Remy—and especially my

brother—can't see me. Of course we're looking at him as a suspect. Remy straightens in his seat with a smug grin, happy that Jax just called him an expert on Elle, and I keep myself from groaning my disagreement out loud.

"It was nice to see you on Saturday; I enjoyed talking with you." Jax butters him up. "But is it normal for you to attend a Swank event that isn't sports related?"

"Yeah. Kind of. I ran into Daniel when he was settling some stuff with one of his clients. It's hard not to notice his banged-up face, so I asked him about it. He told me what happened and said he was worried that Elle might be in danger. When he said she'd be at an event that weekend, I thought I'd drop by to see if she was okay."

As Remy answers, I lean forward, threading my fingers together with my elbows on my knees.

Jax goes for a more direct approach, shocking even me.

"Or did you drop by hoping she would be grateful enough to go home with you?" Then he swings from bad cop to good cop. "Listen, I don't think you're the one stalking Elle—"

"WHAT? No. I mean, I'm into her, but I'm no stalker. I didn't even know she had a stalker until now when you just told me. My money says it's him." He points at me. "I mean, that night at the charity thing, when we bid on Elle, someone slashed all four of my tires. It cost me a fucking fortune to replace them. I thought he was mad that I drove the price up so high."

Jax and I exchange a glance, and he shakes his head before looking up to the ceiling.

This just keeps derailing.

"How did you first meet Elle?"

Remy takes a little too long to answer the question, and I ball my hands into fists.

He's hesitating, which means he's thinking. He's breaking

down why he's really here, and sooner or later, he's going to bow out of the interview.

"I met her through Daniel Hawkins, one of her employees. Daniel and I graduated at the same time."

"So you know Daniel pretty well then?"

"Not really. We were never close. He latched on to the first girl who fucked him in college. Got married and settled down. I'm more—outgoing and social."

Jax stares at him in silence for close to a minute before he excuses himself and asks to speak to me outside.

When he closes the door that now separates us from Remy, he squares himself on me and steps close to keep his voice low. "It isn't Remy. I'm almost sure of it. I'm leaning toward Gregory Pasternak. It's plausible he was stalking Elle before they met at the club. He could have sought her out and waited for his time. Now he's been released early, and all of a sudden she's with you."

"It's not Gregory." Kill steps up from behind me. "He's no longer a person of interest. According to his lawyer, his mother fell, and he was with her in the hospital—two hours away—during the attack."

Jax looks like he's going to rip Kill's head off. He points at him. "Verify it. That's your priority."

"So it is Remy." I rub my temples, trying to calm this growing headache.

"I really don't think it is." Jax doubles down. "Neither of these two fits. I'm trying to make them fit now, and that isn't how profiling works."

"It has to be one of them." I look at my brothers.

"Does it though?" Kill asks, and a wave of nausea rolls through me.

"I'm missing something." Jax rarely shows his frustration, but he's so many shades of aggravated. "Okay, shit. I was running the profile against those two and focused on one side of Elle's personality."

Kill points at Jax. "Run your profile again, but take both of them out of it. Just focus on Elle's complete victim profile. Who is after her?"

I swivel my head to Jax, who's nodding hard, trying to recall what he's learned. Then he closes his eyes to focus. "Elle is submissive—privately. Publicly, she is controlled, organized, and focused, making her dominant. Whoever sent those messages to Elle is deeply devoted to her. She will be their every thought. Outwardly, their commitment to her is seen as supportive, protective, but inwardly, it's obsessive and chaotic. This person believes that Elle is theirs simply because their feelings for her are so strong, and they would do anything for her. It is most likely someone who sees themself as in service to her."

Kill spins to me, pointing a finger in my face. "No thinking. Who does that sound like? Say a name right now."

"Daniel." My answer is unexpected, and it rattles me to my core.

Jax seems to agree with me. "Is Elle still at work?"

I shake my head as I pull my phone out of my pocket and dial Elle's number. It goes to voicemail.

"She's out with Lexa."

Jax looks at his phone, then taps at the screen as he says, "No. She's not."

"Yes, she is. Elle emailed earlier and said Lexa dropped by and they're going out for dinner."

Jax's phone dings, and he glances at it before responding. "Marcus, I'm telling you, she isn't out with Lexa. I have plans with Lexa tonight, and we're still on." He turns his phone to me, and Lexa's text message confirming that she's still at Ravenous punches me in the gut.

Jax opens the door to the conference room. "I have a couple more questions for Remy."

I leave him to it and run back to my office.

The room tilts and spins as I circle the desk and pull up Elle's office phone number.

I was just there.

I was just holding her in my arms.

I was with Elle and Daniel only hours ago.

He stood right beside Elle as I comforted her and told her we were getting close.

The phone rings four times before Nat picks up. "This is Swa—"

"Nat, it's Marcus Wolfe. I need to speak with Elle, and she's not picking up. Is she still there?"

"Elle left a couple of hours ago. She drove Daniel home."

CHAPTER 32
ELLE

Pushing my chair away from the desk, I roll backward and swivel in my seat to look out over the city.

My stalker is out there somewhere, and the butterflies in my stomach refuse to rest.

Something as simple as a knock on the door startles me, where once it was welcome.

"Hey, Elle. Do you have a minute?" Daniel peeks through the gap in the door.

My mind is going a mile a minute, and I'm not getting any more work done today anyway.

"I do. Come in." He closes the door behind him and takes the seat in front of my desk as I roll myself back from the window. "How was lunch? I'm sorry I missed it."

"It was good. We all missed you too."

"And how was your first full day back in the office?"

"Well—um, that's what I want to talk to you about. I'm—it's a little rougher than I thought it would be. I—had to grab some files and...everything kind of came rushing back."

"Oh, Daniel. I'm so sorry. You should have asked me to get

it for you." My stomach drops at how he must have felt. I didn't experience the attack firsthand, and I can barely go near the file room.

"Thank you, but I shouldn't have to. I think maybe you were right. I came back too soon."

"Do you need to go? Daniel, I completely understand. Why don't we talk about some additional paid vacation. Off the books. Just take all of the time you need."

"I appreciate you taking care of me, Elle. This has been really difficult. I don't even want to walk outside to catch the train." Daniel takes a deep breath, blowing it out on a shaky exhale.

I know I'm not responsible, but I still feel awful.

"I can drive you home. You're not far from here, right?" I check the time on my desktop.

"I'm in Forest Glen. About twenty minutes by car. If it isn't too much trouble." When he shifts in his seat, he hisses, cradling his arm across his lap. He's more injured than he's letting on, and the sight gnaws away at the guilt I carry.

There's no way I'm going to let him walk out of here alone. I can easily drop him off and be back here before Nat leaves at the end of the day.

"It's no trouble at all. Do you have your things?"

He smiles, seemingly relieved that he'll be able to get away from here.

The houses in this part of town are farther apart, with single-family homes pushed back on heavily treed lots.

"I don't think I've ever seen your place, Daniel. These are gorgeous homes."

He keeps his attention on the street and tells me to take the next right. "Thanks. It's my family's home. It's this one—with the long driveway."

"Is it just you here?" I know his parents died in a plane crash when he was little.

"For now. Can you help me with these things?" He points to the gift our team pitched in to get him. "I'm still a bit weak in the arms. Will you grab the plant?"

"You should have left this with me in the office. The sun would do wonders for it there," I muse as I lift it out of the back seat.

"I thought about that." He glances at the plant in my arms with a somber frown. "But I'd rather have it here with me, so I can enjoy it on my own."

He gathers up the small stack of get-well cards, and I follow him to the front door.

He fishes his keys out of his pocket and finds the one he's looking for. Once we're inside, he slides some of the locks into place as I look over the main floor.

The two-story home is completely furnished, but it doesn't seem like something that would fit Daniel's style. He's always kept his workspace organized, and this place looks like a whole family lives here. He must have inherited the place and all of the furniture as well.

"I like your place." I hold up the plant I'm carrying. "Where do you want this?"

"If it's no trouble, could you put it in my office? It's upstairs." When I look up the stairs, he adds, "It gets the best sun."

"Sure." I smile.

It's the least I can do for him.

He follows behind as we take the steps up, each one reminding me of the little creaks in my parents' old house.

When we reach the top of the stairs, he points to the left. "It's just off of my room."

He stops in front of a closed door and pauses, deep in thought. For a moment, I think he's going to walk away from the door, but he reaches for the handle. "This is it."

He opens the door and steps back to allow me to enter.

"Okay. Where do you want th—"

Everything stops when I see my jacket spread out on one side of the bed, positioned as though someone might be sleeping in it. It's the jacket that went missing at the charity auction.

"I don't understand." I set the plant on a shelf beside me and approach the bed, running my fingers along its soft threads. "Did you find this?"

My question is wrong. Nausea rolls in the pit of my stomach as soon as I ask it.

Daniel takes a step toward me to answer, and I instinctively take a step back, holding up my hand as everything collides around me.

"It's you."

Marcus said this would happen. He told me *a predator will always wait until they have an advantage.*

Daniel set this all up.

He isn't even as hurt as he made it seem in my office. I hadn't noticed until now, but he's standing up straight. His arm moves without effort. He's not the weakened man he made himself out to be.

"I tried to tell you—so many times." He takes another step forward, and I scan the room for the door leading to his office.

My stomach sinks as I realize there is no door other than the one Daniel is blocking, and Marcus's next lesson comes back to me: *Never trust anything a predator tells you. You are prey. You are meant to be trapped.*

I think I'm going to vomit.

Daniel steps far enough to the side, opening a slim path to the door, and I lunge toward my escape.

He jumps back into place, wagging his finger at me, and I stumble back farther into the room. "Ah, ah, ah. Not until you listen to me."

I can almost hear hindsight laughing at my expense as I think about all of the questions I should have asked Marcus and his brothers about protecting myself. I would have asked Jax how I was supposed to talk myself out of this situation. Do I try to pacify Daniel? Agree with everything he says? Or will that make him mad? Do I answer truthfully and appeal to my friend?

There's just one problem with that last part: my friend is no longer staring back at me.

"Daniel, I don't understand."

"You will. I'll tell you everything, and you'll understand. It'll be like it was before."

Before?

"Daniel, Nat knows I drove you home."

"It doesn't matter."

"Marcus will come looking for me. He's supposed to pick me up soon."

His expression sours as soon as I say his name. But as quickly as his disgust came, it's gone, and he holds up his finger while he removes his phone. "That reminds me." He taps away on the screen before securing his phone in his pocket. "I have the time I need."

"What did you do?"

"I sent him an email from your account when we were in the car. It says he opened it. He won't worry about you for a while."

Daniel, Julie, and Nat all have access to my main work email.

Now that I think about it, Daniel has access to so many things. He offered to watch my house a few months ago, when Barb and I were out of town at the same time. He probably had my key copied, and I never changed my alarm code.

Vertigo rises up, and I sway, taking a step backward and slamming my ass into the dresser at my back. When I reach behind me to steady myself, my fingers skim along the neck of something solid and metal.

Which reminds me of Marcus's last lesson: *there are no rules.*

Daniel rushes to me to see if I'm okay, and I don't give him a second to make this worse for me.

Rock the fucking boat, Elle. I hear Marcus as if he's standing right here with me, and I don't hesitate.

Grabbing a fistful of his shirt at his chest, I swing without knowing what I'm holding. It turns out it's a lamp, and the base connects with the side of his head. The cord whips around with my force. The prongs on the plug catch me on the side of my face, slicing my cheek with a sharp sting, but I pay no attention to it.

He's still in between me and the door, except now he's on the floor. I jump over his body and sprint for the hall. Missing a couple stairs on the way down, I run straight for the front door. As soon as I'm outside, I'll scream bloody murder.

I remember Daniel locking the front door, and I immediately go for the first lock when I slam into it. I even out my breathing, trying to keep my wits intact as I turn the first lock, then a second, then a—

My fingers fail to grip a latch.

The last lock is a keyed dead bolt, and I don't have the key.

Footsteps thud on the floor above me, and I step out of my heels. I push off the door, throwing myself deeper into this house I've never been in before as Daniel reaches the main floor. I turn around and tiptoe backward down a darkened hall as I listen to the sound his shoes make on the hardwood floors. He slows down.

The light in the room I just ran through is turned on, and I scurry backward into a different room.

"You were supposed to be mine, Elle." Doors are opened and closed as I imagine he's looking for me in any hiding space he can think of. "I did everything for you, and I thought we were happy."

None of this makes any sense. Daniel has never approached me about anything beyond a working relationship, and I'm thrown off by confusion.

Glassware crashes to the ground, startling me. I feel around in the dark for an escape when a curtain opens. The bright afternoon sun pours into the room, and I push against the window to slide it open. That's when I notice the nails driven into the wood along the frame, blocking the window from opening.

I am trapped.

The light in the room exposes another door off to the side, and I open it to step through, then pause. Every room in this house has the curtains drawn, and the doors are all closed. He'll know I came this way if I don't close the curtain.

Daniel's voice is just down the hall. "I just want to talk to you, Elle. Come out, and I won't hurt you."

Lies.

I leave the door open and run past the sliver of light still pouring into the room to a door on the other side, hoping he'll follow in the wrong direction.

I hope I'm right, because this is a closet. If he opens this door, I'm done.

I wait. The floorboards in the room groan with each of his steps. My heart hammers into my chest, and I will my breathing to slow.

The small amount of light filtering in from under the door shines bright for a moment before dimming. I assume he's opened then closed the curtain before I hear him moving out of the room, following the path he thinks I took.

With shaky hands, I pull out my phone to call Marcus. My nerves are shot, and I don't remember Daniel's address, but at least he'll know I'm in trouble.

As if he could sense my thoughts—and at the worst possible time—my phone lights up with Marcus's call information. A split-second later, the phone starts ringing at full volume, and I burst out of my hiding spot and run as fast as I can away from the direction I'm sure Daniel went in. I fumble and drop my phone and waste no time trying to retrieve it.

I enter the front hall at the same time as Daniel, who came from a different direction. His dead eyes burrow through me as he runs straight at me and knocks both of us into the front door.

I scream at the top of my lungs as I go down.

"I did everything for you! Anything you needed. We were good!" he yells at me as we push and pull against each other. There is nothing wrong with the arm he cradled earlier.

He lifts me to standing, then slams me against the front door, and my head rattles as the back of my skull connects with solid wood.

His spit flies against my face. "Then *he* came along and ruined it."

"Marcus," I whisper. It's more of a plea, a pathetic hope that Marcus will know I need him.

"No. Greg. I was supposed to be yours at the club, not him. I took you there to show you how good we could be together. You were always so strong, but there, you were weak and pathetic, and he took you away from me." He spins around and tosses me into the room, then closes the distance between us just as Marcus did at the self-defense center. "And now this guy. I won't let him take you away from me."

I don't back away in defeat. My mind settles on the last piece of advice Marcus gave me that night, and I put all of my faith into it.

When he leans over to haul my ass off the floor, I angle my wrist back and stand up fast, driving my palm up and straight into his already fractured nose.

This is the only move I have left, and if it doesn't work, then I'm dying here today.

When Elle's number goes to voicemail, I give up on trying to reach her.

Kill makes a sharp turn onto a backroad, citing rush hour delays and telling us he knows a shortcut. Jax braces himself in the back seat.

"Should we call local PD? Someone has to be closer than we are." I prop my hand against the glove compartment to steady myself as we fly over a bump in the road, and Kill doesn't slow down.

Kill shakes his head, his eyes on the road as he honks and blows through a red light. "I have a call in to a friend of mine. He's a detective, good guy. He's going to meet us at the address with backup, but I think we'll be there first."

Jax points to something up ahead, alerting Kill before he adds to his answer. "You know how it is if a general call comes in for backup. They take over and set up blockades. It wastes time. With this new profile, I'm positive Elle is in immediate danger."

"Fine. Run through it again. I'm going to lose my shit if I don't focus."

Jax reaches up from the back seat, clapping his hand on my shoulder. "This is my assessment based on what we know now. It didn't start with Greg; he was just the catalyst. This goes all of the way back to Daniel's divorce. He mentioned that Elle helped him through a difficult time. I don't think she did. He sees it that way because he traded one obsession for another. Daniel isn't dominant, he's submissive. When Elle is at work, she's in control, she runs the company, she's—"

He raises an eyebrow at me, and I answer. "Dominant."

"Exactly. Remy confirmed that Daniel's ex-wife was controlling, and he made Elle his surrogate dominant. It was never primarily sexual for him, and that is why he was able to hide it for so long. Daniel thrives in service, but he went about it in an unhealthy way, pushing his needs on Elle without her knowledge or consent. She saw him as an employee who loved his job and worked hard, and she praised him for it. That's what drove him. Then Greg came along and triggered her submissive side, which was counterintuitive to Daniel's core beliefs of how his perceived relationship with Elle was supposed to be. Now it's obvious that your relationship with Elle isn't going to fizzle out, and it's probably leached into how she acts at work. This is all going to make him feel as though his relationship with Elle, which is only real up here"—he taps his temple—"is threatened."

Kill mutters a profanity under his breath as we close in on our destination. The map on my phone tells me we're only five minutes out.

"So Daniel busted his own face and left that bloody mess?"

"Yes. And it was intentional that he did it in the Swank offices. I remember Elle saying they were supposed to be there together that night. Those times, as irrelevant as they might be to everyone else, will mean everything to someone like him. That would have been the equivalent of a date, and she canceled to go out with you, and meet your family, nonetheless, abandoning everything he offered her."

A chill runs through me, carrying a vision of Elle with it. She's in trouble, I feel it in my bones. Daniel has known Elle for years, and during that time, he used her as a crutch, building a one-sided relationship to fulfill his needs until he believed his feelings were returned.

He's one of Elle's closest friends, and she trusted him.

Daniel played us at the hospital on the night of the attack. He told Elle he was worried about her personal business getting out and that's why he didn't want to open a file. In reality, he didn't want to open a file because he knew it was only his blood in the file room. He also knew that once I took his clothes from the officer, the evidence would be considered contaminated.

I was so blinded by trying to protect Elle that I walked right into it.

The houses are larger in size and set farther apart in this area. Kill turns down a side street and unbuckles his seatbelt in preparation, and Jax and I follow suit.

We're getting close.

Once it comes down to finding the right house number, time slows down.

Then Jax points between us, up the street. "Is that Elle's car?"

Kill steps on the gas to get to the address, and it's the one we're looking for.

I'm out of the car before it stops moving, and I sprint to the front door, turning the knob and already knowing it won't open.

Sirens cut through the quiet neighborhood from off in the distance. I take a step back and a deep breath, then I put everything I have behind my weight and kick the door open.

The old wood splinters open, and a battered and shocked Elle spins around as Daniel lies unconscious at her feet.

It takes her a split second to snap out of her hell, and I run to her, scooping her into me as she breaks into sobs, clutching at me in terror. "Marcus—I thought—it's Daniel. He was going to—"

Jax and Kill round us, securing Daniel as I turn and lead Elle out of the house and walk her down the steps to her car.

Two squad cars pull in, and Kill runs past us, holding up his badge and pointing at the house as he shouts details at the first responder.

Everything after that fades into the background as I spin Elle to get a better look at her. She's fisted my shirt on either side of my torso with trembling hands, and she won't let go. She winces when I trail my finger over a cut along her cheek.

When I calm her enough that she stops hiccupping her sobs, she looks up at me with devastation in her eyes. "I don't understand. Daniel was doing all of this. Why?"

"I don't know." I pull her into me, combing my fingers through her hair as she shakes in shock. I could share all of Jax's theories with her right now, but this isn't the time, and we don't have all of the answers yet. "You're safe now. Focus on that."

Commotion at the front door catches our attention. Daniel yells Elle's name, and she goes rigid in my arms.

His face and shirt are bloody. "Please, Elle. Just listen to me." He tries to jerk himself free, but the officers on either side of him double down, and Jax steps in front of Daniel, blocking his view.

When Daniel leans to the side to look around Jax, I block Elle with my jacket. The officers drag him toward the first squad car as he yells disjointed sentences, trying to appeal to Elle's good nature.

The door closes, cutting off his pleas, and Elle exhales a deep breath. Her words are muffled by my chest.

Hooking two fingers under her chin, I tip her head up. "Pardon?"

"You saved me." She gazes at me in awe.

"I didn't save you. You saved yourself."

She shakes her head as I speak, denying every word. "Yes, you did, Marcus. I listened to everything you said; I followed everything you taught me. You told me my move to his nose would work, and it did. I wouldn't have tried it. I wouldn't have rocked the boat." Her chin trembles as her eyes fill with a fresh wave of tears. "I wouldn't have known what to do."

She rests her head against my chest once more, and her body relaxes, growing heavy as her adrenaline leaves her. Jax circles the car and glances at her before making eye contact.

"There's an officer here who needs to speak with you, to get an initial statement so they can hold Daniel at the station." A female officer stands five feet behind Jax, waiting to approach. Jax points at an ambulance at the end of the driveway. "We also want to check you out."

Elle looks up at me. "Will you stay with me?"

I brush a stray strand of hair from her puffy face, cup her cheek in my palm, and respond with an answer that goes deeper than she'll ever know.

"Always."

Elle cried herself out about half an hour ago, and she's running on fumes now. She was checked out, bandaged up, and given the all clear as she gave her preliminary statement and answered some questions.

Once the police had what they needed, they let us go. They

arranged a time for Elle to come down to the station to speak with them further after she got some rest.

By the time we arrive back at the Wolfe Security office, Kate and Alexandra are already there and sprawled out across the couches near the entrance. As soon as they see Elle, they jump up, rush over, push Jax, Kill, and me out of the way, and crowd around Elle, guiding her to the couches to sit down.

"Where the hell did all of this food come from?" Kill asks as he reaches for a container.

Kate swats his hand away. "That's for Elle. We didn't know what she might want, and the longer we had to wait, the more places we kept ordering from." She returns to Elle with a caring smile on her face. "Here. Sit down. How are you?"

As Elle says she's okay for the hundredth time today, Jax steps around the far side of the table and approaches Alexandra. Their voices are hushed, but judging by their body language, they have been spending more time together than any of us have realized.

It also wasn't lost on me that he called her Lexa earlier.

I guess he leveled up with her.

"Maybe we can save this for leftovers. I'm not sure I can eat anything right now. Guys, please eat something." Elle doesn't have to tell my brothers twice, and they circle the table.

I grab a soft, crusty roll from a bag and tear it open. Grabbing a mini packet of butter, I slather it on the bread and crouch in front of Elle, holding it out to her. "You need something in your stomach."

She smiles as her fingers wrap around mine. She takes it from me, and I reach back to the table for a bottle of water and break the seal before leaving it near her.

Kill has one hand on a slice of pizza and one on his phone. He chews and reads, then he looks up at all of us around the table. "Daniel is being charged as we speak, and he's being held without bail. It turns out his family was rich, and he inherited everything when they died. He never needed to work a day in his life. The prosecution is arguing for a mandatory psych eval because this shows that he's been targeting Elle for a long time. He's going to remain in custody until his trial." He looks at Elle as he continues, "You should know that they found a lot of other items in Daniel's room, along with your coat. You will most likely be asked to identify some of them when you go in to give your statement tomorrow."

Elle lowers her hand holding the roll to rest on her lap, and I nudge her before glancing down and silently urging her to eat.

"What about everyone at work? How do I even start that conversation?" She stuffs the roll into her mouth and chews, seemingly more out of frustration than actual hunger.

"You let us handle it." Jax steps forward with Lexa at his side. "Wolfe Security has an arm that manages survivor's services. Daniel took advantage of you and everyone he lied to. We have a team of counselors, therapists, and other support staff that you can access to work through this."

"Those support services, can you offer them to Daniel? I mean, to get him help?"

Her guilt is going into overdrive. She'll mourn the loss of her friend for a long time.

"Absolutely, if that is something Daniel and his lawyer would agree to."

Elle looks like she's hit her limit, and I step in.

"Elle needs to rest." I stand and exchange a glance with her. She attempts a smile, but it doesn't reach her eyes. Extending my hand to her, I assure everyone that she is fine and I've got her, then I lead her out of our building and toward her car, which Jax drove back for us.

I slide the key into the ignition, and she leans forward, placing her hand over mine.

"I don't want to be alone."

"You won't be. I'm staying with you for as long as you need."

She gazes sheepishly at me out of the corner of her eye as she twists the strap of her purse between her fingers in her lap. "And what if I need you—forever?"

I drop my hands into my lap and lean into the seat in surprise.

This is Elle surrendering.

I once thought I preferred the hunt, but I was wrong.

I definitely prefer this moment right here.

I reach across, gather her hand in mine, and bring it to my lips, kissing her gently.

"Then that is how long you'll have me. Let's go home."

CHAPTER 34
ELLE

The night I was attacked was the night Marcus moved in, and he never moved back out.

I didn't ask him to stay with me because I was scared. I asked him to stay because when I was scared and alone at Daniel's, Marcus was the one I thought about. I realized the life I hadn't lived with him yet was what I would miss the most if I didn't make it out alive.

Barb eventually came home from her vacation and announced she was thinking about moving into a senior's apartment, to be closer to the friends she travels with. Five weeks later, she and the cat were gone.

Marcus kept most of his things at his place while we renovated the main floor of this house. He's been slowly showing up with boxes over the last month.

At the office, everyone who had worked closely with Daniel was traumatized by his actions. We held many company meetings, and I brought in counselors like Jax suggested, and eventually we grew beyond the hurt.

While we still don't know what will happen, Daniel did

end up accepting counseling as part of his remand before his case goes to trial. With the money he has, the guy could have easily exhausted the system, but he's actively sought out therapy and medication instead.

Although he's asked, I have not visited him, but I'm sure I will one day. I'm just not ready to say goodbye to the friendship I thought I had.

Wolves crave the hunt. Marcus once told me that, and I'm sure it's still true, but we've both been so busy that I haven't had a chance to scratch that itch—until now.

I'm supposed to be at a work event for another three hours.

Instead, I've decided it's time to go on a Wolfe hunt of my own.

Today is the day Marcus is officially moving in.

He took the week off to finish some things around the house, and he's going to be picking up the last of his boxes by the time I'm done at this appreciation dinner.

The clanking of tools travels up through the vent as I pad lightly on bare feet through our empty living room. There was no point in keeping my heels on, as he'd definitely hear them clacking against the wood floor.

Less than a minute later, footsteps thud up the stairs, heading straight for me. I take three careful steps around the old dining table and tuck myself away, hidden behind a partial wall that separates the dining room from the kitchen. I push myself into the dark corner and screw my eyes shut.

The door to Barb's old area opens, and I clamp my own hand over my mouth to stop myself from jumping out of my skin.

Glass jars and food containers rattle as the door to the fridge opens, and a soft glow covers the entrance of the room I'm in. Then comes the telltale *pffft* of a beer bottle opening, followed by a few gulps.

I release a steady breath as he returns to his work in the basement, and a giddy knot tightens in the pit of my stomach.

I'm starting to understand the appeal of hunting. The thrill of being caught before I set my trap is making me deliriously dizzy.

As soon as the clanking starts up again, I step out of my hiding spot in search of another.

We've been fixing up the place for a little over a month now, and I've been paying attention to where the creaky floorboards are.

I consider hiding in the only bedroom on the main floor, but the door sticks in the frame, and opening it will bring Marcus right to me in a matter of seconds.

My body trembles when I realize the best place to hide will be upstairs, and that means opening the back door and making it up the stairs while Marcus works away downstairs. I'll be dangerously close to him for a moment, and there's a good chance I'll blow it.

By the time I reach the back door, I've decided that if he finds me out, I'll pretend I just got home and was coming down to see him, and I'll try this again another time.

One of the first things we did was replace all of the old locks, so the handle moves without sound, but I have to twist it painstakingly slow. The basement door is open, and the light dims briefly as a shadow moves across the floor.

He's right there.

I glance up the stairs, then back down, and I consider chickening out and abandoning my wicked plan. Adrenaline floods my system as the stress of completing my mission builds.

Rock the fucking boat, Elle.

His challenge often surfaces when I need a little push, a reminder that I am a badass and I can do tough things.

I'll rock his boat. A hysterical giggle almost escapes me at the thought, but I clamp it down. I am not getting found out like this.

I brace my hands along the railing that leads up to the second floor. The first step is solid, and the next two are quiet as long as I tread lightly. I skip the fourth step. That one is a pain in my ass. I step to the right on the fifth step, then to the left on the sixth. The rest are all dead center.

I'm so proud of myself by the time I reach the top of the landing—then everything falls apart.

I left the keys to our second floor downstairs, in my bag by the front door.

Just when I think it can't get any worse, heavy footsteps climb the stairs again. I have nowhere to go, but the small alcove before the door makes this landing dark, and if I stay still up here, he may walk on by. But if he's coming up to this floor for anything, I'm done. I can't even try the handle now because Marcus will catch the movement for sure.

He disappears into the kitchen on the main floor again and turns on the tap. I use the sound of the running water to try the handle, and it opens.

I slip through and close the door before the water stops running, but I stay where I am on the other side, waiting to listen for where Marcus goes next.

It's harder to hear him from all of the way up here, and I'm ready to crack the door open when he descends the steps to the basement.

I snicker all of the way into our bedroom for the second part of my plan as he hammers away at something in the basement.

My phone vibrates in my pocket. I take a deep breath, smugly satisfied with myself for turning the ringer off before I stepped through the front door.

Marcus's name flashes across the screen. We have two

floors between us, so I should be able to get away with answering if I keep my voice low. "Hey!"

"Hey yourself. Listen, Kill just got off the phone with his contact in corrections. Daniel's lawyer applied for a pretrial release late yesterday, and it was granted."

I freeze beside my nightstand as my heart beats anxiously against my rib cage. "What does that mean?"

"It means he won't be held in remand before his court date. There are stipulations to his release. He can't go anywhere near you, Swank, its employees, or anyone else involved in the case, and he had to surrender his passport. The judge agreed to the terms because Daniel accepted psychiatric help without a fight. It shows remorse and a willingness to comply."

"Why are you telling me this? Aren't they supposed to let me know?"

Marcus sighs heavily. "They will let you know—eventually. Look, it isn't the best system. Your call is sitting in someone's to-do pile, and it's Friday night. You'll probably get a call next week."

I suck in a deep breath, steeling myself for what this means. I know I shouldn't have become complacent, but I can't live my life in fear. I shouldn't have to look over my shoulder. At the same time, I feel guilty. Daniel has made an effort to talk to a counselor.

"So when will they be releasing him?" I reach out, wrapping my fingers around the pull chain on my glass lamp to turn on the light.

"He was released last night."

His answer surprises me, and I instinctively recoil without letting go of the thin metal chain. My lamp tips off my nightstand and crashes to the floor, shattering around me.

"Shit." I stare at the glass shards scattered around my feet.

"Are you okay?" Marcus's tone has lost all of its kindness.

"Yeah. Just surprised."

"I'm coming to get you. I'll stay with you at the event until you're done, and we'll figure this out."

I groan into the phone, slouching my shoulders in defeat. "Ugh. I'm not there. Just come upstairs. I came home to surprise you," I confess.

He's quiet on the other end of the line before he says, "I'm not at the house. I'm on my way back with my last load."

The room tilts as my stomach twists in on itself.

"That's not funny—you're in the basement." I close my eyes, summoning the courage to whisper, "I hear you down there."

My body goes numb as I open my eyes and look at the broken glass. The same broken glass that would have alerted anyone in the house that they weren't alone.

Dread creeps up my spine when I don't hear anything in the basement anymore.

Marcus swears as a horn blares through my phone. "GET OUT OF THE HOUSE! I'M TEN MIN—"

I disconnect, then freeze as the telltale creak in the fourth step catches my attention. A moment later, the sixth step whines. Whoever is approaching is doing it slowly and with extreme caution.

There is only one way in and out of here.

My phone lights up with a notification from an unknown number. It's like a beacon in the dark room.

I don't answer it.

Instead, I bend down and slide my phone under my bed. Then I leap toward the edge of the glass shards and haul ass on tiptoe, as quietly as I can toward my closet.

It's the only hiding spot I have up here.

The door to the second floor opens just as I get inside the

closet. I take a step back, blending into the darkness as I watch through a crack in the door.

Nausea rolls through me when he finally speaks.

"I asked to see you, but you never came."

Daniel.

He makes no attempt to mask his footsteps as he walks around the apartment. Clearly, he knows it's me here and not Marcus. For one thing, Marcus wouldn't hide.

"You said you needed me. You told me you didn't know what you would do without me."

I see our relationship through his eyes now.

What I saw as employee appreciation, he gleaned as a different type of praise altogether. If I'd only known what he was struggling with, I would have handled him differently.

My guilty heart wants to step out from my hiding spot and tell him how sorry I am, but my feet won't move because I know that the man I thought I knew is gone.

Daniel gets louder as he approaches the room I'm in.

"I just wanted the chance to show you how good I could be for you—in all things."

The bedroom door sighs on its hinges as he pushes it all of the way open. It's usually a soft sound, but now it's deafening in the silent house. Daniel enters the room in darkness, moving like a shadow.

The first jagged pieces of glass grind under his shoes as he stops in the middle of the room, muttering to himself, "This wasn't here before." Then he turns.

While I can't see the features on his face clearly, I know he's squared himself on the closet I'm hiding in.

"I know you're in there, Elle. I've missed you."

The sadness in his tone sends chills across my body. He's made himself into the victim, and I'm the one at fault. None of his counseling has helped, and a sudden wave of anger floods my veins. He used our offer of help not as a way to get better, but as a way of pretending he wasn't the threat he so clearly is.

Slowly, in the dark, I raise my hands and fist them in front of me, just like Marcus showed me during our training sessions.

Marcus must be only minutes away by now.

"Fine." His face is lit by the glow of his smartphone as he taps away at the screen. "Have it your w—"

It's so dark and quiet in the room that it's obvious when my phone lights up with a notification. It vibrates against the floor under the bed.

Daniel turns to face the soft glow, then pockets his phone, plunging him into the shadows once more.

TAKE THE BAIT! My thoughts scream at him, but I remain frozen and ready.

He turns away from me as he takes a step closer to the bed.

"You are not where I thought you'd be," he taunts as he takes another step away from me.

He's buying it.

I am nowhere near strong enough to lift both the mattress and box spring on my own without making a sound, but he doesn't know that.

"I'm going to enjoy this."

My time has run out. As soon as he sees I'm not there, he'll find me in the only place left to look.

Bending over, he first tries to look under the bedframe, but the sides are too low to the floor, making the space underneath dark. He kicks at the glass shards littering the area, knowing they will cut him if he kneels. Returning to his full height, he braces his legs in a stance and lifts both the box spring and mattress with ease before grunting in confusion. That's when I push out of my closet and make a run for the door.

"You—"

There's a commotion behind me as my mattress falls

against the bedframe, and I slam into my bedroom door, jarring my shoulder before pushing myself off of it and toward the steps.

Halfway down the stairs, I realize the back door is locked up tight. That isn't the door I came in through, and if I stop to unlock everything, he will be on me before I get out of the house.

I push through the already open door to the main floor as Daniel charges down the stairs.

I make it through the kitchen and around the dining room table just as he enters the room.

"STOP!" The rage in Daniel's tone vibrates through me, and I stop, but not because he told me to.

I'm trapped behind the table, unable to make it to either door before he does. The only thing between us is this heavy slab of wood, and I intend to keep it that way until Marcus gets here.

He slows his movements, taking a step and watching as I match with a step of my own on the other side.

"You're not supposed to be here." It's my intention to sound firm, but I'm sure there's a tremble in my voice.

He ignores me.

"Why didn't you come to see me? I needed you."

"Daniel." He flinches at my clipped tone. "You need to leave. You're scaring me."

Another step.

"I wasn't going to hurt you."

Wasn't.

I have to be down to only minutes before Marcus gets here. I freeze when a set of headlights comes into view, turning my attention to the window facing the street.

The car doesn't stop, but Daniel notices my reaction.

As though he knows we won't be alone for long, he dives

under the table, grabbing my ankles and pulling hard, taking me down to the floor.

I flip onto my stomach and claw at anything to stay away, but the legs on the table are too large to hold on to.

My sweaty palms squeak against the polished floor as he jerks me to his side, then climbs on top of me, pinning me with his weight.

A scream locks in my throat as he grinds his hips. His erection pushes against my thigh, and I curl my fingers, turning them into claws and drawing blood from his face.

We roll together until I'm on top, and I throw myself off him, landing on all fours in an attempt to crawl toward the front door.

My scalp burns as I'm lifted and pulled back by his fist tangled in my hair. Daniel wastes no time wrapping his arm around my neck, and my next scream is cut off before it gets out. Then he releases my hair to clamp his hand over my mouth as he drags me toward the back of the house.

He's no longer talking, which means he's spiraling, and I'm unable to speak to reason with him. I decide to wait until we get to the stairs going up to fight. He'll probably make me go first, and I'll have a height advantage.

My hopes crash down when we clear the kitchen, and he shoves me hard down the stairs that lead to the basement. My arms fly wide, and I'm able to catch myself on the banister, but the strained muscles in my arms scream as I stumble down the last two steps, landing hard on my knees at the bottom.

When I look up, all of the banging from earlier registers.

"What did you do?"

My question is mostly rhetorical because I can see, with my own eyes, what he's been up to.

"I won't let him take you from me."

He can't possibly be thinking rationally. The sheer

absurdity of it all renders me speechless, and I gawk in disbelief at the hooks that have been hammered into the wall.

"I'll give you what you want." He points at the restraints on the ground that he, no doubt, is about to put me in.

He can't possibly think I want *this*.

"Daniel, this isn't what I want."

His façade fractures, and his expression slips into nothingness. Then his face contorts with rage as he leans over me and yells, "It's *me* you don't want! SAY IT!"

It is him I don't want, along with whatever this is, but I don't say a thing as I reach back and crab walk away from him. He doesn't allow it for long. He closes the door, then takes two large strides, gobbling up the space I put between us. He reaches down, wraps both arms around my neck, and hauls me to my feet, but he doesn't stop squeezing or lifting.

The pressure builds behind my eyes as he lifts me higher off the ground, shouting, "I LOVED YOU!" My feet barely scrape the ground. When I close my eyes, he shakes me. "LOOK AT ME!"

Torn between trying to get his hands off me and scratching his eyes out, I go for his face, but he's ready for me, and he holds me away from him, tilting his head back so I barely brush his jaw. His own face is tinged red with fury.

I return to his hold on my neck, scratching at the skin on his hands. But my strength has already left me, and darkness seeps in along the edges of my vision as I open my mouth to suck down air that isn't getting in.

Thudding echoes in my ears, and it takes me a second to realize it isn't inside of my head. The basement door bursts open, and a furious Marcus charges across the room, taking Daniel down in a tackle. Since he's still holding me, I go down with them, wheezing in a deep breath of air when Daniel releases his hold on my neck.

"GET OUT OF HERE! NOW!"

I roll away from the two, then stand, rubbing my throat before I freeze when I notice Marcus is looking and yelling at me. He turns back around just as Daniel comes at him, and I stumble back toward the door, falling once before I run up the stairs on my hands and feet.

I've learned to trust Marcus, and I do as he says without question.

I'm through the kitchen and heading into the dining room before I realize I have no idea what the hell I'm going to do once I'm outside by myself.

It sounds like an all-out brawl is going to crumble the foundation of this house. Then a wide-eyed and panicked Cillian runs up the front steps shouting, "WHERE'S—"

I point through the kitchen toward the back step. "In the basement. Please hur—"

A single gunshot shatters my world, and I trip over my steps before my legs give out from under me.

NO!

I'm unsure if I've screamed that out loud as I push myself off the floor and run toward the back of the house. Cillian grabs me, pulling me back, and I fight his hold, pleading, "Let me go. I have to help him."

He jostles me to grab my attention before leveling his gaze on me. "Help is right behind me. Go outside and wait. I've got this."

I open my mouth to argue, but footsteps coming up the back stairs makes me snap my lips shut. Cillian turns, drawing his gun and tugging me behind him before raising his voice. "IDENTIFY YOURSELF. I'VE GOT A GUN."

"It's Marcus." His tone is laced with pain and exhaustion, and Cillian hunches forward in relief.

Marcus waits a full two seconds before stepping into the

room with his empty hands stretched out in front of him, and Cillian secures his firearm.

Pushing Cillian out of the way, I rush to Marcus and barrel into him. My tears leave me in desperate sobs against his chest as he cocoons me in his arms, resting his chin on the top of my head and shushing me.

Cillian steps closer, and an unspoken question passes between them before Marcus says, "He's dead." Then his lips brush along the strands of my hair as he kisses my head, muttering, "I'm sorry, Elle."

He's not sorry that he protected me; he's sorry that I lost my friend. But I don't share his regret because Daniel was never the friend I thought he was. That person never existed to begin with.

I think, deep down, I didn't go to visit Daniel because I knew that he wasn't there anymore. I felt it in my bones. I still felt unsafe—until right now.

Marcus holds me at arm's length to look me over, and it's just now that I see him in the light of the main floor. The collar of his shirt is torn, his eye is bruised, and he's bleeding from a cut on his lip, but none of it seems to faze him.

When he lifts his hand between us, I catch the smear of blood on his knuckles he tried to wipe away.

Brushing his fingertips along my cheek, he tilts my head. His eyes narrow in on my neck at the same time I swallow. It's forced and painful. Reaching up, I try to rub where he's looking, but he wraps his hand around mine and holds me still. Then he leans down to kiss where Daniel tried to strangle me. When he lifts his head to look at me, his features have softened. "This will take time to heal."

He's right about that in more ways than one.

CHAPTER 35
ELLE

I've been distracted all morning.

It's been three months since Daniel passed away, and he crosses my mind every day.

In one final blow, Daniel's will named me his sole inheritor, leaving me with the future he should have had. I struggled with the guilt of not seeing the signs earlier.

It turns out, Daniel did not have to work a day in his life. Bits and pieces of his past came to light—parts I should have known about—and it sent me into a tailspin.

At first, I wanted to give everything of his away. I didn't even want it to pass through my hands, but I still couldn't let go of the man I called my friend. I owed that friend more.

Had I known about his torment when I first met him, I would have done so many things differently.

A couple of weeks after his will was read, Marcus held an intervention of sorts. His brothers, Kate, and Lexa showed up to our house one night, with Nat in tow, and we all sat around and talked over a couple of bottles of wine.

First Jax and Kate talked about how things played out from

their perspective, how Marcus struggled with his guilt when he failed to notice a woman in trouble. Then I listened as Marcus told me about the morning Jax showed up and gave him a way to pull himself back from the hollowness that was slowly dragging him under: the self-defense center.

Cillian, Lexa, and Nat listened quietly, offering firm nods of support every time I looked their way.

Two hours later, I joined the conversation, sharing my grief, guilt, and disappointment in both myself and Daniel—which made me then feel more guilt since he's no longer with us to defend himself.

Finally, when all of our wineglasses were almost empty, Marcus slapped his palms against his thighs and leaned forward, asking, "So, what are you going to do about it?"

He took my blank stare as an invitation to continue, and he shuffled his ass closer to me on the couch and covered my hand with his. "I've always told you, you have three choices: fight, flight, or fright. Look around." He gestures to everyone I love with his free hand. "We're all here to fight for you. What do you choose?"

I chose to fight.

I decided to hold off on my plans to expand Swank into another city for the time being. Instead, I promoted Julie into my position and created a new section at Swank for myself, working pro bono to help nonprofit organizations raise money through events and fundraising activities.

Nat followed me into my new role as my assistant, and our first team member was a tenacious new intern who is every bit the force I thought she'd be when she tried to bid on me at the charity auction.

The intercom buzzes on my desk.

Nat clears her throat on the line. "Your eleven o'clock is here."

I tap at my keyboard, pulling up my calendar. Then I shake my head as if she can see me from the other side of my closed door. "I don't have an eleven o'clock."

The door opens before I finish my sentence. "Knowing I'm coming defeats the whole point of a surprise attack."

Wolves crave the hunt.

The corner of Marcus's lip twitches up in amusement as he enters, closing then locking the door behind him.

I forgot Nat was on the line, and I jump in my seat when she sighs. "Damn, woman, that ass. Your man looks just as fine going as he does com—"

"You're on speaker! Goodbye now!" I jab at the phone, missing once, then disconnect as she bursts into laughter on the other end.

Marcus only smirks as though he's fully aware of his attributes, and I bury my face in my hands.

He moves like a phantom, so fast and silent that I don't realize he's already crossed the room and made it to my side by the time I lean back in my chair and sigh to catch my breath.

He pushes my knees open and kneels on the floor between my legs, his large palms sliding my skirt up the length of my thighs.

"Busy day?" His hands rest just before the apex of my thighs, his thumbs massaging my tender flesh as he waits for my response.

I reach out, combing one hand into his hair. "Nothing I can't handle."

With a smirk, he lowers his face, his lips caressing along my inner thigh. "We'll see about that." After three more careful kisses, he adds, "Are you ready for tonight?"

Tonight.

Ravenous's second club officially opens tonight, and all of

its new members have been invited out to celebrate—Marcus and I included.

After many talks, we joined last week, to Lexa's absolute joy. Marcus sent in our questionnaires anonymously, and he asked that Ravenous only process them against each other.

We're a ninety-seven percent match.

"I am." I shift my hips, silently hinting for Marcus to keep going, but he chuckles against my skin, sending a shiver down my legs.

"We'll see." Lifting my skirt, he settles his lips against my silk panties and hums in approval, the vibrations tickling my clit. When he nips at my pussy through the fabric, I suck in a desperate breath. "That's my good girl. I want you needy by the time I get you alone in one of those rooms."

He settles my skirt on my thighs, and I huff my disappointment, which earns me a pleased grin.

Ravenous's new venue bears a stunning resemblance to their flagship location. We're sitting on our own sofa in the lounge area, which is decorated with the same comfortable seats we sat on during the self-defense presentation back when I first met Marcus. Lexa mentioned that the place was designed to be similar, so members who move between the two clubs aren't disoriented.

Knowing Lexa isn't here tonight has settled some of my nerves. She has her own club to run.

"How are you?" Marcus runs his finger along my hairline over my forehead. His gaze follows the path he draws before settling on my eyes, waiting for my answer.

"I'm good—really good."

The hint of a smile reaches his eyes. Satisfied with my

answer, he trails the back of his knuckle along my jawline and down my neck, hooking it under the soft, plunging neckline of my dress.

I hold my eyes on his but shudder under his touch as goosebumps whisper across my exposed skin. I'm not used to going without a bra, so every move, every touch, pushes me out of my comfort zone.

Marcus licks his lips. "You are beautiful."

My stomach coils at his praise because I know he isn't talking about my appearance.

He's talking about our history, the precious moments we spend together now, and our future. He's talking about who I am and how we fit together.

"Thank you." My gratitude goes far beyond his compliment, and for a moment we pause, lost in each other.

There is nowhere I would rather be.

Marcus stands, takes one look around the darkened room, and extends his hand to me, palm up. "It's time, Ms. Sinclair."

There's something about the way he looks at me that wraps its tendrils tight around my heart and squeezes until the air turns thin, forcing me to take a deep breath, to steady myself for what's to come.

He stands still, waiting as though he has all of the time in the world.

I slide my fingers into his and allow him to lead me across the room and into a hall near the back. His grip tightens when a man steps into the hall and glances at me with an approving smile, and I lower my gaze to the floor.

I'm not here for anyone but Marcus.

Marcus slows, then stops in front of a door with a sign that simply reads, Reserved: Wolfe. He slides a plastic card along a scanner and pushes as soon as the lock clicks open. Then he leads me inside.

Our safe word always remains the same: bowling. Marcus shared that he likes the familiar word because it carries happy memories for him. He says it centers him to us, allowing him to step away from his headspace faster. I've needed to use it a few times since Daniel's attack while we figure out what is now triggering for me.

Some things I once loved now walk a fine line, but we've met each one head-on, and we've had lots of fun working out alternatives. My eyes still roll into the back of my head each time Marcus wraps his fingers around my throat and holds me down; however, we discovered that my limit is one hand. Two hands around my throat brings back painful memories.

We do, however, use two hands when we train together because Marcus says if I am ever in a position where I'm attacked like that again, I need to get used to that possibility so I don't freeze up.

The lights in the room are dim. Nothing looks particularly ready for us tonight, and I take a few steps into the center to look around. A made bed with lush, black sheets sits off to one side, along with an oversized armchair and a table. Hooks decorate the walls and ceiling, but none of them are set up, and curiosity creeps in at what Marcus has planned.

I turn and watch him as he crosses the room to one of the walls that's covered by floor-to-ceiling curtains.

"Safe word?" This is Marcus's way of asking if I'm ready, and I tell him I am:

"Bowling."

A wicked smile spreads across his lips as he licks them. Butterflies flutter furiously in my stomach at his confidence.

Closing the distance between us, Marcus circles one hand around my waist, then stands flush against my back. He tucks his hand into the deep collar of my dress and tickles his fingers over my nipples. They harden instantly at the direct contact, and he pinches them as he groans into my ear.

When Marcus takes a step toward the curtain, I have no choice but to follow since he's tightened his grip around my waist. He continues to tug at my nipple. The sensation goes straight to my core, making my legs weak.

"Do you know what I wanted to do the first night I met you?" he growls against my ear as he moves his hand from my waist to cup me between my legs.

Saliva fills my mouth, and I swallow my nerves as he licks the length of my neck, waiting for me to ask, "What?"

Warm air washes over my fevered skin as Marcus straightens, creating a sliver of space between us, and unfastens my dress behind my neck. That's all it takes for the whole thing to slip to the floor, leaving me in only my shoes and black panties.

He returns to me, steps us out of the fabric pooled at my feet, and takes another two steps toward the curtain. As we approach, he fists my hair in one hand and covers my pussy with the other, massaging me through my panties.

He leans over me, blowing a cool breath of air over my nipples, and they go rock hard for him. "I wanted to tangle my hand in your hair and drag you down the back alley, hide you away from everyone, and make you mine. I wanted to push you up against the dirty wall and fuck you right there, taking you for myself while everyone sat inside learning how they could protect themselves—from men like me."

I groan. I don't mean to, and he chuckles into my ear.

The muscles along my spine go taut, forcing me to arch my back and push my chest out for him. He doubles down, slipping his fingers under my panties and sliding through my wet folds with ease. Then he goes straight for the sensitive spot along the side of my clit. "I won't stop taking what I want from you, Elora."

I'm close, so close to coming that I moan and writhe under his touch. My senses are so overwhelmed that I act on a delay when he grips my panties in his hand and tugs hard, tearing them from my body.

"YES!" I step my legs farther apart for him, but he doesn't return to me just yet.

Gripping the curtain in front of us, he pulls the heavy fabric hard to the side, then steps us up to the mirror as he works his fingers back into me.

"You belong to me, and by the time I'm done with you, everyone will know it."

It takes a moment too long for me to realize that it isn't a mirror, but a floor-to-ceiling window facing into the main area of the club—and I can see everyone out there.

Marcus doesn't relent. He knows how to touch me to draw things out, and he knows what to do to set me off.

I'm too far gone. My orgasm is coming at me too fast to care about anything but the two of us.

I grip his hand between my legs with my own to steady myself, and he allows it because I'm not stopping him. I'm pushing him into me, and he grinds his hips into my ass, his erection pushing hard into my side.

His low timbre at my ear sends shivers through me. "That's it, Elora. Scream for me."

And I do.

My body convulses around his fingers, and I toss my head back, yelling his name as he finishes me off.

By the time I ease out of my orgasm, Marcus has released my hair. His arms are wrapped around my front, holding me to him, and I'm thankful because I'm not sure I'd still be standing otherwise.

"Hey." He brushes his fingers over my breast. "You know it's a one-way mirror, right? They can't see us."

I chuckle. "Yeah. I figured it out." At least, I was about ninety percent sure it was.

He kisses my shoulder and loosens his grip, and I spin, dropping to my knees with the memory of his hard cock pushing against me.

I go to work unfastening his pants while he slips his jacket off and tosses it to the side. And he groans from above me when I lick his tip before sliding my mouth down his length as far as I can take him.

His fingers tighten and loosen on either side of my head as his hips jerk forward when I fall into a rhythm he enjoys.

Then he goes rigid, tightening his hold on my head and telling me to stop.

I let him go with a pop, and he hauls me up, facing me to the window once more and circling around behind me.

He palms his big hands over my ass and squeezes my cheeks before releasing them and slapping me. The contact is meant to sting, and it does. I sway a little to the side, and he steadies me before slipping my heels off and holding my hips so I have nowhere to go when he bites the fleshy part of my ass before standing.

He bends me forward. "Put your hands on the glass."

I brace myself as he lines up behind me, digging his fingers into my hips and driving his length forward in one solid thrust until he's buried deep inside me, and I cry out at the overwhelming sensation.

"Fuck. You always feel so good." Marcus slides out, then thrusts deep again.

He settles his palm on my lower back, then spanks my ass as he rides me, making me moan, and I let myself sink into my position against the glass.

We slip into a rough tempo. I focus on my palms, which are now sweaty against the glass, as Marcus takes control of us, pounding into me from behind.

I'm drifting in my own euphoria when he slides his palm up my spine and into my hair, guiding my body up by his hold and stepping us closer to the one-way mirror.

He sandwiches me between him and the glass, and my breasts flatten against the cold surface. Once I am braced on my own, he slips his hand out of my hair and under one leg to lift it off the floor, spreading me to the room in front of us. His free hand goes for the most sensitive spot on my clit, and I buck my hips at the contact.

He heaves me back into the position he wants me in and continues to pound into me, forcing me to take every sensation.

I open my eyes and stare into the room on the other side of the glass. Men and women go about their lives while we are cut off, separated into our own time and space. He's caught his prey, and he is reaping what he desires from my tired body as he claims his reward.

"Are you going to come for me like this? While I take everything I want and fuck you in front of everyone out there?" Then he turns his full attention on me, growling into my ear as though he's trying to outright possess me. "No one will help you, Elora. You belong to me. You are mine to do with as I please."

My vision goes white as all sound is sucked out of the room.

I shatter, breaking apart around him and letting go.

I couldn't tell you if I screamed or fainted. I'm not even sure I'm still standing.

All I know is I'm safe—because I'm with Marcus, and he's got me no matter what.

THANK YOU FOR VISITING RAVENOUS

The Ravenous series is a collection of standalone novels set in the Ravenous world. Characters from these stories often overlap into others within the series.

This series is ongoing and new stories will be added as they are written. There are no cliffhangers in these books.

ACKNOWLEDGMENTS

I want to mention the amazing members of our Ravenous group on Facebook for providing support and encouragement while I wrote this book. Your excitement for Marcus's story was an immense motivation.

I also want to acknowledge and thank everyone who gave their time and talent to this book:

Cover design: Kirsty Still (Pretty Little Design Co.)
Editor: Caroline Knecht
Photographer: Wander Aguiar
Cover Model: Michael Martin

Until next time...

ABOUT LUNA

Luna Kayne is a multi-genre romance author located in Canada. She writes dark, explicit, romantic suspense with a hint of humor and angst. Her men are dominant and often stubborn, and her women are usually underestimated. As for tropes and sub-genres, nothing is off the table.

In 2021, she won an IPPY (Independent Publisher Book Awards) award with her novel, *Step Darkly,* which earned a bronze medal.

Luna Kayne is the pen name of author *Sheri Landry* who writes non-romance action thrillers and has won awards for her writing under both names.

You can find a complete list of books and learn more at LunaKayne.com.

BB bookbub.com/profile/luna-kayne

facebook.com/lunakayne

instagram.com/lunakayne